P9-DDH-571

Would Rindo take the money if he showed it to him? No, the question was did he ~~Back up~~. ~~Do you~~ have to show it to him? ~~No.~~ And the answer to ~~You're sure.~~ that was no. He had no obligation, even, to suppose, now, that the money belonged to anyone else.

~~Of course. You have no obligation, None at all, to show him that money. It was given to you not to him.~~

Then why, he thought, do you keep bringing Rindo into it?

Where the red glow was now would be the center of the church. The crucifix--that could be suspended, hung from the ceiling, eh?

"Bless me Father for I have sinned." Again the whispered sound. A man's voice. Familiar? Yes; but he did not try to ~~place~~ identify the voice. He listened. "It's been over two years since my last confession and since then I missed Mass about all the time and I stole things."

"What kind of things?"

"Money."

"~~A lot of~~ Much money?"

"Over three thousand dollars." ~~U. S. currency."~~

Father Schwinn opened his eyes. His elbow was on the ledge of the basket-weave screen and as he ~~raised his head~~ looked up his hand moved from his forehead to his beard. "That's the total amount? From different places?"

"Nuh-uh. All from the same place."

"Did you cause physical harm to anyone?" He spoke slowly, quietly, knowing what the man would ~~say~~ answer.

"We liked to killed one."

There you are, he thought. He felt disappointment, but relief at the same time. "This was at Rindo's, wasn't it?"

"That's right."

"Did you--" He stopped. "What are you going to do about it?"

"That's what I come to find out."

CHARLIE MARTZ
AND OTHER STORIES

ALSO BY ELMORE LEONARD

FICTION

Raylan
Djibouti
Road Dogs
Up in Honey's Room
The Hot Kid
The Complete Western Stories of Elmore Leonard
Mr. Paradise
When the Women Come Out to Dance
Tishomingo Blues
Pagan Babies
Be Cool
The Tonto Woman & Other Western Stories
Cuba Libre
Out of Sight
Riding the Rap
Pronto
Rum Punch
Maximum Bob
Get Shorty
Killshot
Freaky Deaky
Touch
Bandits
Glitz
LaBrava
Stick
Cat Chaser
Split Images
City Primeval
Gold Coast
Gunsights
The Switch
The Hunted
Unknown Man No. 89
Swag
Fifty-Two Pickup
Mr. Majestyk
Forty Lashes Less One
Valdez Is Coming
The Moonshine War
The Big Bounce
Hombre
Last Stand at Saber River
Escape from Five Shadows
The Law at Randado
The Bounty Hunters

NONFICTION

Elmore Leonard's 10 Rules of Writing

CHARLIE MARTZ AND OTHER STORIES

The Unpublished Stories

Elmore Leonard

wm

WILLIAM MORROW

An Imprint of HarperCollins*Publishers*

This book is a work of fiction. The characters, incidents, and dialogue are drawn from the author's imagination and are not to be construed as real. Any resemblance to actual events or persons, living or dead, is entirely coincidental.

HarperCollins books may be purchased for educational, business, or sales promotional use. For information please e-mail the Special Markets Department at SPsales@harpercollins.com.

FIRST EDITION

Library of Congress Cataloging-in-Publication Data has been applied for.

ISBN 978-0-06-236492-0

15 16 17 18 19 OV/RRD 10 9 8 7 6 5 4 3 2 1

CONTENTS

FOREWORD

MORE THAN ANYONE, YOU'LL see Hemingway's influence in Elmore's early prose. When my father was just starting he told me he would put a blank piece of paper over the page of a Hemingway story and rewrite the scene his way. It's how he learned to write.

I remember when I was seven or eight, going down the stairs to the basement, seeing my dad at his red desk, a cinderblock wall behind him, concrete floor. He was writing longhand on unlined, eight-and-a-half-by-eleven yellow paper. There was a typewriter on a metal stand next to the desk. Across the room was a red wicker waste basket with balls of yellow paper on the floor around it. Scenes that didn't work. Pages that didn't make it.

In retrospect, the room looked like a prison cell but my father, deep in concentration, didn't seem conscious of his surroundings.

I said, "Dad, what're you writing?"

"A short story called Charlie Martz."

I think I said something profound like, "Oh."

Elmore got the name from his best friend, Bill Martz. Bill didn't work as well for the character, so he changed the name to Charlie.

While my father was writing the stories in this volume he worked at Campbell-Ewald, an advertising agency, writing Chevrolet ads. For almost a decade he got up at 5:00 A.M. and wrote two pages of fiction before he went to work. His rule: he couldn't turn the water on for coffee, until he wrote a page. This routine continued until Elmore quit the advertising business. One day he said, "I'm gonna make my run." Which meant he was going to write fiction full time.

These stories also remind me of growing up with my father. Eating beans out of tin plates while we watched a Western on TV. My dad said beans tasted better on a tin plate and he was right.

They remind me of playing hide and seek with guns. My brothers and sisters and I would hide somewhere in the house and when Elmore found us we'd shoot him. He loved the game as much as we did; he was a kid at heart.

They remind me of the bullfight poster that hung in our family room, a dramatic shot of Manolete holding his sword and cape ready to finish off a charging bull. Elmore loved the idea of the matador, dressed in his outfit, putting on a show, knowing any mistake might be his last.

And they remind me that my father was always writing. I can picture him in the family room, lost in thought, working on *Hombre* while I was twenty feet away with two friends, listening to the new Jimi Hendrix album. Elmore said he wrote eight pages that afternoon.

I can picture him on Easter break in Pompano Beach, Florida, sitting by the pool filled with kids playing, and surrounded by their parents talking and drinking vodka and tonics, Elmore, once again, oblivious to his surroundings, writing on a yellow pad.

In these early stories you'll see Elmore experimenting with

style, trying to find his voice, his sound. You'll see him start a story with weather. You'll see him use adverbs to modify the verb "said." You'll see him describe characters in detail, breaking several of the famous *10 Rules of Writing* he developed almost fifty years later. And you'll also see glimpses of Elmore's greatness to come.

Peter Leonard

CHARLIE MARTZ
AND OTHER STORIES

One, Horizontal

THE JOINT ON BEAUBIEN was a semi black and tan, more black than tan. Any lighter element in the place, disregarding a few beboppers, was sure to be overdressed, on the greasy side, and usually carrying a gun. Since it was of the lower order, and because I was familiar enough with his lower habits, I was willing to bet my last buck Marty Carrito would be there.

Inside the door I fought off the check girl who had my raincoat half unbuttoned before I could tell her I just wanted a quick warmer, and got a blast full in the face from five pieces—mostly brass and bongos.

Everybody in the place was beating his own time to the jazz—feet, hands, wooden knockers, and any part of the anatomy near something strong enough to take the beating. The check girl said it was "Honeysuckle Rose," with not a little enthusiasm. Quite a surprise, but I didn't have time to discuss it with her. I spotted my man at the bar.

He was slouched on the stool, elbows on the bar, looking like a teddy bear made out of black pinstripe. He was talking to a girl; blond, looked real, not bad, but not the kind you'd take home to mother. If you could judge by his gestures and the "baby stick with me and you can go places" look, she'd better have her snowshoes on. Laced tight.

I'm the kind of guy that gets lovey and buddy-buddy after I've had a few. Only this wasn't the time to be lovey or buddy-buddy, or even the least bit nice for that matter. All evening I had been buying bottle courage for what I was going to do, and now I felt like kissing the guy . . . instead of killing him. Right then, along with the cute feeling, and probably because of it, I got an idea. It added a little color to a drab job.

Off to the right I spotted MEN in yellow neon, went in, picked one of the more private compartments, of which there were three, closed the door, and pulled a .45 from the left pocket of my raincoat. For the first time since I entered Jade's I relaxed my grip on the handle. My hand was sweating.

I glanced at a couple of jingles and smutty words on the wall and found out that Kilroy had been there. Ordinarily I wouldn't have laughed, but I was in a peculiar frame of mind. What makes a men's room bring out artistic talents? I decided to think about it later and took the clip out of the gun. I slid the top slug from the clip, put the gun back together and in my pocket again, but kept the slug in my hand when I stepped out.

The men's room attendant gave me an unenthusiastic look, saw I wasn't the hand-washing type, but figured what the hell and tried to brush me off. However he wasted his time. I brushed him instead.

Out front I noticed that "Honeysuckle Rose" had withered away and now "How High the Moon" was being rasped to death by a skinny little colored boy with a great big tenor sax. Everyone was still going nuts. Including my man. The stool next to him where the girl had been was now vacant. Either he had missed out or else she was powdering her nose. I knew he was the type who generally got what he wanted, one way or another, so I threw the first guess out and decided I'd better work fast.

I squeezed in next to him and put one leg over the empty stool. It took about ten seconds to get the bartender's eye. I ordered a double, paid, and placed the shot right in front of me. Carrito was so intent on the music—beating on the edge of the bar with his ring turned toward the palm—that he hadn't noticed me yet.

I tapped him on the left shoulder, gently. No response. I tapped him again but with a little more knuckle. Still beating, bouncing, but without taking his eyes off the sax player, he reached a fat, perspiring paw over and held my hand. It took him almost a minute to realize that the hand he held had never used Ponds, wasn't lovely, and sure as hell didn't belong to the doll with the blond hair.

I thought he'd spin around and that he might even throw one, but he turned toward me very slowly, probably trying to get his fat brain to turn over fast enough to say something Richard Widmark would if he were sitting there. He looked me right in the eye with his still half closed, took a drag on his cigarette, and blew the smoke in my face, slowly. I had planned on being the smooth apple, but he was out-smoothing me. I tried not to blink, put my left hand on the bar, and placed the .45 slug sitting straight up. He didn't notice.

"I already got a date, pal."

I beckoned to the bullet and he followed my glance.

"She can have you, Marty." He didn't show surprise that I knew his name. "I just want to make a prediction for you. I'm going to kill you with something just like that."

I picked up the hooker and took two gulps to kill it, turned from the bar, and walked toward the entrance as naturally as I could. At the check window, I stopped and turned up my collar. Part of the show. Then I left fast, without looking back. Not part of the show.

A Checker cab was in front of the place and I grabbed that. If it hadn't been there I probably would have taken off like a 220-dash man right down the middle of the street. As soon as I left the bar I knew I was scared. I hadn't counted on it, but there was nothing I could do about it.

All the way across town I kept looking back, got a few scares, but finally decided that I wasn't being tailed. Then I began to wonder why I wasn't. I had just told the guy I was going to kill him and he didn't even come after me.

"I'll bet he didn't hear what I said!"

"What did you say?" The cabby was looking at me through the rearview mirror.

"I said don't you care if the light's red?"

He jammed on the brakes and I almost ended up next to him. We were on East Adams, downtown Detroit. Since it was close enough, I told him that this was fine, paid, and got out. I stopped in the Brass Rail to see if you could still get a shot for thirty-five cents. It didn't take long. Thirty-five cents lighter I was back outside again. Within five minutes I had picked up the Chevy that I had parked in a lot around the corner, and was heading for Grass Lake.

It was raining again and the windshield wipers squeaked a monotonous beat on the downward motion. I opened both of the front window vents wide. The moist air felt good on my face. I relaxed, and for the first time in over a week, since I had left Tampico, I breathed more slowly and began to think with a little logic. A year ago I'd only drive out this way for a swim, and now . . .

I HAD BEEN IN Mexico almost a year when I got the wire telling of Cliff's accident. I was just scrounging around trying to make a fast, easy buck, but legitimately, when the bad news reached me. My brother didn't send it himself. He would have made it look better.

The guy that sent it was either drunk or not past the third grade, because a baby could figure from the way he said, it it wasn't an accident. Nobody gets shot in a hunting accident when the hunting season isn't open. That was enough. I gave up starving to death and headed for Detroit. That was Monday before last. Two days after I got here, Cliff left the hospital and moved out to a little cottage on Grass Lake, confined to a wheelchair, knowing he'd never walk again.

He was evasive at first and hard to get along with. He just sat there with a chip on his shoulder continually bawling for a drink. He had changed a lot. A year ago he had just finished high school—a football star, popular with the girls, and even pretty good in school. Sometimes I thought he dressed funny, but that was all in the age. If I had kept my job in Detroit and an eye on Cliff, everything would have been all right; but I was a little too unsettled for my own good. Maybe he got some of his wildness from me. But where did I get it? From what I can remember, the folks couldn't have been better—doing everything right, and contributing to the old saying that only the good die young. I wish Cliff had remembered them better. If he had, he wouldn't have fallen in with the pool-room crowd who filled him with the easy-money idea. It was through one of them that he got the job in the local numbers bank. That was the start. In a few months he moved farther uptown, dressed better, but now carried a revolver. He was an easy kid to like, so I can see how he moved up fast. But in that racket you don't push too hard if the guys in front of you are heavy. Cliff was ambitious and liked to push.

A state cop found him in the bushes alongside US 16 about a mile this side of Farmington. He had been badly beaten and shot. They probably had every intention of killing him, I'm not sure, but the bullet only chipped the spine—went right through. If they had done a good job, he'd been better off.

It took just a few days of watching him break up a little bit at a time before I decided what I was going to do. I thought about the cops and a dozen other things a member of the Better Citizens League would do; but I wasn't a better citizen and I couldn't see how going to the cops would do any good. To them he was just another mug who got what he deserved. If the guy who did it was picked up, he'd be out within twenty-four hours. No evidence. A dozen guys would swear they were having a beer with him the exact second that Cliff was shot. If anything was going to be done, it would have to be done by me. I didn't have any delusions of wiping out the whole racket, or even the Detroit branch, but one guy was going to get it. The one who decided that Cliff was no longer useful.

Finding out his identity was no easy job—even when I poured everything except aftershave lotion into Cliff to make him loosen up. I'd drink along with him to make it look like a party, but either he'd pass out too soon, or else he'd just get talking good . . . and I would.

Last night I was pretty disgusted with my progress, and was trying to think of where I could lay my hands on a torture wheel, when he opened up out of a clear highball and gave me the whole story. He was really feeling sorry for himself, and it made me a little sick. But at the end of the story I found out my man was Marty Carrito.

At first I was going to shoot him on sight. Nothing fancy, and to hell with the consequences. I found out where he hung out most of the time, took the better part of the afternoon and evening to drink some courage, and arrived at the black and tan about eleven. I was planning on getting him outside, somehow, and on his back in the gutter without further ado, when the cute idea hit me. It was prescribed to prolong the agony, and make him sweat. What a dreamer. The first part was over, and I knew damn well if anybody was scared it was only me.

IT WAS GOING ON 1:00 A.M. when I turned up the narrow, muddy drive leading to the cottage. I turned sharply off the drive about a hundred feet from the cottage and drove as far into the bushes as I could, which was only about twenty feet off the drive. Before going inside I pulled some loose shrubbery around behind the car and tried to hide it.

I went through the back door into a kitchen that looked more like a bottling plant and smelled more like a distillery. Twenty-three men of distinction props were on the sink and on the kitchen table. All thoroughly used. I took the ones off the sink and placed them on the table with the others, arranging them all in two neat rows. Dressed the place up a little.

Cliff was on the couch in the living room, a couple of pillows propped behind him and his right arm resting on a card table next to the couch. There was a half-full bottle on the table along with two shot glasses, a tumbler, and a dozen or more cigarette stubs that had been butted on the tabletop.

"What do you think ash trays are for?"

He picked up a crumpled cigarette pack and tore at it nervously. He looked up at me, throwing the empty pack on the floor.

"Gimme a cigarette. I'm out." He looked more nervous lighting it, but seemed to relax after the first drag. "Did you bring a bottle? This is the last one."

"No, I didn't have time," I said. "You'd better cut down anyway. Bad for the liver."

"You found out all you wanted to know, so now I'd better cut down. You think I'm going to sit here and go nuts? I'll beat the damn liver to death first!"

"Cliff, you have to have patience. Soon you'll be—"

"Start one more of those sickening lectures and I'll vomit right on the floor. Have patience . . . read . . . get interested in a hobby . . . do something constructive! What'll I do, weave baskets or sell pencils? Stan, you got to either keep your mouth shut or get the hell out. You stopped being the big brother a long time ago!"

His face was very red and he was getting more and more excited. Without knowing it he was trying to pull himself up from the couch. I pushed him down gently and arranged the pillows behind him more comfortably.

"As a martyr you make a good drunk, Cliff. You're going to do something for yourself and stop feeling sorry whether you like it or not. One thing is sure, we're not staying here. As soon as you're a little stronger we're going west. This burg is too cold."

He looked at me quickly. "Sure it's not because it's too hot?" He thought that was clever, and what he said next even more so.

"You look kind a pale, Stan. See a ghost, or did you almost become one? I told you monk around and you'd get more than you could handle."

"Go to sleep, Cliff."

"Go to sleep, Cliff." He imitated my voice. "You really think you're God Almighty, don't you? Go to sleep, Cliff!" He did it the same way. "You're just too goddamn smart for your own good." He was pulling himself off the couch again. "I hope they put you to sleep! Even if you are my brother."

I turned out the lights and went into the bedroom without answering. He kept it up for a while, but I couldn't make out what he was saying. I knew he wouldn't have spoken that way if he were sober, but I still couldn't help liking him a little less, and went to sleep wondering if what I was doing was worth the time and effort.

I expected Cliff to be in a better mood the next morning. Maybe if he had gotten some sleep he would have been, but I noticed the bottle on the table was empty. Cliff was still half drunk, but now the other half of him was hungover, and he was in an uglier mood. I told him I was going out for a while and he told me to GET THE HELL OUT . . . so he could have the last word.

I drove to Henderson's Corner, about two miles down the road, had two cups of coffee, got cigarettes, and then went across the road to the post office.

I bought one stamped envelope, and had to tell the clerk three times that I thought the weather stunk before I could get away from the window and over to an addressing table near the door.

You don't have to be too sneaky about dropping a .45 caliber bullet into an envelope. It isn't that big. So I didn't worry about anyone being a witness to my breaking the law. I addressed it to Carrito in care of Jade's, the joint on Beaubien, and dropped it into the box.

I was more than halfway home when I realized my mistake. The Grass Lake postmark would stand out like muscles on a snake dancer! For Carrito not to notice it, he'd have to be as dumb as I was when I pulled the stunt.

I raced the rest of the way, trying to think of how to get Cliff out of town in the shortest possible time. I turned into the drive, pulled up behind the cottage, and then noticed the gray, '49 Buick over to the left and partly among the trees. I took it for granted who the visitor was, but I didn't take for granted he'd have a friend along. Not until . . .

"Out of the car, Jack. No tricks."

I turned fast. The right front door opened and a young, good-looking guy in a drapey gray flannel suit was standing there with his left hand on the handle. I couldn't see the other hand because it was inside the coat—where a shoulder holster hangs. I got out his side.

"Let's go inside, Jack." That's all he had to say.

Marty Carrito was straddling a chair turned backward, his elbows on the back and his chin resting on both hands. He didn't raise his head when we came in, but his eyes moved up from the floor and rested on me. The same slow, half-closed eyes.

"Who's your friend, Buddy?"

Before the gray suit could answer, Carrito lifted his head with a jerk, recognition all over his face.

"Oh, it's MY friend. Yeah, we're old friends. Even hold hands."

The gray suit came around and stood in front of me. "You mean this is the guy at Jade's last night?" His right hand was out of the coat and he was holding a snub-nosed .32.

"Yeah, Buddy, this is the guy who gives his shells away." He turned to me, still straddling the chair. "We're sure glad to see you. Thought we'd have to give Cliffy another lesson. Cliffy hasn't been minding lately." He turned his head toward the couch. "Have ya, pal?"

Cliff wasn't on the couch but right next to it in a mess of cigarette butts and broken glass. The card table was on its side next to him. I started to go over to him, but didn't get two steps—under my own power—something hard and flat, like a cut-down revolver, smashed against the side of my face and I landed in the mess next to my brother.

"I thought he wanted to sit down, Marty, so I give him a seat." Buddy thought it was very funny.

Carrito didn't pay any attention to what he said, just smiled and looked at me. He said, still smiling, "Check me if I'm wrong. You're Stan Ellis. You've been down in Mexico for the past year or so. Left just before Cliff got his position with us. Heard about his little accident a couple of weeks ago, and decided to play the big brother." Now he was laughing. "See, we've got to know all about our boys. Even about their brothers."

He stopped abruptly, jumped up, and threw the chair aside. For the first time I saw his eyes open all the way.

"You think I'm a too-big mug who takes that kind of stuff offa somebody's big brother! There're a dozen guys in the river wearing cement shoes who didn't do half of what you tried. You think I'm punchy or somethin'!"

He calmed down a little, but his eyes were still open wide. I took that as a bad sign and didn't say a word. Buddy started to laugh.

Carrito looked at him. "Shut up!" Then down at me and pointed in my face. "You take that gimpy brother and get out of town fast. If I ever hear of you around here again, I'll blow your head off . . . after Cliff gets his. If you think I'm bluffing, stick. You'll stick for good under this goddamn ground!"

He looked at me for about ten seconds without moving. You could see that he was relaxing. He pulled a silver case from an inside pocket and took out a cigarette. He kept his eyes on me while he lit it and took a long drag. As he blew the smoke, he turned and walked out. Buddy walked out backward.

I heard the Buick start and pull away before I got up. My face ached and I felt a little blood, but I know it didn't hurt as much as Cliff's. Blood was smeared all over his face and down the front of his T-shirt. Both of his cheeks were badly bruised. Buddy's gun had been working overtime.

I made Cliff comfortable on the couch, cleaned him up, cleaned up the mess and then myself. When I got back to him he was wide awake, but not feeling too good. I told him the whole story, including what Carrito had said. Without making too big a chump out of myself I told him Carrito was probably right and we'd better go someplace else. Cliff was able to swear at me only once before he passed out again.

I thought we'd be able to pull out the next day, but in the morning Cliff was feeling worse. Pretty sick to his stomach. So I put off the departure and planned it for the next day. There wasn't much preparing to do—no tickets to buy—because I thought everything would be easier if we drove. So all afternoon I moped around, smoked two packs of cigarettes, and lost two thousand bucks to myself playing Canfield. About seven I was ready to blow my lid. Cliff was sleeping—much needed—so I elected to go out for a while. Out of cigarettes anyway.

The room adjoining the general store of Henderson's Corner boasted of a short mahogany bar, stained, and about a dozen tables marred with names, initials, and intimate ads like J.H. loves M.M. It was fairly crowded. Mostly farmers and a few of their wives, but not many cottagers this time of the year. I sat at the bar, minding my own business until a little after nine. It was at this time that I noticed a fellow at a table close to the bar tearing into a very rare-looking steak. This inspiration, plus the fact that I hadn't eaten all day, moved me to a table where I had the same, plus two beers. At after dinner drink time, I was back at the bar, feeling much better, and even ready to put up with any farmer who wanted to discuss girls, wheat, the new calf, girls, beer, sports, or even girls. Twenty minutes later I was right in the middle of all of them, and didn't finally pull myself free until going on twelve. I'd had it.

A little more than halfway back to the cottage I noticed the red glow in the sky. A few people were walking hurriedly down the road in the general direction. I had never chased a fire before and didn't plan on starting now.

I didn't plan on starting, but when I turned into the cottage drive, I saw that I had chased it whether I liked it or not.

I wasn't able to get more than halfway up the drive. The volunteers were out full force, along with a few dozen ardent fans blocking the drive and doing everything they could to get in the way. It took me fifteen minutes to get a straight story out of someone. All the watchers were eager to relate the details, only they all talked at once and every story was different. But I did find out that no one had gone into the house since the fire was discovered . . . and no one had come out.

I felt numb and kinda drained. Cliff couldn't have dragged himself out without help. I thought of the cigarettes mashed out on the table, matches thrown on the floor, I even toyed with a defective wiring notion. But I wasn't even close.

It was close to me though. I felt the nudge and looked around.

"Nice homey fire, huh Jack?" Buddy. His hand in the usual place.

I let go with all I had. Brought both fists up under his chin and a knee into his groin. He staggered back, went down, and the momentum carried me over him. I landed on his face with both knees, rolled over him and kept going. I ran down the drive a few steps, saw that my car was blocked, so I cut to the left and raced for the woods and thick bushes.

I ran, stumbled and staggered through the foliage, the branches tore at my face and clothes, but kept going. If I stopped I was as good as dead. A guy with a gun was behind me, somewhere, itching to pull the trigger in my face. I was breathing hard, and the hot, fast breaths seared inside my chest. It kept going through my mind that I had to get away . . . get far enough then out back to the road . . . bum a ride to Detroit . . . but why did they do it? . . . Then it dawned on me. The bullet I mailed! Carrito got it after he had talked to us, so figured I was still playing the hero. Why hadn't he looked at the post date!

I stopped short and sunk to my knees. Slowly I fell back in a sitting position. I was thinking what a hopeless mess it all was when I heard the faint crackling noise from the direction I had just come. He was near. He wanted to kill me.

Buddy was about twenty yards away when I picked up the rock—as big as two fists. I crouched in the brush and held my body close to a tree.

I wanted him to get a few feet past the tree, then let him have it in the back of the head. But when he got even with the tree, he stopped. He was so close I could have touched him. His gun hung at his side. He glanced around and then took the decoration handkerchief from his breast pocket and began wiping his forehead and eyes.

He was looking into plain white when the rock smashed into his face . . . with my hand around it. Before he went down I let go with three more. I don't even know where it hit him, or if he was dead before he hit the ground; but when I knelt beside him to check, he was very dead.

A GUY IN A gray flannel suit, a little on the long side, walked into the Avenue Hotel on Michigan about two hours later. He registered as Stan Conway. The clerk wasn't surprised that he didn't have a bag—very few did—but he did eye the suit with some curiosity. The clientele of this fleabag rarely owned a suit, much less one with the pants and coat matching. I wasn't going to explain, so I left him to figure it out for himself and went up to my room.

The room was dingy, old, and depressing. The only bright feature was the pint I had just placed on the dresser. I took one long one to get my feet on the ground, then went through the pockets of my new suit. I pulled out the wallet. The driver's license described one Angelo Di Vico, born Oct. 11, 1925. Buddy was even younger than I thought. Still, he hadn't done bad. If money's the judge. He was carrying over two hundred bucks. Now I was.

In the inside breast pocket I found a little black book. *The* little black book. And from the amount of names inside, Buddy Di Vico was no slouch with the ladies. Thumbed through, not looking for anything in particular. Then I stopped. Gloria Tatum, Jade's. Imperial Hotel. Room 220. I looked at every name in the book, but Gloria's was the only one with Jade's under it. I thought of the blonde sitting with Carrito at the bar. She could have been working there that night. It was a hunch and maybe just the lead I was looking for.

I went down the hall to the phone, looked up the Imperial, and dialed the number. The desk clerk, or whoever answered, had kind of a fruity voice.

"Miss Tatum, please," I said.

"Miss Tatum isn't in yet." Sort of a singsongy voice. "Any message?"

"Miss Tatum still work at Jade's?"

"Yes, I believe so. May I ask who's calling?"

I told him that he may not, hung up, and went back to my room.

It was two-fifteen then. The bars close at two. If Gloria wasn't the type that frequented blind pigs, she should get home by two-thirty. I decided to give her an extra half hour, picked up the *Times* and looked for the crossword puzzle.

I filled in a few but got too tangled up in female sandpipers, Egyptian sun gods, and Latin prepositions. I decided to wait for a brighter mood, tore the puzzle out of the paper, and put it in a side pocket. I had been ignoring the pint.

At a quarter to three I checked Buddy's gun, combed my hair and was ready to go.

The corner to the left of the hotel entrance was pretty bright, so I waited there until I saw a cab and a cab saw me. At five to three I walked into an all-night drugstore next to the Imperial and ducked into a phone booth.

"Miss Tatum, please."

The same singsongy voice, but this time: "One moment, I'll connect you."

The phone rang exactly seven times. Finally she answered.

"Yeah?"

"Sorry to disturb you, Miss Tatum. This is the night clerk," I said. "There's a fr—"

"Why, Donald, baby, you're beginning to almost sound like a man."

I remembered the singsong, kicked myself, and boosted the pitch. "Er . . . thank you, Miss Tatum, but there's a friend of Mr. Carrito's here who insists he has an important message for him." It was a long shot.

"Marty isn't here yet," she answered. "Wait. Have you ever seen him before?"

"Oh yes, I think it's Mr. Di Vico."

"Buddy?" She seemed pleased. "Why didn't you say so. Send him up."

I entered the Imperial through the side entrance and went up the stairs without the night clerk spotting me. I did get a glance at him. Looked just like his voice.

Room 220 was three doors from the stairs. I knocked gently and tried to feel like a Buddy Di Vico.

"Just a sec, honey." From within.

As soon as the knob started to turn I pulled my gun, threw a shoulder, and was in the middle of the room before she knew what had happened. I covered her with the .32. It was a good thing because the black negligee was falling down on the job.

"Aren't you cold?"

"Brother, that's a new one." She wasn't the least bit flustered and made no attempt to cover up. "If it wasn't for the suit, I'd hardly recognize you, Buddy."

"I have a confession to make," I said, "that was me on the phone. I want to see your boyfriend pretty bad, so I thought I'd wait here."

"I've met funnier guys." She was turning on a bored look, but still didn't adjust her uniform.

"I'm not joking, Gloria. This is official business. You're looking right into the eyes of the grim reaper."

She didn't get it. "You wrestle?"

"Are you propositioning me?"

"Now you're getting funnier." She laughed, low, but at me, not with me. "You're in the wrong ballpark, sonny. You couldn't even tie Marty's shoelaces."

"I'll bet I could untie yours though."

We probably would have waltzed around a couple of more times, but two sharp raps on the door ended the bout.

I grabbed her by the wrist. "Open it, but act nice. No signs." I moved to the right of the door and flattened myself against the wall.

Gloria had been in the game much longer than I had. She opened the door without a word, but not more than three inches before she was telegraphing like hell with her eyes, with a faint nod in my direction. The door slammed. Pulled from the outside. With the bang of the door there was a louder noise. In fact, a few, but they all mixed together and sounded like one big bang. Something ripped through the door, and the lamp on the end table shattered. Gloria broke from the door, took a few steps and then jerked, clenched her fists tight to her sides and fell next to the lamp.

For a second it was quiet. In almost one motion I had the door open and was out in the hall expecting to see Carrito's back heading for the stairs. That's when I made my mistake.

I felt the hot, sharp pain between my shoulder blades the same time I heard the shot. I turned on my way down and opened up; I don't know how many times. Carrito was running down the hall, his back to me, and was almost at the end when I fired. I expected him to freeze and fall backward. Then I thought I had missed . . . until he crashed into the wall. He lay sprawled on his back and didn't move.

I was on my hands and knees. I tried to move my arms, but couldn't. I felt paralyzed and sick to my stomach. Then I don't know . . .

A GUY IN A white coat was looking down at me like he was trying to figure out what I was. Cops were all over the place, but mostly around me. I moved my hand up to my chest, underneath the blanket, and was surprised that I was stripped to the waist. An elderly man in a blue-gray suit bent over me.

"You've done us a favor, son, but I don't know if you've done yourself one. Want to tell me about it?"

I looked up at him. "It's a long story. How about later on?"

"Suit yourself, son." He turned to the white coat. "Get him in a talking mood as soon as you can, Doc." He yawned, walked away, and the policemen around him followed.

The doctor said, "The wagon will be here soon. Just lie still."

Next to him another guy was standing with my coat on his arm. For some reason I tagged him for a newspaperman. He waited until the doctor walked away and then said:

"You don't have too much to worry about. Self-defense written all over the place. By the way—this your coat?"

I nodded.

"You doing the puzzle?"

I nodded again.

"No wonder you couldn't get going. You had the first one across filled in wrong."

I heard him, but didn't pay much attention. Fine time to discuss crossword puzzles.

He was still talking. "I guess it was a natural mistake, though, with you. Must have had a lot on your mind."

Another guy, with a camera, came up to him then.

"Got 'em all, Jerry. That all?"

"Yeah, that's all. Hey, wait! Want to see something funny?" The reporter brought the crossword puzzle out of the pocket.

"See this guy is doing the puzzle, then he finds that he's stuck. Know why? Look at the first one, across. It's a one- two- three- . . . seven-letter word for corpse. You know what this guy has written in? CARRITO! The guy's a prophet!"

Charlie Martz

IN MESILLA IT WAS the hour of the siesta. The small square that marked the center of the adobe settlement was void of any sign of life. Only the glare of the bleaching southwestern sun danced about the dry fountain in the middle of the square, and against the crumbly, baked-sand walls of the adobe buildings fronting the square. The tall, sandstone Mission bordering the eastern end stood desolate and alone. Occasionally could be heard a faint, hollow clang as a hot wind swept though the arch of the Mission belfry to nudge the massive bell. The bark of a stray dog, the slam of a screen door—only these sounds broke the bright-glare stillness.

Across the square, directly opposite the Mission, stood the Exquisita, Mesilla's only saloon. Its adobe surface was the same bleak structure as the other buildings in the solitary row, except that above the wide doorway, and the width of the building, a supported tin-roof structure extended, awkwardly, eight or ten feet, providing the only shade on that side of the square.

A thick, untidy man wearing a collarless shirt and white apron lounged in the doorway of the saloon. His body was loose and relaxed, leaning against the doorframe, but his face bore a puzzled expression. His eyes were half-closed, squinting against the glare, in the general direction of the Mission. He was the first and only one to see the rider walking his horse slowly up the middle of the narrow street bordering the Mission.

As the rider reached the square, his horse balked slightly, but the rider urged the horse along at the same slow pace. The man in the doorway squinted harder, but there was no recognition on his face. He walked out the few paces to the end of the shade as the rider reached the rail in front of the saloon.

"Howdy, mister. You sure pick a hot time of day to come callin'. You come far? I see you must've come from Orogrande say . . . that's a killin' ride this time of day. Come on in and fresh up. I got a boy that'll take care of the sorrel."

The rider had only nodded his head in greeting. He dismounted stiffly, unbuckled his chaps, and threw them over the saddle horn before he looked up again. "Just have your boy give her some water. I'm not sure if I'm through ridin' or not. I know I'm ready to have a drink, though."

"Sure thing, mister. Hey, *niño*! *Aquí*!" He waited a few moments and was about to yell for the boy again, when the young Mexican came running around from the side of the building. The man in the apron said a few words in Spanish, then followed the rider through the doorway, eager to be of service, yet not sure what kind of man he was going to serve.

"Finest saloon in Mesilla."

"The only one, ain't it?"

"Well, yeah, but that don't make it not the finest. Just ask Smitty there." He beckoned to the sole customer in the saloon. A heavy, balding man in a tight, tan-bleached coat was standing in the middle of the bar. One hand was on the brim of a limp Panama lying on the bar, the other hand was reaching for a bottle in front of his empty glass. He eyed the stranger curiously, but answered the man in the apron.

"I cannot argue with you, Martin, when you are the only saloon within thirty miles." He spoke with a faint German accent. "Come over, my friend, and let me buy you a drink. Every day I have to look across the bar to Martin's homely face. A change will do me good."

"Set it up, mister. You got a taker," the rider said as he walked over.

The German studied him eagerly as he approached the bar. He saw a sun-scarred, dust-streaked face beneath the dirty, narrow-brimmed, white sombrero. The face was young, but at the same time old. Maybe just past thirty, but more likely closer to forty. A sandy-colored mustache drooped around the corners of his mouth. The middle part was stained slightly from tobacco juice. His arms hung limply, his left hand almost touching a holstered revolver that hung low on his left hip. As the rider came up to him, the German saw part of the butt of another revolver protruding from his open buckskin jacket. The second gun was under his right arm. Approaching the bar, his strides were long, slow, but noticeably stiff . . . he'd been riding for a good many hours.

"Friend," said the German extending the bottle, "you walk like you have been riding for a week straight. Come far?"

The rider shifted his position at the bar, facing the German more, but only poured another drink.

"If you have been riding far, from the east, like you came into town, then you must have come through Mescalero country. Word reached town the other day that some of the bucks jumped the reservation and got themselves up a little war party."

The German stopped and waited eagerly for the stranger to take up the conversation . . . but he had not even looked up from his drink.

"I don't blame you for wearing all those guns, friend. If I went riding through Apache country this time of year, which you can be sure I would not, I'd even get me a few more. Now, what did you say you—"

The rider slammed his glass down on the bar with a loud rap that made the German jump back with surprise.

"Mister, for all them questions you're asking you're going to have to pour a whoppin' lot more drinks down me to get all the answers."

The German relaxed visibly as he saw a slight smile under the rider's straggly mustache . . . then he smiled himself as he saw the rider's grin broaden.

"And I might just let you pour all you want," the rider finished.

The man in the white apron had been standing still just inside the doorway while the German had unsuccessfully tried to open the conversation. He had taken the rider's silence as a sign of hostility, so he had been more than reluctant to approach the two men and take the chance of getting in the way of an argument. Especially the kind he had seen so many times in front of the same bar. Now he hurriedly stepped around behind the bar to serve the two men. He let go with a hearty laugh, but it wasn't very convincing. His nervousness had not altogether subsided.

"Take another, gents . . . on the house. Seeing my patrons enjoying theirselves is worth a drink any old time." He filled the two thick glasses almost to the brim. The bartender was feeling more sure of himself now.

"And so's we won't be strangers drinking together . . . this old dude here is Adolph Schmidt. My name's Martin Huber. Mr. Schmidt meet Mr. . . ."

"Bill."

"Mr. Bill?"

"No," said the rider with the same faint smile, "just Bill."

"Kinda short, isn't it," said Schmidt, his curiosity returning.

"Smitty, it's long, short, or any way you want to look at it . . . but you ain't given me near enough likker yet. Bill I guess'll be good enough as long as I always come a runnin' when the cook yells it out."

"Smitty sure is curious about you, Bill," put in the bartender. "Bet he thought you was some gunny when you first come in, but I could tell right away that you was . . ."

"Look, Mister, you don't know who I am . . . you probably never will know. I could be Billy Bonnie's daddy and you'd never know one way t'other. Now if I was a gunny like you say, you'd be sure using an unhealthy way to find out. What you say we just all stick to our own business?"

"Don't mind Martin or me, we're just kind of starved for knowing what goes on outside the Territory. Like I said before, we heard about the 'Paches jumping reservation, but haven't heard what's happened since. Charlie Martz was in—"

"Charlie Martz!" The rider stiffened and almost shouted the name, but relaxed immediately, as if to hide his excitement. "You mean to tell me old Charlie holes out around here! Well, I'll be go to hell!"

The German again eyes him with interest. "You a friend of Charlie's?"

"Hell, Charlie and me are real old friends. Known each other since about '71. Why he's one of the reasons I'm around this part of the country. Found out he was in the south part of the Territory, but didn't know where for sure. Hell, old Charlie . . . what's he doin' now anyway?"

Martin broke in before the German could answer. "Charlie Martz is the law around here, Bill. He lives up to Doña Ana, but you never find him home. Most time he's up in the hills huntin' or fishin' or somethin', but he comes—"

"Charlie Martz is the law! You don't tell me." The rider smiled broadly.

"He comes in quite regular lately," Martin went on, "about once or twice a week for the past month. He does enough movin' around, but he sure don't do much tendin' to the law. Bet the folks up to Doña Ana get rid of him pretty soon."

"I'm afraid Martin is no respecter of age. Charlie is getting along in years and doesn't have all the enthusiasm that Martin has. He doesn't have all the worthless talk either."

"What do you mean, worthless—"

"Never mind what it's worth," interrupted the rider. He looked back to the German. "I've come a long way to see Charlie. Think you can tell me where he'd be about this time?"

"My friend, you are in luck. I can tell you exactly where he is. As a matter of fact, he is coming to my place sometime this afternoon. If you'd care to accompany me home I'll present you to Charlie in the flesh."

"Smitty here's makin' over a gun for Charlie," Martin put in eagerly.

"Makin' over a gun?"

"If you please, Martin," said the German with a show of dignity. "Most of my life I worked as a gunsmith . . . in the east . . . now I have a few cattle, very few, and some crops I raise. Just enough for Flora and me to get along on, and maybe a little more. But my first love is still guns. It is a pleasant pastime, and I take great pleasure in my work. Just ask anyone if my work is not the best."

"What's Charlie want with a new hawg leg?" the rider asked with more than a little interest.

"Must want it just for huntin', as far as I can see," drawled Martin. "He sure don't do no work. Like I said, the folks up to Doña Ana are goin' to have his job if he don't do a little sheriffin' once in a while. I bet he ain't throwed down on a wanted man in three, four years."

"Ach, Martin, you talk and talk and talk!" The German turned from the bartender disgustedly. "Come, Bill, it is time we go . . . thank God!"

The two men walked their horses across the square in the direction from whence the stranger had come. They passed down the street bordering the Mission, then turned right abruptly as they reached the open plain, urging their horses to a trot. In the distance could be seen the alkali flats. The heat still clung forcefully to the bleak, dry land. Both riders pulled their brims down closer to their eyes to afford as much protection as possible from the glare.

"It is only three miles and a half to my place. There I know it will be cooler. We have a stream close by, dry only a month or so of the year. The stream starts up in the peaks of the Tularosas and then slowly . . ."

For the last few seconds the stranger had been looking back over his shoulder toward the town they had just left. The Mission bell tower could still be seen, just over a slight rise in the ground behind them. The rider turned to the German. The faint smile was on his mouth again.

"Charlie ever go to that church back there?"

"I think . . . yes, I am sure he has. I have seen him go in more than once. But what he does inside is something I do not know." The German chuckled at his own attempt at humor. "But why do you ask?"

"Well, Smitty, I just thought it would be right nice if old Charlie was familiar with the church he's goin' to be laid out in."

"Ach, Charlie is not that old. He has many good years ahead of him. Charlie will not lie in state for a good while yet."

"Mister, if you call tomorrow a good while yet, then you'll be right." The rider no longer wore the smile. He unconsciously shifted the position of the gun and holster under his arm and stared hard at the German. Not a muscle in his face moved.

Adolph Schmidt knew at once that it was not a joke. Still, he tried to smile. Tried to laugh. Better to let the rider believe he thought it a joke. But his pretense collapsed. His companion's eyes were too cold. This was not the atmosphere for laughter.

"What are you goin' to do about it, Smitty?"

"You ask me what am I going to do, and I don't even know what I'm supposed to do about what?"

"You *sabe* English, Dutchman. Don't play dumb. I'm goin' to throw down on our old pal Charlie Martz and old Charlie's goin' to drop dead right at your big feet." The rider seemed to relax slightly. "No reason why I shouldn't tell you now, seein' as you're goin' to be there anyhow. I got no fight with you, Smitty, long as you act well brought-up and don't do nothin' dumb. I've had my picture in the Express Office too many times to waste words on you if you do somethin' dumb . . . like reachin' for one of your hobbies."

The German looked at him, bewildered. "But you said that Charlie was an old friend; that you used to know him years—"

"I knew him years ago, but I only met him one time. That was about thirteen years ago up in Colorado. Durango. Sure was sleepin' that day. I come backin' out of the Wells-Fargo Office with an armload of dust bags, and I back right into Charlie's shotgun. Charlie was right pleasant takin' me to Canon City, but the ten years I had to squat there wasn't so pleasant. Yep, Charlie sticks a shotgun in my back one fine day and I lose ten years of my life. Well, I'm goin' to stick my Colt in Charlie's middle this fine day and he's goin' to lose ten years of his life."

"Ten years?"

"Yeah, I figure Charlie ain't got much more'n ten years to go anyway. Too bad I didn't find him sooner . . . taken me almost three years." The rider looked up suddenly and saw that they were only a short distance from a small cluster of farm buildings. The house was neat, clean-looking, freshly whitewashed; but the outlying buildings were in a state of dilapidation.

"Looks like you spend most of your time in the house, Smitty." The rider spoke cheerfully. "Let's you and me take the horses around back right away. But leave them close together 'cause yours is comin' with me as soon as Charlie says good night."

Flora Schmidt greeted the two men with a warm smile. It wasn't often that Adolph brought visitors home. She was hurriedly beginning to plan in her mind a nice supper when the two men reached the porch. Her smile faded abruptly. Adolph acted as if he was walking with a ghost.

"Go in the house, Flora."

The woman turned and went into the house immediately; both men right behind her.

"That's no way to talk to a lady, Smitty, even if she is your wife." The rider swept his sombrero off in the imitation of a gallant gesture. "Ma'am, the pleasure of this meetin' is all mine. My name is Billy Bushway, ridin' out here on a very important mission." The rider laughed hard, without restraint, and slapped his sombrero across his thigh. "Ain't that right, Smitty?"

The German had jumped when he heard the rider's name. "Flora, this man is wanted by the law. He has come to kill Charlie Martz."

Inaudibly the woman said something that turned into a low moan. She sat down slowly in a rocker as if to brace herself for what was to come.

The man called Bushway was all nonchalance. He sat on the edge of the table watching the couple. He was taking a great pleasure in their anguish, knowing that they both were trying to conceive a way to help Charlie Martz. Maybe a shout of warning . . . maybe a gun.

"Say, Smitty, where's that hawg leg you're fashionin' for Charlie?"

The German turned without answering and started to leave the room through the door leading toward the back of the house.

"Hold it! I don't want you to come walkin' out holdin' it in the wrong direction. We go out together, huh?"

Bushway held a short-barrel Colt .45 in his left hand when they returned. His fingers curved around the bone handle of the revolver in a way that showed they were more than accustomed to this position. "This is a fine gun, Smitty; only thing wrong, you ought to file the front sight down, almost off. Makes for liftin' it out of the holster easier. But then Charlie's only goin' to be drawin' once more in his natural life, so it probably won't make no difference."

He studied the gun intently, then looked up suddenly. "I just got a fine idea, Smitty. Why don't I shoot Charlie with his own gun?" The idea broadened the smile beneath his stained mustache. "It's only fittin' that a fine gun like this gets a successful start. It would be a failure"—he chuckled—"if Charlie was to go and use it first."

Bushway was sitting at the table putting the last one of five cartridges into the pistol when they heard the horse approaching. The gunman pushed the cylinder back in place so that the hammer fell on the empty chamber. He warned the couple again that if they interfered, they were as good as dead, then took a position against the wall next to the front door. When it opened he would be behind the door. To the German he said, "Don't open it yourself, just tell him to come in." He nodded toward the table. "You two sit over there on the other side and be quiet as little gophers."

Charlie Martz hobbled into the room stiffly, rubbing his backside with both hands. "Boy, have I been riding! Too far for these old bones." He stopped abruptly and stared at the couple. "What's the matter with you two? I ain't no rattler." He realized then that they were not looking at him.

"Hello, Charlie. You got your back to it this time."

"Bushway!" Charlie Martz still faced the old couple. "I only seen you once, Billy, but that voice of yours has stuck with me." The lawman turned to face the outlaw.

"Come to settle an old score, eh, Billy? Well, at least it don't surprise me. Kind of a natural undertaking with boys like you.

The lawman's eyes smiled beneath the stiff brim of a sweat-stained sombrero. A full, drooping mustache—the fashion of the day—similar to the gunman's, graced his upper lip. But Charlie's was pure white and well trimmed. He stood before Bushway tall, very thin, and just a little tired-looking. His pistol was on the left hip, but well toward the front with the butt facing forward.

As he spoke, Charlie was lifting his left hand slowly, an inch at a time, toward the gun.

"Tryin to throw me off, ain't you, Charlie? You're movin' the wrong hand. You don't sling your iron in that backward cradle so's you can draw with your left." Both men smiled, but Bushway's was the broader.

"You'll get your chance, Charlie, but I'm goin' to call the turn." He beckoned to the German. "Lift his gun, Smitty, and put mine in his holster in its stead. Then you and the little woman get over to the side there where them pans are hangin'."

He had not taken his eyes off the lawman. "When you're set, Charlie, back over to the other side of the room right across the table from me . . . and for the time bein' I'll thank you to keep your hands even with your hat."

The gunman holstered the new pistol, but kept his left arm limp at his side. "Case you don't know it, you're goin' to get shot dead by your own gun—the same one that brought you here this afternoon. You got mine and I got yours, and as soon as we get a signal . . . let's see . . . I got it!"

His eyes shifted to the woman for a split second. "Florie, you fetch that big spoon from the table, and whenever the fancy strikes you, you bang it agin' that dish pail hangin' behind your head. Get it. Charlie . . . when you hear the gong—go for your gun."

Charlie Martz lowered his hands slowly until they were hanging at his sides. He swallowed hard, but there was no fear in his eyes. He had never run out on a showdown before. And he couldn't now if he wanted to. He knew that. One step in any direction and he'd be cut down in a second.

"Guess you got me, Billy. When I woke up this morning I never thought this would be the day. How about lettin' me say a few words to the Schmidts before the gun goes off?"

"Old-timer, you're goin' to have me cryin' in a minute." The gunman was cold now, with no trace of a smile. "You just keep your lips tight and tend to your business." He shouted to Mrs. Schmidt, irritably, "Come on, woman, give the signal!"

Mrs. Schmidt held the long-handled spoon as if it were an object of evil. She bit her lower lip, not making a sound, but her eyes pleaded in the direction of the gunman. Bushway was about to yell at her again when she closed her eyes and, with a shudder, swung the spoon behind her with all her might.

The sharp CLANG of the dishpan vibrated no more than a second before the room was filled with the explosive bark of a Colt . . . a split second . . . then the same crashing short bark as a Colt jerked fire from its barrel.

The dishpan lying on the floor gave a sharp, hollow ring, stopped. And then quiet.

Billy Bushway held the pistol in front of him at arm's length. He still stared across as he brought the gun onto the table . . . then he stumbled backward a few steps, jolted against the wall, and slid down slowly until he was in the sitting position. His eyes were wide open, unblinking, staring across the table, still. Then his hand dropped forward and his chin rested against his chest without moving.

"Charlie, you did it! You did it! You outgunned him!" Schmidt jumped around excitedly and then over to the fallen gunman. He touched the still outlaw lightly on the shoulder. The crouched figure slid slowly across the lower wall and sprawled on the floor.

"He's dead as a stone, Charlie. You got him clean through the chest, twice."

Charlie Martz had only then relaxed his position. He holstered the pistol and made his way around the table.

Siesta in Paloverde

IF YOU'D HAVE ASKED all of the boys in the Four Aces that afternoon if they had a feeling something out of the ordinary was going to happen, you'd probably have gotten some pretty sour replies with a few colorful oaths thrown in. But all the answers, regardless of the tone, would have added up to one thing: Paloverde was a hot, dusty, adobe cow-town with one saloon and a reputation for being the deadest community in southern New Mexico Territory; and that day it was even hotter, dustier, and deader than usual. And even if it was the Fourth of July, what the hell could ever happen in Paloverde!

Four cowhands from the Spanish Hat sat at a table and went through the motions of seven-card stud. Nobody had his heart in the game, because most of the time a Spanish Hat rider wouldn't have enough money to affect his heart one way or the other anyway. But they sat around with their hats back, not saying much, nursing a bottle of yellowish-looking liquid called *mescal*. They only had money between them for one more bottle, so they drank slowly, making it last. It was a long day.

Count Rudolph Von Bock leaned against the bar with a thumb crooked around a suspender strap and a scuffed boot perched on the brass floor rail. He lifted his glass of beer as Mickey Tigh passed the bar rag along the shiny, wet surface in front of him. And when he raised the glass to his round, rosy, beard-stubbled face, his elbow poked out of a hole in the red-flannel underwear sleeve. Count Rudolph Von Bock wasn't the most prosperous citizen of Paloverde, but he easily drank more beer than anyone else, and he paid cash, so Mickey Tigh, at least, was always glad to see him. The Count's town attire was his undershirt, with usually a couple of buttons missing, a frayed Panama hat that alone would make the Count stand out in a crowd, without his other eccentricities. All the boys laughed at and with the Count, and thought maybe he was just a little loco . . . even if he was the best, and only, gunsmith in Paloverde. One thing for sure, he was the only Count in New Mexico. All you had to do was ask him. But that's another story.

Mickey Tigh pulled his big belly from the mahogany edge and dragged the rag down the length of the bar toward the front of the saloon, and looked out the window. Mickey, fat and fifty, didn't particularly care if there was anything to do or not. On quiet days people drank more.

It was glaring hot outside, and still. The stillness seemed to make it all the hotter. He turned back to the contrasting dimness of the barroom and almost commented on the weather. But they had been all through that before. The heat and boredom of Paloverde had been described six different ways in the past two hours. It was just one of those depressing, hollow afternoons when you'd even look forward to the bark of a stray dog, or a screen door slamming.

And then Charlie Martz walked in, and things began to happen.

Charlie had one thing on his easygoing mind and that thing was ice-cold beer. After a dusty ride like the one from the county seat at Cruces, the first stop was always Mickey Tigh's Four Aces. This even took precedence over any law enforcing that had to be done. And as Charlie Martz, sheriff of Doña Ana County, seldom had any enforcing to do, it didn't matter if he did like an occasional beer at Mickey Tigh's. The only trouble was, Charlie knew he'd always be in for an argument if there were any Spanish Hat riders about, which was practically every time he came in.

The Count and Mickey Tigh were two of the few men in town who didn't underrate Charlie Martz. And that was because they were old-timers and knew him when. They allowed that a man was entitled to take it easy after working hard as a civil servant for more than thirty years.

The Spanish Hat boys saw only a tired old man with a droopy mustache, who wore his gun far too high to be any good with it, and who had been sheriff of Doña Ana County for going on ten years without making more than a dozen arrests a year. And those were mostly picking up drunks. The Count and Mickey tried to tell them about Charlie's younger days in Tucson and Prescott, but the Spanish Hat boys mostly believed what they saw. If he was so all-fired good, how come he never threw-down on any wanted outlaws? These same boys had never in their lives seen an outlaw in Paloverde, but that didn't stop them from asking the same question over and over. Charlie was just right to poke fun at . . . and there he was again!

Vance Roman usually started the Charlie-baiting. Hell, he was twenty-seven! Been punching cows for a dozen years. Had to lead off because the other boys were just stretching out of their teens. Cocky, but still a little wobbly when it came to razzing an old-timer. But that Vance knew how to start things off!

"Hey, Charlie," Vance yelled across the room. "Round up any *bandidos* on your ride down?" That really brought a laugh from the boys.

Charlie usually ignored the cowhands the first couple of rounds. He'd wait until he felt the relaxing effects of a few schooners of beer, then he'd let go. This day, he looked a little more tired than usual when he propped his elbows on the bar next to the Count's.

From the Spanish Hat table a few more remarks floated over. Vance was getting wound up. But they passed right by Charlie's head. It was still too early.

"Charlie, don't pay no attention to those kiddies," the Count consoled.

"Hell, I don't really mind those youngsters, but one of these days I'm going to surprise 'em and run the whole bunch in, just on general principles," he grumbled. He had thought of it before, but with no jail in Paloverde, it would be a helluva lot of work to drag those waddies up to the calaboose in Cruces just for a general principle.

"Maybe they'll grow up someday and I won't have to bother," he thought aloud. "Boy, this is good beer!" he said, smacking his lips. Charlie forgot things very quickly.

The Spanish Hat representatives went back to their seven-card game, not being able to get a rise out of Charlie.

The Count was toying with his schooner halfway up to his face, sloshing the half glass of beer around, trying to develop a head. Suddenly he banged the schooner down on the bar, some of the beer slopping over the rim of the glass.

"Hell, Charlie, I almost forgot the reason I came here! Sort of a secondary reason though, to be honest. I got your gun." He stretched his body over the bar to look at Mickey Tigh down by the front window. "Hey, Mickey! Where's the gun?"

The fat man waddled up slowly on the squeaky duckboards, and stooped with a grunt a few feet from the two men. "Got it right here, genius. You did a nice job on it." He held the pistol with a light, awkward grip, eyeing it suspiciously as if it were alive.

"Give it here, Fatso, before you faint dead away," the Count said with a very straight face. That meant he was being funny. "You see that, Charlie? Mickey still ain't sure which end the lead comes out."

Charlie winked at the New Mexico nobleman. "Count, you got to remember that Mickey here is a clean liver and don't have no truck with the sources of evil . . . outside of this drinking hell he runs. Here, let me heft it," he said, reaching for the gun.

"How she look to you, Charlie?" the Count asked with a pleased smile on his face. He hadn't had a complaint against his gunsmithing yet and wasn't expecting any.

Charlie balanced the heavy Colt .44 in his hand deftly. His tan, freckled fingers curled around the ebony gun-butt as he spun the cylinder.

"The old iron looks like new, Rudy. I wouldn't have known it. You know I had in mind to chuck it, when I remembered how you make over old irons. Yes, sir, I think this is just fine." Charlie inspected the revolver with a broad smile on his face. "Just fine and dandy."

"Glad you like it, Charlie," the Count said. "Only I ain't finished yet. Just brought it in to show you the external ornamentation, you might say."

"*You* might say," Mickey Tigh put in. "But we wouldn't."

The Count shot Mickey a quick glance. "Just stick to your beer drawing, Fat Boy." He returned to Charlie. "As I was saying, the finish is finished, and the bullets fit the cylinder as you probably noticed. There are five in there now and the hammer's on the empty chamber. Only trouble is when you squeeze the trigger, the cylinder moves around too far and the hammer falls in between the chambers and jams. Doesn't do the hammer any good either. It's getting all bent out of shape with my testing it to fall right. Yep, it looks fine, but the way it is, it ain't worth a tiddly-do."

"You don't tell me! Well, I'll be damned!" Charlie was more disappointed than surprised.

"Oh, I'll fix it, Charlie. Like I said, I just wanted you to see how far along with it I am."

Charlie looked at the shiny pistol sadly, reluctant to give it back to the Count. "Rudy, what you say I just hold on to it awhile and kind of get the feel of it? Been a long time since I used this girl." Charlie was a little boy with a new toy. He wasn't very subtle about it either.

"Sure, Charlie. It's your gun," the Count answered.

The Doña Ana sheriff lifted the pistol he was carrying from the worn leather holster and handed it to Mickey Tigh. "Here, put this one behind the bar, Mick, and I'll get it when I go." He slipped the renovated Colt into the holster and patted it lightly. "Feels good."

"Want another beer, Charlie?" said the bartender.

"Don't mind if I do, Mick," Charlie answered him, shaking his head. "That's a killin' ride from Cruces."

The Count glanced over his shoulder just then and gave Charlie a poke with his elbow. "Look out, Charlie, here comes that rough rider, Vance Roman."

A few heavy, high-heeled footsteps, accompanied by the jingle of Mexican spurs, and Vance Roman was at the bar.

"What you got there, Charlie? Looks like new iron. Let's have a look."

Before the sheriff could prepare for anything, Vance Roman jerked the Colt from Charlie's holster with a howl of laughter and pointed it in his face.

"What are you doing with one of these, old-timer? They shoot real bullets, you know!" Vance threw his head back and howled again, and then waved the Colt in the direction of his *compadres*. "Hey, boys! Look what Charlie's got! Think we ought to tell him what it is?"

Charlie made a wild grab for it over Vance's head, but the cowboy jerked it out of his reach. "Give me my gun, you crazy kid!" Charlie was dead serious.

Vance wore his usual silly, superior grin. He held the pistol high over his head and held Charlie away at arm's length. "Aw, does the sheriff want his gun? Well, let's see him try and get it! Hey, Sid, catch!" He glanced over to the table and tossed the pistol in the general direction.

One of the cowpunchers scrambled out of his chair and caught the pistol on the fly.

"How you like it, Sid?" Vance yelled over, still laughing.

Sid examined the gun with a big grin on his hollow-cheeked face. "This here's a big gun for such a little man. Hey, lookie here, Vance! There's three, no four notches on the butt! How you suppose they got there?"

"Probably slipped out of his hand while he was rabbit huntin' and got scratched on a rock," Vance yelled back.

"All right, that's enough," Charlie said quietly. He pushed Vance aside and walked over toward Sid, slowly.

"You're gettin' kind of uppity, ain't you, Sid, for a green kid who ain't even shaved his whiskers yet? Give it here."

Sid held the gun away from the sheriff, ready to throw it back to Vance.

"Come on, son. Hand it over." Charlie spoke very softly.

"Don't let the old coot buffalo you, Sid. Heave it back," Vance said excitedly.

And that was the timely encouragement that Sid needed. He grinned again. "Here you go, Vance!" He feinted a toss over Charlie's head, bent quickly and scooted the gun between the sheriff's legs across the board floor to Vance.

Charlie Martz's thin shoulders sagged to match the tired look on his face as he turned to face the cowboy bully. His mustache seemed to droop even lower.

"Look here, Vance. I ain't playing with you. Hand over that iron or you'll find out fast how I get notches on the butt. The fifth one's liable to have your name on it."

Vance just grinned. "You threatenin' me, Charlie. Why I thought—"

"Shut your mouth, Vance!" Charlie's face was full of fire. He'd never been madder in his life. "Looks like I'm going to have to paint you a little picture, Vance. Though it's something I've never enjoyed talking about a whole lot." He pointed to the gun in the cowboy's hand.

"See that first notch? Well, that represents Wyn Scallon. He held up the Butterfield Stage Line seventeen times. Seventeen times successfully. Then I caught up with him in the Blue Bell in Prescott. I only shot once, Vance, and Wyn Scallon never robbed another stage. The second one's Billy Bushway. He went loco from too much bad whisky in a saloon down in Wittenburg. I forget which one it was. Anyway, he shot five unsuspecting customers dead before the rest could get out into the street to safety. He turned around from shooting bottles off the bar when I walked in. He turned around, Vance, so I could plug him between the eyes. The third one belongs to Kurt Masselon. I know you heard of him. He was the fastest gun in West Texas . . . only he came too far west and he wasn't the fastest no more. At least he wasn't the day outside of Red Healy's livery stable in Tombstone. I shot three times before old Kurt dropped. He was tough." Charlie lowered his voice slightly. "Course, toughness don't mean a damn thing on Boot Hill."

"That fourth one belongs to Reb Spadea—"

A shrill peal of laughter broke from the front of the bar. Charlie wheeled around with the rest of the Four Aces' customers to see the tall, dust-caked rider standing in the doorway. His thumbs were hooked behind two, low-slung gun belts that crossed below his waist and tapered around thin, straight hips. Two revolvers, butts forward, rested loosely in holsters attached to his thighs at the lower ends with rawhide ties. His knee-high boots were almost white from alkali dust.

He wore a sweat-stained sombrero that had a silver concha band, and his lips formed a smile that turned them down at one corner.

"Charlie, you trying to sell these boys a big bill of goods? The first part sounded all right. Could have happened. But I thought I'd better stop you before you found yourself in a fish story. I'm just gettin' at how come you decorate your gun with a notch when that notch is standing right in front of you?" The stranger bellowed with laughter. "Don't you know me, Charlie?"

The rider's spurs chinged in rhythm to his heavy stride as he took a few steps to the bar and leaned his elbow on the edge. Mickey Tigh shuffled down to him to be of service, but the rider waved him away.

"This is strictly business," he said, without taking his eyes from Charlie. "Maybe one later." He pushed his hat back from his forehead and leered at the sheriff.

Charlie blanched and lurched a half step forward.

"I come in at the wrong time, Charlie? Did I wreck your yarn?" The corner of the gunman's mouth drooped even farther and he shot a glance at Vance Roman holding the sheriff's pistol.

"You pointin' that at me, son?"

"No, sir," Vance stammered. "This is Charlie's. I was only lookin' at it."

The gunman had an amused smile on his face. "Oh, that the gun Charlie shot all those outlaws with? Say, I'd like to take a look-see at such a famous iron as that. I'm especially interested if it's the one Charlie used on Reb Spadea."

He walked up to Vance slowly, swaggering with the confidence of two heavy pistols on his hips, and took the Colt out of his extended hand. There wasn't any sign of resistance from the cowboy. He inspected the gun carefully, spinning the cylinder, and then looked up at Charlie.

"This the one you got Reb with, eh?"

"You know that as well as I do, Reb. You were on the receiving end!" The sheriff spoke with just the slightest nervous edge to his tone, but if nervousness was there his face showed no sign of it. "I thought you were up to Fort Harrison for good, Reb?"

"Can't keep a good man down, Charlie. About three months ago I got kinda sick of choppin' rocks and seein' blue coats every place I looked, so I decided to hit out and look up my old *compadre,* Charlie Martz—the one who bought my ticket to Harrison." Reb still wore the sneering smile on his lips, but there was no gleam in his eyes. They were lifeless. Dead serious. "After ten years of lookin' at stone walls, you'd get a little tired, too, wouldn't you Charlie?"

"Been ten years already, Reb? Yeah, I guess it has," Charlie reflected. "It was in '78 when we got you."

"When *you* got me, Charlie. I ain't about to forget those ten years, and that piece of lead in my side—and I still don't think you deserve a notch on your gun for a wound. Big or little.

"Well, that all depends on how you figure your scoring. I figured catching a man of your reputation deserved a notch . . . whether you were underground or just in the calaboose. Don't forget, you were supposed to be in there for good," Charlie argued.

Reb Spadea was silent for a moment.

"I just got an idea, Charlie. And it's in keepin' with why I'm here. I just figured out how we can make that a legitimate notch. Long as you don't care in particular whose name it belongs to."

"What you pushin' at, Reb?" Charlie asked. It would be a lot better if the outlaw just spoke out plain. Charlie didn't trust him, but with the distrust, there was still curiosity.

"Well, Charlie, to be perfectly frank with you, I came here to kill you." Reb Spadea was just stating a simple fact. Nothing to get excited about.

But there was a natural commotion in the Four Aces when this was announced. No one moved too deliberately. Actually, it was like the room being filled with one long gasp. Charlie, the Count, and Mickey Tigh stood perfectly still. Vance Roman edged innocently over to the safety-in-numbers circle of Spanish Hat riders. Although at that time this group looked something a bit less than formidable. Sid, especially, looked as if any minute his knees would buckle and he'd faint dead away. Vance Roman's mouth hung open as he watched the outlaw with wide eyes of disbelief. He couldn't believe here was the notorious Reb Spadea.

The outlaw was visibly pleased with the shocked expressions. It was no little satisfaction to him to be able to walk into a saloon and with just a few casual words turn everyone's blood to ice water. Reb Spadea would liked to have just stood back for a while longer and watch the faces filled with fear and awe staring at him: but there was business at hand to be taken care of *pronto.* There was no sense in hanging around too long. No one's luck lasts forever.

"Here's how it is, Charlie. It's very simple. You want to make that notch good and I want to take a shot at you. So we'll draw ag'in each other; only I'll use your gun and you can use one of mine. That way I'll get you and your gun will get a notch."

The Count started to say something, but cut the word off before it was all the way out when Charlie shot a glance at him. The sheriff's face was impassive, but to the Count it told a story.

"Looks like you're leading the band, Reb," the sheriff drawled. "So I can't very well contradict you. Only I would rather use my own iron."

The Count's eyes almost popped out of his head. In his excitement he fumbled around for words of objection, but the outlaw cut him off before he could say a word. Reb had made up his mind how it was going to be, and nobody was going to change it.

"I told you how we're goin' to play it, Charlie, so ain't no use of you thinkin' of something else," Reb stated. "Besides, how we goin' to make that notch good if you're usin' the gun?" He chuckled.

"It was just a thought."

"Well, get those thoughts out of your head and start thinkin' what you're goin' to do with this," the outlaw said, drawing a pistol and handing it to the sheriff. He slipped Charlie's Colt into the empty holster and stepped back two feet. "Watch you don't shoot yourself in the foot now. That's got a hone-trigger on it. 'Course, that's if you last long enough to get your hand around the butt. I don't figure you will." Reb was speaking for the benefit of the crowd. They'd have a better story to tell their children if he flavored it up a little bit. Reb was dead set on making a legend out of himself—no matter what it cost.

"And we'll stand pretty close, Charlie. I figure your eyes ain't what they used to be." That ought to give them something to talk about!

The sheriff and the outlaw stood no more than four feet apart. Spadea wore a broad, confident smile. His feet braced and his arms hanging limply. He'd done this before. More than once. Charlie looked a little nervous, but around the eyes there was an expression of a kind that might have been considered amusement. Reb was too full of his own confidence to notice it.

Reb crooked a thumb on his gun belt. "You can commence anytime you want, Charlie."

And Charlie commenced while the words were still fresh on Reb's lips.

Throughout the border country you're likely to hear the story a hundred different ways, but they all agree on one thing—the main thing. Both men jerked their guns at the same split second. Maybe Reb was a shade ahead, but when the guns came up, Charlie came out of his crouch, leaped at the gunman, and smashed his Colt across the outlaw's face. One story states that the gun crashed against a face that wore a very surprised look.

Reb Spadea sagged to the floor. The force of the blow knocked him backward a step, and he went down full on his back and lay still. His outstretched hand still clutched the Colt.

Charlie stepped over to the sprawled form and with the toe of his boot pried the pistol from the outlaw's hand. He glanced at the Count and then kicked the revolver in his direction.

"Here you are, Rudy. I don't guess I do deserve that notch."

But if four cowhands from the Spanish Hat spread had not been too dumbfounded at that moment to speak, Charlie Martz might have gotten quite an argument.

Time of Terror

ALMOST NOTHING WAS KNOWN of the Chinese-Malay girl Ah Min before the murder of Police Officer Harold Crowley. The day she was brought in, a number of soldiers from a Suffolk regiment identified her by name. A year ago, they said, she had been working in a Kuala Lumpur dance hall; and they remembered her because in all of K.L. they'd never known a girl who looked so inviting, yet acted so believably innocent. They claimed to have seen her frequently at that time; but aside from her name, they knew nothing about her.

With the Crowley incident Ah Min was rediscovered. This time in a Communist jungle camp—technically, a camp of the Thirteenth Regiment, Malayan Races Liberation Army—ten miles north of the village of Ladang.

According to the news item in the *Singapore Straits Times*, Crowley's jeep, with three Malays from his police jungle squad aboard, was ambushed on the main tarmac highway not far from their Ladang post. A grenade stopped the jeep as they scrambled for cover, Sten guns opened up from the secondary jungle growth close to the road. Crowley and his three Malays were killed instantly.

Within the hour a company from the Suffolk regiment was on the trail of the terrorists. The *Straits Times* account called it pure luck that they were able to locate the jungle camp late the same afternoon. That may be. At any rate, a brief skirmish took place; no one on either side was hit; the terrorists melted into the jungle, safe from effective pursuit with night closing in. And only the Chinese-Malay girl was found in one of the attap huts.

For two full days Ah Min was questioned by Military Intelligence. It can be said that she was treated exceptionally well during this period. Perhaps because she did look rather forlorn and helpless, sitting quietly in her khaki shirt and trousers—faded and torn and several sizes too large for her—answering politely, never complaining of the long hours of repetitious questions.

Where were her father and mother? Both dead. Closest relative? A widowed aunt living in Ladang. But Ah Min lived in K.L.? Only to be able to work to support her aunt. Was she a member of the Malayan Communist Party? No. Even though she was found in a Communist camp?

Ah Min answered that a man she had met in K.L., a Chinese of apparent means, had asked her to come care for his children as an *amah*. She consented, went with him and soon found herself in the jungle camp, closely guarded. Was the man who had deceived her the leader? She thought he was.

So she was shown a photograph of Tam Lee, the most wanted terrorist operating in the Ladang area. Was this the man? Ah Min nodded. Though it must be an old photograph, she said. Tam Lee was much thinner now and he seldom smiled. Intelligence seemed pleased with this.

Finally they gave her back to District Police with a somewhat vague recommendation. The girl hadn't been armed when she was taken, so they couldn't very well execute her. She could be placed in a detention camp. However the poor girl was cooperative enough. She seemed the sort who'd been kicked around and taken advantage of all her life. Perhaps it was time someone treated her decently. Which could mean simply letting her go free. Still, it wouldn't do to take unnecessary chances.

So Ah Min was sent to the Communist rehabilitation school at Taiping. The School of Great Peace and Tranquility.

During the morning at Taiping, beginning the second week, Ah Min attended required courses. One explained the necessity for resettlement as long as the terrorists relied on the villages for their subsistence. Another stressed the need for Malay and Chinese to live together in an atmosphere of mutual respect and understanding. Still another course dealt briefly with the responsibilities Malaya would soon face as an independent nation. Ah Min's eyes would remain on the instructor, but her thoughts were elsewhere.

Most frequently she relived the six months in the jungle with Tam Lee. The camp had been comfortable, fairly large for being so close to a village, and there had always been enough to eat. The idle times had been the best, when they simply rested or talked or planned ambushes, and when there were no pamphlets to read. The Malayan Communist Party was forever providing dull, political-sounding literature.

There were other girls in the camp, most of them married and happy to be with their husbands. Ah Min was certain Tam planned to marry her. Why else would he want her near instead of working for him in K.L.? He enjoyed her company, she knew. And he respected her ability to plan. A number of times, setting up ambushes, he had acted on her quietly offered suggestions. The way they stopped Harold Crowley's jeep, for example, had been Ah Min's idea.

She could picture it clearly, seeing Tam Lee step out to the road as the jeep approached. He had clutched the grenade to his stomach, bent almost double, dragging his feet and waving feebly as if for help. And as the jeep came to a stop, she saw him lob the grenade underhanded onto the flat hood of the vehicle and dive for the side of the road. There was the explosion and the men struggling to free themselves.

Ah Min could feel the Sten gun in her hands again, the frame stock pressed against her side. She rose with the others and fired point-blank at the jeep, keeping the trigger squeezed, feeling the vibration and hearing the exhilarating clattering sound of the automatic weapons on both sides of her.

The rest was not worth remembering.

In the afternoon—every afternoon while she was at Taiping—Ah Min studied shorthand and typing. This course, an elective, was not taken simply to pass the time. Already a plan was forming in her mind: a way to aid Tam Lee that could be exceptionally interesting, yet required only a normal amount of luck to put into practice. And if it failed she would simply rejoin Tam Lee in the jungle.

Each evening she read the *Straits Times* for news of Ladang. This was the sixth year of the Emergency in Malaya and now only major terrorist incidents were considered newsworthy. Still, at least once every two weeks there was mention of Tam Lee. He now had 15,000 Straits dollars on his head and his organization was fast gaining notoriety as the Ladang Gang.

During the early part of March the gang ambushed two lorries of special constables, killing six men, wounding thirteen, and escaping with two bren-guns and four hundred rounds of ammunition.

In mid-March a police-lieutenant, A. B. Clad, who had replaced Harold Crowley at Ladang, reported the capture of three of the gang. Clad had lain in ambush six days with a handful of his police jungle squad to do it—"demonstrating patience and jungle fighting ability learned while serving with a Gurkha regiment during the war," the newspaper account said of Clad.

Tam Lee was mentioned again in early May when the Ladang Gang stopped a Kuala Lumpur–bound bus and unloaded all the passengers except three men—later identified as police informers and one-time Communists. They tied these three to their seats, doused the bus with gasoline, and set it afire. The passengers failed to identify any of the terrorist photographs the police showed them.

That same month Police-Lieutenant A. B. Clad was in the news again. Returning from a visit to a nearby rubber estate, Clad had roared straight through a bandit ambush doing seventy miles per hour and taking a curve at just under fifty while the Sten-gun slugs slammed against his car.

There was a somewhat blurred photograph of Clad standing next to his bullet-marked Riley sedan. The incident was newsworthy because Barney Clad only two years before had been a member of the Jaguar racing team. It was noted that Clad had finished second in the famous Le Mans 24-hour sports car race in 1953.

In June Tam Lee's gang slashed 540 rubber trees in the Ladang area. He led a night raid on the newly established resettlement camp at Seremban, blowing up over a hundred feet of barbed wire and injuring two constables. Twice that month he destroyed the water pipe and telephone lines leading into Ladang.

Barney Clad, it was noted during this same period, had organized an interpolice post badminton tournament for the entire sate of Selangor. Finals to be played the first week of July in K.L.

This last item was unusual enough to rate a close-up photograph of the tournament organizer. Ah Min studied the youthful face of Barney Clad. His age was given as twenty-nine, but he looked much younger. He was smiling—apparently proud of himself, Ah Min decided—and showing very white teeth against his deeply tanned complexion.

Ah Min clipped the photo and studied it for days, comparing it to the picture of Tam Lee in her mind. Comparing this man who organized badminton tournaments with the man who attacked well-guarded resettlement camps. The smiling one who drove fast motor cars and used his life only to amuse himself. The unsmiling one who had been in the jungle eleven years now, fighting first the running-dog Japanese and now the red-haired devil English.

Soon perhaps everyone would see who was the better man. It would require only ordinary luck.

Ah Min was released from Taiping near the end of June. The Malayan Chinese Association, after interviewing her, requested she be given a civil service position to make use of her newly acquired skills of typing and shorthand. "Since she must live in Ladang to support her widowed aunt," the M.C.A. report stated, "perhaps she could be given a position in the office of the police post—"

BARNEY CLAD WAS DELIGHTED to have a girl who could take shorthand. At least that was the word he used. Ah Min saw little evidence of his delight. Clad smiled the white smile of the photograph and seemed friendly, though far from enthusiastic, sitting low in a canvas chair with his feet crossed on the corner of the desk.

She was more surprised than disappointed that he didn't study her more closely. She knew very well that few girls, even in Kuala Lumpur, could wear a white, tight-fitting *cheongsam* dress as she could. Few had her softly lighted eyes, or knew enough to comb their hair straight and shoulder length so that it would gleam and move subtly as you looked over your shoulder. Yet Clad hadn't even got up.

He asked only a few questions about Taiping before saying, "We can begin right now if you're ready."

Ah Min nodded. "Certainly. If I may get my book?"

Clad returned her nod. "I'll be right here."

In the outer office, Clad's Malay police clerk watched Ah Min closely. *What was his name?* she thought. *Yeop. Yes, that was it.* She could feel his eyes on her, but she picked up her notebook and returned to Clad's office without looking at him.

The police lieutenant still sat with his feet on the desk; but now he was intently writing something on a small notepad. Ah Min's eyes rose to the wall map of Malaya behind him. But within the moment her eyes lowered to Clad again, seeing his short-cut brown hair and deeply tanned face and arms. That was a curious thing. The white man was darker than the Chinese and Malays, darker than anyone in the village except the few Tamil Indian people. This smiling, slow-talking, unexcitable Englishman who raced motorcars and organized badminton tournaments—

"Ready?" Clad looked up. "As soon as I file this."

Ah Min was about to sit down, but now she stopped. Clad had taken a feathered dart from one of the desk drawers. He punched the point through the note he'd written, half turned in the chair, and threw the dart across the room, still with his feet on the desk.

The girl watched him with open astonishment, then looked around. On the wall behind her, pinning their notes to a four-by-five-foot corkboard, were at least a dozen darts.

"My file of things to do," Clad said. "Notes in plain sight aren't lost." He saw Ah Min look at him curiously again.

"You might just as well become familiar with it now, Minnie," Clad said then. "The ones on the right are things to be done soon." He pointed his pencil in the general direction of the darts. "The ones on the left are things to be done anytime. But sometimes my aim is off and the things to be done soon become things to be done anytime."

She nodded thoughtfully. "I see."

"For example," Clad said, "that note I just filed. That's to remind me—" He paused. "You know about the badminton thing?"

"I heard some about it."

"It's next Sunday. Here." Clad's dark face showed momentary concern. "That's something we have to get on right away. Get the word about that it's going to be here instead of K.L."

Ah Min said, "And the note is to remind you to write letters of explanation "

Clad shook his head. "I don't have to remind myself of that. No, the one I just filed is a reminder to invite an old friend to the thing Sunday." He nodded toward the board. "Read it. You can begin getting used to my handwriting."

Ah Min hesitated. "Which one is it?"

"Somewhere on the right," Clad said. "To be done soon."

She moved to the board now, pulled off one of the darts, and read the note aloud. "Phone Rad to bring up a case of Scotch from the Selangor Club Friday."

"No, not that one."

She tried another. "Find out where five-four Gurkhas are. Call Mitch for b.t." Then looked at Clad questioningly.

Clad nodded. Then asked, "You don't understand it?"

"I'm not sure."

"Mitch is Lieutenant Colonel Gordon Mitchell. Fifth Battalion Fourth Prince of Wales's Own Gurkha Rifles. I served with him during the war. So, when I heard he was somewhere down around K.L., I said to myself, get him to the badminton thing."

"The b.t.," Ah Min said, still hesitantly, but nodding her head now.

Clad smiled. "Minnie, my system just sounds complicated. If it wasn't absolutely simple, I wouldn't have any part of it."

Clad dictated fifteen letters that morning, and during the afternoon, Ah Min typed them. All of them announced the badminton tournament's change of location and urged contestants to arrive early Sunday morning. All were identical but for the last paragraph. Clad varied these, adding something personal and for the most part mildly insulting to each.

At four o'clock Ah Min left the police post. She walked past Clad's green Riley, noticing the bullet marks from front to rear fender where Tam Lee's Sten gunmen had swept the car. Perhaps they had been overanxious. Or Clad had an overabundance of luck. But luck couldn't last for a man as lazy as he was. A man who never moved from his chair or noticed her dress. A man who threw darts and called her Minnie.

She followed the main road through the village to her aunt's house, a one-story structure made of plywood, bamboo, and roofed with attap; and as soon as she was inside, while her aunt silently prepared the rice, Ah Min composed the message to Tam Lee.

She had planned to wait at least two weeks before contacting him; but that was out of the question now. If Clad was having her watched, which she doubted, then she would have to be that much more careful. But regardless of the risk she had to see Tam Lee within the next two days.

It wouldn't be necessary to tell him she was working at the police post. He would know that already. Nor would she have to sign it. She wrote: *Fifteen villages will be left without police officials Sunday. I must see you. Please come to me or have me taken to you. Please.* That was all.

At dusk she left the note in the hole beneath the mangosteen tree beyond the north end of the village. Returning home, she saw Yeop, Clad's office clerk, standing in front of his house watching her. As she passed him she looked up and smiled and Yeop seemed to lose his poise. *As if he had been caught stealing,* Ah Min thought. She continued on unhurriedly. Yeop would be less trouble than Clad.

Before dawn Ah Min went to the mangosteen tree again. The note had been picked up.

Clad was out of the office most of the day, seeing to the building of stands for Sunday, so Ah Min's time was her own.

She pictured Tam Lee reading her note, deliberating over it, convincing himself that it wasn't a police trick. And finally he would contact her. She was certain of that. He would remember their months together in the jungle camps and hurry to her. He would be delighted and show his delight and ask her to return with him. That was something else to think about and decide.

When Clad came in later in the afternoon, Ah Min reported that she had nothing to do.

Clad shook his head. "I don't have any letters."

"Or forms or things to be typewritten?"

"No forms or things." He looked beyond her. "Unless you want to give me a report on my 'things to do.' "

She looked at the corkboard. There were seven darts there, all grouped on the left or *things to do anytime* side. "Just list them on a sheet of paper," Clad said. "We'll call it our weekend report. All right?"

Ah Min gathered the notes, carrying them to her desk in the outer office. But a moment later she was back.

"I'm afraid I made a mistake."

"What?"

"This note with 'things to do anytime,' but it should have been with 'things to do soon.' I think yesterday when I read it—when you were explaining this system?—I replaced it on the wrong side."

Clad unfolded the note. He was on his feet at once, studied the wall map behind him, then sat down again and picked up his telephone.

"Operator . . . yes, Clad . . . I want to contact a Colonel G. A. H. Mitchell, fifth-fourth Gurkhas, either at Kajang or Seremban . . . Yes, I'll wait."

Ah Min went to her desk in the outer office. She sat looking at the notes but listening to Clad. She heard him say, "Mitch!" almost shouting it, and who this was and how long it had been and something about India. There was frequent laughter. Finally Clad brought up the badminton event, inviting him, and after that there was a long silence.

The man on the other end of the line was doing most of the talking now. From Clad there was only an occasional yes or no or mumbled two-syllable sound. Ah Min began to lose interest. She took out memo sheets and placed carbon paper between them carefully.

Yeop was still watching her, she knew. But she was already growing accustomed to this. As if, because his watchfulness was so obvious, there was nothing to fear from it.

Clad's voice came to her again.

"Of all the days to pick for a field problem . . . I know, I should have phoned before but . . . Mitch"—she pictured Clad suddenly straightening up—"Mitch, why not march them up here? It would be perfect! . . . Uh-huh . . . No, let them bash about in the woods for the day and march back Sunday afternoon . . . Yeah . . . Mitch, you're the C.O., you know . . ."

Ah Min shook her head very faintly, thinking, *the most important thing in his life is a badminton contest. That followed closely by drinking Scotch whiskey stengahs* (which she assumed must be one of his habits), *or just sitting with his feet up and doing nothing.*

It was some moments before she realized Clad had rung off.

Tam Lee came late that night, though not the way she expected he would.

There was no sound. She opened her eyes in the darkness feeling someone close to her sleeping mat, and as she stirred, a hand closed dimly over her mouth. She was pulled to her feet; a gun barrel pressed into her back, yet there were still no sounds; none from her aunt in the next room, not even of footsteps as they left the house, keeping close to the shadows, or as they darted across the open yard to enter first the scrub brush then the tangled, clawing darkness of the jungle.

They moved hurriedly, one man in front, one behind, and now

there were swishing, rustling sounds and after minutes of this she heard the in-and-out gasps of her breathing. But no one spoke; not during the entire half hour of their travel, not until they had stopped in a clearing and stood listening for perhaps a full minute. Then one of the men cleared his throat, a short grunt of a sound, and said, "We have her."

They came into the clearing from three sides, a dozen men, no more than that; all of them heavily armed, all of them looking at Ah Min. She watched them, her gaze moving carefully from one to the next, then stopped.

"Tam—"

He was hatless, in plain, faded khaki, a carbine under his left arm pointed to the ground; but now, as Ah Min moved toward him, the barrel rose abruptly.

"Tam?"

"Say what you have to say."

She hesitated. "You don't trust me?"

"I have no reason to."

"No reason!" She paused to let her tone become quiet again. "After the months we were together?"

"You've been to Taiping since then," Tam Lee said flatly.

"Do you think I wanted to go there?"

"People come out of Taiping with our cause washed from their minds."

"I thought only of you," Ah Min said quietly.

"And now you work for the police."

"In the office of the police. There is a difference." She had sensed the change in him, the holding back, the distrust; just as she knew his face was more drawn, starkly hollowed and impassive now, even though she could not see him clearly in the darkness.

"Do you think I inform on you?"

It was then, when Tam Lee said nothing but continued to stare at her, that she became afraid and could feel even the presence of fear inside her body. *But don't show it,* she thought. *Or cry or scream or run or try to hide—*

Quietly, continuing in the Hokkien dialect they were using, she said, "Would I send you the message of the villages if I worked for them?"

"Fifteen villages, each one with its police officer gone for the day." For a moment Tam Lee seemed to smile. "They make it inviting, don't they? 'Take your pick,' they're saying. 'Look, it's Sunday and no one is alert. The Malay policemen sleep or visit friends because the head one is at Ladang.' "

Ah Min watched him. "Well?"

"But they wait with grenades and heavy weapons," Tam Lee said. "One or more of the fifteen could be raided, so all will be ready."

Now the girl frowned. "They want you to attack?"

"To show ourselves. A plan to draw us out."

"But why assume that?"

"I assume nothing. Our source in Kuala Lumpur warned us weeks ago. It was the idea of the man you work for. They put it in the newspaper so it would look authentic. 'But how do we make certain they know about it?' someone asks. And this man you work for says, 'I send my girl out to them. Even if they don't read the newspaper, or even if they miss the significance of fifteen unguarded villages, the girl will see to it that they know.' "

Ah Min shook her head. "That isn't true."

"How do you prove it isn't?"

"How can I prove it? I came here in good faith. Beyond that I can say nothing."

"You can confess; admit your guilt."

Ah Min watched him closely, holding his gaze. "You've changed," she said after a moment. "No longer sure of yourself. You would even kill me because you're not sure what else to do."

"Or perhaps," Tam Lee said, "because you mean less to me than you imagine."

The bluntness of his words took her by surprise. But she said, still quietly, still controlled, and not taking her eyes from his face, "Then there is no reason not to kill me, is there?"

The terrorist shrugged and the barrel of the carbine came up. "None I can think of."

"Let me ask you something first."

"Ask it."

"What will you do about the fifteen villages?"

"Stay out of them, what else?"

"But do nothing in turn?"

"I haven't thought about it."

"Truthfully?"

Tam seemed annoyed. "I don't lie to anyone. Not even you."

"Then you have changed," Ah Min said. "A year ago you would have a counter plan. Something to make the plot blow up in their face."

She was thinking quickly, picturing the villages ready and waiting for a terrorist attack; then picturing Clad and Ladang and the badminton court and the newly built stands to hold more than a hundred people.

The stands filled with police and army people—

Of course! *But be careful,* she thought, keeping her excitement in check and making herself gaze at Tam honestly and straightforwardly.

"The obvious plan seems to have escaped you," she said.

His expression did not change, but she imagined his mixed feeling of curiosity and suspicion.

"What plan?"

"To attack Ladang."

"A village filled with soldiers and police."

Ah Min nodded. "And all of them watching the games. None worried you would dare come."

"How many of them?"

"Sixteen contestants. As many as a hundred spectators. Perhaps more." She paused, her eyes remaining on Tam. "Can you picture coming out of the rubber trees on the east side of the field, coming before they know you're there, then throwing grenades and firing into them?"

She waited expectantly. "Can you picture them, some on the ground, others running in panic?"

Tam was staring, his eyes on her but not seeing her, and she thought, *You have him. Now put the top on.*

"Tam"—her voice soft, controlled—"kill me if you have to. But kill them too. Go to Ladang on Sunday and kill them as they sit unsuspecting and foolish. Do that and my coming here, my dying, will be for some good."

He was studying her again. "This could just as easily be a trap."

"Tam," she murmured, "trust me. I ask for nothing more. Not even my life."

He walked away from her slowly, beckoned to two of his men, and squatted down to talk. After only a few minutes he was standing before her again, this time much closer.

"I can trust you now," he said intently. "I can trust you at this moment. But remember—and remember it well—I can kill you at any time."

SHE DECIDED THAT THE best place to watch would be from the police post. Here, sitting at her desk and looking out past Clad's Riley and the lines of cars now parked along both sides of the road, then beyond and through the thinly scattered palms that edged the parade ground, she could see the newly erected stands and a portion of the badminton court. This was also the safest place. When the firing began, even though over a hundred yards away, she would drop to the floor.

For a while she watched the villagers filing by on their way to the spectacle. Some of them would be killed, no doubt. Well, they deserved to die, Ah Min decided, for supporting the recreation of these English.

Even the weather supports them, she thought disgustedly. Today the usual afternoon rain had held off.

Soon then, from the reaction of the crowd, she knew the games had begun. It was shortly after this that Yeop came into the office. A carbine was slung over his shoulder.

"Work on Sunday?" the Malay said from the doorway.

Ah Min rolled a sheet of paper into her typewriter. "I must practice this every day to be worth my wage." Looking at him then she sensed his self-consciousness and almost smiled.

"Is watching me your idea or Mr. Clad's?"

"Watching you?"

"Isn't that what you're doing?"

"I guard the cars."

Ah Min smiled. "Then we can be sure none will run away."

Yeop fumbled the screen door striking his head against it as he left and again Ah Min smiled. *Watching me must be his idea,* she thought. *Only Yeop would think of so stupid a reason for being here.*

An hour passed, then another. Her anxiety began to mount and more often now she faced the window, her gaze held on the stands and the corner of the badminton court that was visible.

Still, when the door opened, she knew instantly that no one had passed the front of the office or had come directly from the road. She turned, still expecting to see Yeop again; but the thin, unsmiling, tight-faced man in the doorway was Tam Lee.

She saw the revolver and parang in his belt. She saw the unwavering unblinking expression of his eyes, and she knew why he was here. He moved past her, looking into Clad's office, then motioned her inside.

"They failed," he said.

"They?"

He moved toward her. "There is no time for that today. Just do one last good thing and don't scream."

"You ran into an ambush and you think—"

"Almost. My forward men found them. We tried first one way around, then the other, but their lines protect Ladang on three sides. No isolated patrol; an entire battalion of Gurkhas deployed and waiting."

"Gurkhas! There are none of those here."

But even as she spoke, as she heard Tam Lee say, "I know those animals when I see them," she remembered a note on the wall and remembered a Colonel Gordon Mitchell and remembered Clad talking to him on the telephone, remembering part of it, not all, but enough—his words about a field problem.

"Mitch, why not march them up here? Let them bash about in the woods for the day . . ."

Of all the days—Ah Min stopped. She heard Clad again using the same words over the telephone. "Of all the days to pick for a field problem . . . I know, I should have phoned you before but . . ."

She provided the rest herself, though it was still Clad's voice in her mind: *But my girl misplaced my note to call you.*

On the left side of the board, she thought dully, *instead of the right.*

They had come, perhaps arriving sometime during the night; but up early and already maneuvering, their lines dug in, firmly established in time for Tam Lee. Of course he would think it was an ambush. Anyone would. And there would be no convincing him otherwise.

She was aware of Tam again, the parang already in his hand, the blade not glistening but hard and cold looking. She closed her eyes and let him come to her.

I won't scream, she thought. But she sucked in her breath, gasping and tightening as the parang went into her. She was already dead when, moments later, three rapid-fire reports of a carbine came from the front of the bungalow.

THE *STRAITS TIMES* HEADLINED the incident in its Monday edition.

LEADER OF LADANG GANG SLAIN!

A three-column picture showed Tam Lee lying in the doorway of the police post. There was a smaller photograph of Constable Yeop, obviously posed, standing at attention with carbine at his shoulder.

The text of the write-up inferred that Tam Lee had come to the police post to assassinate Clad. It told how the alert Constable Yeop shot him as he attempted to flee. Halfway down the column Ah Min was mentioned: civil service typist, an innocent victim, murdered in cold blood simply because she had been in the office.

The story even told how the reporter and photographer happened to be on the spot; but other than this indirect reference, there was no mention, not even on the sports pages, of the Selangor State Badminton finals.

Clad stood in the outer office. Lowering the newspaper, his gaze went to Yeop's desk.

"Well, you were wrong about her."

The Malay nodded.

"Still," Clad said, "if you hadn't suspected Minnie you wouldn't have bagged Tam Lee." He folded the newspaper under his arm. "There must be a lesson to be learned from this." He was thinking of the fifteen villages, all likely targets as far as Tam Lee was concerned; yet the man had come here. And only because one Malay constable had kept his eyes open was Tam Lee now a past concern.

"But what the lesson is," Clad said then, "I'm pretty sure I don't know."

At his desk, his feet up on the corner, Clad opened the newspaper to the sports pages. His eyes went over the columns carefully. But no, there wasn't even one inch devoted to the badminton finals. Perhaps if the games had been finished—

He jotted down a reminder on his notepad: *Why not play off b.t. anyway? Even if it didn't work—at least something to do!!!*

He folded the note double, attached it to a dart, and apparently without aiming hit the center of his file board.

A Happy, Lighthearted People

1963

"What we try to do," the American said, "my wife and I, we watch the people as they come in the dining room and we try to figure where they're from. You know, like that couple, he's very tall and looks like Sinclair Lewis and she's blond, kind of nice-looking."

Paco, the day clerk, standing behind the lobby desk, had never heard of Sinclair Lewis, but he nodded pleasantly.

"We thought sure they were British," the American went on, "and they turn out to be Dutch."

"Yes," Paco said. "We have the Dutch couple . . ."

"Hey, and the Italian countess, with the monkey."

"She has a ranch in Kenya," Paco explained.

"Is she really a countess?"

"They say she is."

"Now the Norwegian couple we knew weren't English."

"You knew them before?"

"No, no. I mean you can tell by looking at them. And as soon as you talk to her you find out her husband's a ship owner. Every other word: 'We have a big house and a chauffeur because my husband is a ship owner, you know.' Or: 'I was skiing last week in the mountains . . . my husband is a ship owner, you know.' But the one that really fooled us is the fellow with the cane and the little Pekingese. We call him The Duke. He wears an ascot, duck shorts, kneesocks, and we find out from that couple from London, the Grahams? . . ."

"The Grahams. Four seventeen."

"Now they could pass for American."

"Yes, they could."

"But the fellow with the cane and the ascot, we find out, he *is* American and his wife, who looks American if anybody does, is *English*."

"This time of year," Paco said, "our guests are almost all English."

"I'll say. Really English. You know that older couple with the son that's tall and kind of bald and never says anything?"

Paco nodded. "They went to Tangier today."

"Right. Well, they usually sit next to us at the swimming pool and every day the old man . . ." The American grinned. "Every day he wears this sort of blue-on-blue dressing gown that reaches almost to the ground. He lies there in the sun and after a while he gets up and says, very, very slowly, 'I believe I shall make my way down to the sea.' " The American shook his head, grinning his sincere grin. "Then he comes up, *changes* under the dressing gown and spends the rest of the morning scraping the tar off his feet."

"From the oil tankers," Paco said.

"I'm the only one using the pool."

"I suppose they like the salt water."

"Do *you* like it better?"

"Oh, I don't swim very much."

"Working all day." The American nodded understandingly, looking away for a moment, then back to Paco. "Is Torremolinos your home?"

"Nerja."

"Nerja. I understand it's beautiful up there. The caves and all."

"Very beautiful," Paco said.

"But you live in Torremolinos now."

"Yes, I have a room here."

"You go to school?"

"Do I go now?"

"I mean *did* you?"

"For two years in Sevilla."

"I thought so. You speak very good English. Excellent."

"I think I learn most of my English in Madrid."

"Wonderful city."

"I was in a hotel there three years."

"How old are you now? If you don't mind my asking."

"Twenty-four."

"I see."

What is there to see? Paco thought. He watched the American put a cigarette to his mouth; a Reyno. Paco slipped his lighter from a side pocket and flicked it lit as he reached across the counter.

"Thank you."

"*Nada.*"

He waited while the American looked across the lobby to the wrought iron clock against the white wall. He checked his watch with the clock.

"Almost dinnertime." The American's grin formed again. It came and went, as if actuated by a switch.

"I don't know if I'll ever get used to eating so late. You always eat this late? I mean does *every*body?"

"Nine, or ten perhaps."

"The people in the villages too?"

"Perhaps a little earlier."

"They work hard and get hungry, I guess."

"Or there's nothing to do so they eat and go to bed."

The American took time to grin before looking at his watch. "It's been nice talking to you, but we're supposed to meet the Grahams—the English couple from London?—in the lounge."

Paco smiled politely. "Enjoy yourselves." To tell him the Grahams had not yet returned from Tangiers would only lead to more conversation.

"Thank you. I mean, *gracias*."

Paco stood motionless with his hands on the edge of the counter waiting for the American to cross the lobby. "He did see," Paco said, his tone becoming very serious, "you don't learn about Spain at the Castellana Hilton and taking one-day trips to Toledo and Escorial and hurrying back to Madrid to eat in the good restaurants."

"No," the manager said. "You come to Torremolinos."

"You learn about a country," Paco went on, "by living in one place and talking to the people."

"Ah, the people," the manager said. "Of course."

"He feels the Spanish people are very warm and sincere."

"Unlike the French."

"He feels the Spanish people have dignity."

"But think too much about death."

"He wonders about that."

"They must all read the same book."

"He feels the Spanish people have remarkable poise."

"In the face of appalling poverty."

"He would like to live here."

"With many servants," the manager said.

"He feels the ideal would be to have the temperament of the Spanish and the material convenience of Americans."

"I feel," the manager said, "I should return to my office."

Just before nine the English couple with the balding son and the Grahams, the Londoners, returned from the all-day round-trip excursion flight to Tangiers.

Dennis Graham, who wore checked shirts and large cuff links and reminded Paco of a television announcer, reached the desk first.

Paco was waiting, thinking: He could be Spanish: his height, his hair.

"Did you have a good trip?"

"All right, I suppose," Dennis Graham said. "Messages?"

"No. Nothing."

"The, ah . . ." Graham snapped his fingers trying to remember. "The American couple. Have they come down?"

"In the lounge."

Dennis Graham took his wife's arm and she had to skip quickly, her dark hair bouncing, to move with him. "It was fun," he called to the English couple and the son.

"To do once," the Englishwoman called back. She, her husband, and son moved unhurriedly to the desk.

"You wouldn't have matches, would you?" her husband asked. He wore a canvas sun hat, the brim turned down all around. Paco's lighter came out and flicked once, then again before the flame appeared.

"No. What I need are matches."

"I'm sorry," Paco said.

"Do you know," the Englishwoman said, "in all of Spain I don't believe there are more than several packets of matches."

"No paper bags at all," the son said. "I haven't seen a paper bag since Gibraltar."

"The scarcity of forests," the Englishman said.

Paco smiled. "You had an enjoyable trip?"

"Beggars," the Englishman said. "All we saw were beggars. One chap in the group brought out a peseta and they nearly tore him to pieces."

"Robert," the Englishwoman said, "feels he's caught something."

The son twitched his shoulders. "I've been scratching all day."

"Well," the Englishwoman said. "I think I shall make my way up."

Her husband considered this. "A Scotch first?"

"I think after," she said.

As they moved off, the Englishman turned back to the desk. "When you get the matches, send up a few packs, won't you?" He did not wait for a reply.

At ten o'clock Paco was about to leave when the American appeared again. He raised his arm coming across the lobby and Paco was held at the desk.

"We still haven't eaten. The Grahams came in and we got to talking . . . very interesting . . . but what I need is a match."

Paco brought out his lighter. He offered the flame, leaning forward slightly with his elbow on the counter. The American did not have a cigarette ready, but he brought out his pack of Reynos quickly, pressed against the counter with a cigarette in his mouth, and puffed once, twice, gratefully.

"*Gracias.*"

"*Nada.*"

The American frowned. It was his I-want-to-learn-and-I'm-trying-to-understand expression. "I say thank you and you say 'Nothing?' "

"*De nada,*" Paco explained. "But we shorten it. Like saying . . . it's nothing, uh?"

"I see." The American's momentary thoughtful expression vanished and his face brightened. "Listen, would you join us after dinner? I mean, could you?"

"Oh, I don't think . . ."

"We're just going up to the British Club with the Grahams for a drink or two. You'll be off, won't you?"

"I'm off now."

"Then it's done." He snuffed his Reyno out in the ashtray on the counter and was moving away as he said, "In about an hour then."

The brown suit that Paco wore had been left in room 519 the year before and he had given the manager 450 pesetas for it. The suit did not fit the manager and it did not fit Paco as a suit should; but with the coat buttoned no one could tell that the trousers were too large about the waist and were pinned so that the back pockets came almost together.

He wore a white shirt, which was his own, and a neckerchief knotted tightly and folded over once and showing just two inches of red pattern at the open unbuttoned collar of his shirt. This was for the benefit of the American who would expect something about his dress to be *different*, something the American would feel was *Spanish*, or at least European.

He sat at one end of the couch in the dimly lighted British Club. The American sat in the upright chair across the coffee table from him, leaning forward with his elbows on his knees and his hands folded above the glass of sherry on the low table.

The American's wife sat in the middle of the couch half turned to Dennis Graham next to her, but dividing her attention between Dennis and his wife, who sat on the floor, her legs tucked under her, on the other side of the coffee table. This setting before the fireplace took up nearly a third of the oak-paneled room. Behind them stood a small bar with six stools, a barman, and three waiters. Somewhere behind the bar a record player was playing one of the recent hits of the Beatles.

"You don't hear them in America?" Lizzy Graham was amazed.

"I don't know," the American's wife said. "*I've* never heard them."

"We might've," the American said. "But you're never sure because they all sound alike." He looked up as the waiter approached.

"Let's order another."

"I love that dress," the American's wife was saying.

Lizzy Graham pinched the shoulders of the loose-fitting sweater-like wool, stretched the front out and let go. "It's so comfortable. Especially for lounging around; you know?"

"Mary Quant?"

Lizzy straightened, surprised. "Yes. Do you see her things?"

"Just beginning to."

The American looked around and up at the waiter again. "Silence means consent. That's oon boor-bon, oon Scotch, oon gin and tonic ee dos cloroso."

"I think," Paco said, looking down at the glass in front of the American's wife and lingering on the tight beige-knit of her thigh before raising his eyes, "I'll try bourbon this time."

"Then that's dos boor-bon ee oon cloroso."

"How do you like his Spanish," the American's wife said.

"Listen, I try. That's more than a lot of people do."

"But don't you find," Dennis Graham said, "there's always someone who speaks English?"

"That's not the point. Why should everybody learn our language and we don't bother to learn theirs?"

Dennis smiled his television-announcer smile. "No one's forcing anyone." He raised his glass, put it down again suddenly, and pointed a finger in the startled, upturned face of the American's wife. "I've got one. Greer Garson and Gregory Peck. Coal."

"*Valley of Decision.*"

"Damn—all right, Joan Fontaine and Laurence Olivier . . ."

"*Rebecca.*"

"That's too easy," Lizzy Graham said. "I've got one. Carole Landis, Betty Grable, and Victor Mature. Spooky."

Dennis whistled.

The American's wife lifted the stick from her highball and twirled it thoughtfully between her fingers as she stared into the empty fireplace.

The American said, "I think somebody's finally got you."

Her hand waved, brushing his remark aside. "Be quiet."

"This started yesterday at lunch," the American said to Paco. "Trying to guess old movies just from the people in them and maybe one or two hints."

"Your wife seems to be an expert."

"What amazes me, we don't go to that many movies."

"I can't think when I feel pressure," the American's wife said.

Paco watched both of her hands rise to one side of her face, then to the other, taking off pearl earrings and placing them on the table. His gaze shifted to Lizzy Graham and saw her shoulders moving in time with the music.

"Bonus question," Lizzy said. "What's the name of that piece."

"It's Goodman," Dennis said.

" 'Mission to Moscow,' " the American's wife said immediately. "About 1946."

Paco's gaze shifted from Lizzy back to the American's wife. The Englishwoman had the better figure. At least a rounder figure, which showed well in a bikini. A little stomach. Just enough stomach. The American's wife wore a black one-piece bathing suit or a dark blue one and there were no individual attractions, only the slim clean, delicately firm line of her body from shoulder to ankle. Neither of them could compare to the German girl of last season, God, who wore the white bikini, never touching or adjusting it, and the thin-thin silver chain around her middle.

"Now when the waiter brought the drinks," he heard the American saying, "he poured the sherry and didn't seem sure where to put it because you had a glass there too. I wanted to say, 'For me,' but I didn't know whether to say *por mi* or *para mi.*"

"*Para mi.*"

"I'll have to remember that. You know, something else, it's funny the way you pronounce words differently in different parts of Spain.

Like in Madrid it's the *Platha*. Or *serbithio*. You know, and down here it's just *plaza* and *servicio*."

"You have this also in your country, uh?"

"I Wake Up Screaming!" the American's wife said suddenly. "Betty Grable, Carole Landis, Victor Mature *and* Laird Cregar."

"I'm not sure though," the American said to Paco, "that our dialect differences are the same as yours. Like a southern accent drops the *n* on the end of a word and makes it sound like *ah* or *aw*. But taking a *c* before an *e* or an *i* and making it a *t-h* sound the way Castilian does . . ."

"But taking a *c*," Paco heard, and at the same time, closer to him, heard the American's wife say, "Peter Sellers and Terry-Thomas. Opens in a nudist camp."

Dennis Graham laughed out loud. "*I'm All Right Jack*. You got that in the States?"

" . . . but as far as I can make it out, the *t-h* sound is used everywhere but in Andalusia."

"We get a lot of your films . . . *Room at the Top*. Was that big in London?"

"Oh, yes, but I don't think it was quite the study *Saturday Night and Sunday Morning* was."

"Albert Finney."

"That's right."

"We missed that one. How about *David and Lisa*?"

"No . . . I don't think so."

"Dennis, that was coming when we left."

"It's marvelous."

"How about Ustinov's thing?"

"The one about women?"

"No, naval."

"It could still be about women."

"*N-a-v-a-l*."

"Billy Budd."

"Right!"

Now the American was saying something about North and South . . . different dialects . . . Civil War. Was Spain divided geographically during the Civil War the way the United States was?

"Yes, to some degree."

"Here's Spain," the American said, and was drawing an irregular square on his cocktail napkin.

"The line would be diagonal," Paco said.

"This way?"

"Yes, with the Republican sector including Madrid."

"You weren't in it . . . no, of course not."

"No, I was born the last year of the war."

The beige thigh shifted. "I'll tell you who's big in the United States right now from England. Shirley Bassey."

"Really?"

"Oh, and Georgia Brown. In *Oliver.*"

"What about the Profumo thing, did you get much of that?"

"Much!" It was the only thing in the paper. Christine and, what was her name, Davis?"

"Mandy Rice-Davies."

"Yes. Oh, I *love* that name."

"I can just barely remember newsreels," the American was saying, "of Barcelona being bombed and people running across empty streets to shelter and looking up at the planes."

Paco's eyes dropped to the map and saw Barcelona, the point of the pen forming a dot, going around and around to enlarge it, where Valencia should be.

"But I get confused, you know, with the term *Republicans* and *Nationalists.* We always called them Rebels or Loyalists."

"There would be a picture of either Christine or Mandy coming out of court with the crowd all around."

"Now the Loyalists were the Nationalists, right?"

"No, the Loyalists were the Republicans."

"And the Rebels the Nationalists?"

"That's correct."

"I've got to think of a way to remember that."

"What do people in the States feel Goldwater's chances are?" Dennis Graham said.

"Oh, God, let's not get into politics. I'm lost."

"As a person, though, he's quite charming, isn't he?"

"Well, personally I think he's a little folksy."

Paco heard Dennis's laugh. "That's good." And saw Lizzy Graham's shoulders moving in the strange V-neck dress that was like a long sweater that hung loose and straight to her knees when she was standing, but was not loose now the way she was moving, sitting on the floor and drumming lightly on the edge of the table.

"What's that, the one they're playing now?"

"If the Rebels were the Republicans it would be easy. You'd just have to remember *r-r.* Rebel-Republican."

"The Ray Charles Singers or whatever they're called."

"Un-unh. Ray Coniff."

Dennis Graham leaned forward. "What are you two so serious about?"

"Paco's straightening me out on the Civil War. The Spanish one."

"Oh," Dennis said, and seemed about to say more, but he turned abruptly to the American's wife. "I've got one."

"Time-out," the American's wife said. Paco felt her rising and he stood up quickly, offering his hand. She touched it, her fingers tightening in his palm as she rose, but she did not look at him.

Lizzy Graham pushed up. "I'll join you."

They were gone only a few moments when Dennis said to the American, "Did you see the records? Really an astonishing collection."

"No, I didn't."

"Come on."

The American looked at Paco as he rose. "Join us?"

"I think not." Paco smiled. "I stand all day."

He did not turn as they circled the couch to the bar. He took a Reyno from the pack on the table, lit it, settled back for a moment, then leaned forward, raised his bourbon and sipped it. Still with his back to the two men at the bar, hearing them but not turning to look at them, he put the glass on the table, picked up the pearl earrings the American's wife had placed there, and dropped them into his side-coat pocket.

She wouldn't remember them when it was time to go; he was sure of that. But if she did, he could pretend to find them on the floor.

Tomorrow morning then, at ten o'clock, he would watch the American drive off on his daily trip to Torremolinos to cash traveler's checks or buy magazines or mentholated cigarettes or to do whatever he had been doing every morning since coming to the hotel. Between ten-fifteen and ten-thirty, the American's wife could be expected to step off the elevator and pass the desk on her way to the pool. But at ten-ten, approximately, Paco would be knocking on the door of room 615.

She would open the door in her bathing suit. She would look at him. She would show surprise. He would hold her gaze and in the next moment, in the next five seconds that could seem an eternity, he would make his judgment. If he was the least bit uncertain, he would smile, open his hand, and there would be the pearl earrings. She would say thank you and he would say *nada.* There was still a chance at this point, but it was too unlikely even to consider. It would be there in the moment their eyes held or it would not be there.

How would you bet this one? Paco thought. He thought about it as the two women returned to the table. He thought about it as he rose and smiled and was ignored as the two women continued talking. And he decided in that moment that, if he were to do it, he would bet it even.

Returning to the hotel, they took off their shoes—all of them but Paco—and walked along the beach. In the darkness there was wind and the sound of waves breaking and far out, where the horizon would be, were two pinpoints of light.

"Is that Africa?" the American asked Paco.

"No. Ships. Sometimes from the Sierras you can see the Atlas Mountains, but not lights from this level."

They were walking together, a dozen strides behind the Grahams and the American's wife.

"Listen, something else I've been meaning to ask you."

"What is it?"

"Well, I don't know if you talk about it or not but . . . I was curious to know what you think of Franco. I mean what happens after he's gone? He's not young; he's going to die sometime."

"Yes," Paco said. "But when?"

The American began laughing and his wife and the Grahams turned to watch him.

"What's so funny," his wife called.

"That's wonderful," the American said finally, catching his breath. "I mean, what an attitude to have." He raised his voice then, calling to his wife: "Hey, I told you the Spanish had a sense of humor under all their dignity. Listen to this . . .

Arma Virumque Cano

1954

HARRY MYROLD LEFT THE men's store just across from the building and pulled his hat brim closer to his eyes before walking down around the corner to the parking lot. The early winter drizzle would have been no more than a minor irritation but for the stinging wind that blew the rain head-on against him to make him step quickly across the cinders to the two-tone Chevrolet parked near the entrance.

He threw the clothing-store box on the rear seat and jumped in too quickly, knocking his hat to one side so that his glasses slipped and hung precariously on the tip of his nose, his topcoat twisting beneath him.

Damn! Damn glasses that don't bend around your ears! Damn coat that always bunches when you get in the car!

Harry Myrold placed his hands firmly on the steering wheel, then relaxed his grip slowly against the slender coldness of the wheel. He pushed up his glasses, straightened his gray, narrow-brimmed hat, smoothed the fold of the topcoat beneath him, then very deliberately started the car, pushing the automatic drive lever to the D position. Before edging out onto Woodward, he craned his neck to look at the brown rectangle on the rear seat that bore the squat Gothic inscription ROSE BROTHERS. Only forty-three dollars. He felt better.

But not for very long. In ten minutes he had gone only a few blocks. What was the matter with this damn city! Everybody comes here to make money and they spend most of their time going home.

For a mile or so he was somewhere else. Somewhere where there was sun, and he was only vaguely aware of his stubby white fists on the steering wheel and beyond them grayness, lights, and the shiny bodies of wet automobiles. Horns, brakes, and the monotonous beat of windshield wipers. A streetcar clanged close and someone behind blew with a vengeance the split second the light turned. He smiled and started off as slowly as he could, then drove almost a block less than fifteen miles an hour while the horn continued to blow and the space in front lengthened. A car from the next lane slipped in ahead of him and Harry Myrold swore out loud.

He pictured the box on the rear seat and remembered the suit hanging in the store and remembered the price tag on it.

He hunched a little lower in the seat to watch the traffic light. The red circle stood out bleakly against the rainy grayness, then in his vision the light blended with the white lights of the theater marquee ahead and across the street. Burt Lancaster. *Ten Tall Men* and *That's My Boy.* Dean Martin and Jerry . . . The light changed and he pressed the accelerator automatically . . . Lewis.

The girl walked out to the curb from where she had been standing under the marquee and stuck out her thumb as she stepped off the curbing into the street. Harry Myrold stopped as automatically as he had started, not quite knowing why, and the next thing the girl was in the car. He looked past her, as she got in, to the eight-foot cardboard legionnaire standing beneath the marquee.

"Thanks a lot."

"Don't mention it."

"I've been standing under that show for almost a half-hour."

Harry Myrold couldn't think of a reply that would mean anything. He looked quickly to the left, to the car in the next lane, keeping busy to fill in for the silence.

"It's so wet out," the girl said.

"We're getting our share," Harry Myrold said.

"More, I'd say."

"It's the traffic that gets me," he came back quickly. "A little rain and it takes an hour longer to get home. I don't know what's the matter with this city!"

"It's so big."

"Well, it's not as large as New York or Chicago or a couple of more, and they don't have this trouble when it rains." Harry Myrold had never visited New York, Chicago, or the couple of more, but he attributed an equivalent amount of efficiency to their greatness, and he took it for granted the girl had never been to these cities. "It's a decided lack of foresight in city planning. Traffic Management's dropped the ball," he added.

"Ye-ah, I guess so."

"Just look, three solid lanes of cars, all creeping." Harry Myrold pointed out the inefficiency.

"So slow," the girl said.

He was silent for a few minutes, keeping busy with the traffic because there was nothing to say. Then something occurred to him, but he hesitated and drew and lighted a cigarette first, as if there was always something to say, and in his hesitation he said, "Cigarette?" sort of instinctively, and was sorry immediately. The girl was probably only a couple of years older than Marion, and it would be a long time before he offered Marion a cigarette.

She said, "Oh, no thanks," very quickly, and everything was all right.

For a moment he forgot what he had planned to say. Then it came back.

"How far are you going?"

"Just to Six Mile. I go west then"—and added quickly—"I can get a bus there . . . out to Grand River."

"I go all the way to Thirteen," Harry Myrold said. And it occurred to him that an explanation was necessary. "We've been wanting to get out of the city for a long time, so when our little girl finished grade school last year we moved out near Bloomfield, sort of this side."

"We live kind a out, too, but it's still in Detroit."

"It's the only place," Harry Myrold said vaguely. "I mean, out."

Since picking up the girl he had not looked at her directly. His eyes would shift slightly when the traffic eased, but it was only a shape sitting straight and very close to the door. Something white about the head.

Silence again, and he returned to studying the signs along the storefronts, dancing orange and red through the gray drizzle. New York Lunch . . . Hot Roast Beef .60 . . . then a white sign with five-foot buckeye lettering that blared SALE! Drastic reduction—SALE! SALE! SALE! All suits now only 53.95! His head turned instinctively to the rear seat and the brown box that said ROSE BROTHERS, and he smiled.

When he turned back he glanced at the girl as he pulled his eyes back to the road.

So it was a white babushka. He tried to remember what else he had seen in the part of the second. A dark jacket. Coat? No, it was shorter. And a plain face. A white plain face with a straight nose and deep shadowed eyes. Harry Myrold smiled to himself.

He looked at the storefronts again and edged his eyes toward the girl. She was looking toward the shop windows also. Yes, the nose was straight, but he couldn't see the eyes. Say about eighteen? High school girl going home after a few extra hours at the library. Like Marion would be doing soon. He looked at the gray outside turning to black and frowned. He could pick up the books for Marion.

"How's school?" he asked, after a glance determined that there really were books on her lap.

"Okay."

"Do you like it?"

"It's okay, I guess."

Marion loved it. Marion had mentioned the other night that she had just begun to live. Everybody acted so sort of grown-up and even Latin was fun.

"Do you take Latin?"

"No, I did. I finished up with it."

Harry Myrold couldn't help himself. *"Arma virumque cano,"* he recited. *"Troyae qui primus ab oris."*

The girl didn't say anything. Harry Myrold chuckled, but it didn't help. He was sorry he had said it. "Know that one?"

"No, I don't believe so," she said. Then hurriedly, "My girlfriend does, I think. I think I heard her say that once."

"I go back a long way to remember that one," Harry Myrold said.

He quoted the verse again to himself and stopped at a stone wall after *ab oris.* "Yes, a very long way."

"I've never regretted my Latin, even had two years of Greek," he told her. "Mind stimulators, both of them."

"Ye-ah, I guess so, even if they don't do you any good when you get out."

Harry Myrold cleared his throat. "You work only eight hours a day, but you live with people twenty-four hours a day." He stopped and said it over again to himself. It had sounded good before.

"See what I mean?" he explained. "You have to live with people all day long. You work at a job, but you have to work with people.

You have to be able to get along." He knew clearly what he meant, but it didn't sound right.

He looked at the girl and said earnestly, "See what I mean?"

She nodded and said, "Oh, ye-ah," but he knew she didn't understand.

"See, you can go to trade school anytime. That is, if you have to, but your education is something you should treat with respect. I'll tell you, you'll appreciate it later on, and you'll be sorry if you don't take advantage of it. I never regretted an hour of school."

"Does the Latin help you in what you do?" the girl asked.

"Not directly, no. But as I said before, it's a mind sharpener," and immediately wasn't sure if he had said it before. "Mental gymnastics. You exercise your body to be strong and healthy. You exercise your mind so that it will be agile, quick to respond to a given problem." Now it was sounding better. "So I can say, yes, indirectly Latin has been very useful to me."

"My brother was real good in Latin. Good in everything."

"Oh?"

"That's where I heard what you said," she said triumphantly. "Not from my girlfriend."

"What does your brother do?"

"Works in a shop. He's a turret lathe grinder."

"Oh."

"I wonder if he uses his Latin."

"Some, perhaps," Harry Myrold said.

"Ed says he could do his job with his eyes closed and a bottle of beer in one hand."

"Well, naturally some people have the advantage of using their education more than others."

"Ye-ah."

"In the selling game you have to keep on your toes . . . and . . . keep your mind sharp. You have to be quick with the answers."

They were a block from Six Mile when he made up his mind suddenly, almost without even thinking about it. The girl was squaring her books, ready to get out at the corner. She opened her purse and slipped her hand into it, and looked up at the approaching corner.

Harry Myrold glanced at her pocketbook then saw her standing on the corner with the fifteen cents bus fare in her wet hand.

"Look, I can cut over Six just as easy as not. If we pass a bus without people standing, I'll drop you at a stop ahead of it, and if we don't, I'll take you all the way to Grand River."

The girl looked at him and then toward the busy, illuminated corner. Her hand came out of the purse slowly.

"Thanks a lot. It's so wet out."

"People should do more for people," Harry Myrold said, making the left turn onto Six Mile. "It'd be a lot better world." He felt a sudden warmness and an eagerness to talk. "Why shouldn't I give you a ride? I got all this room here and just one person in the car. Look at all the cars with just one person in them. That's why we have a traffic problem.

"Another thing, I've got a Buick at home for the wife. But she uses it so little, I have to drive it down every so often just to keep the battery charged." He laughed.

The girl said nothing and Harry Myrold found himself being dragged back into the silence. He thought and thought but there was nothing obvious to say. The girl wasn't being much help. The warm feeling began to leave and for a moment he was sorry he had made the left turn at Six Mile. For going out of the way she could say more than *thanks a lot*. God, kids don't have anything that resembles a vocabulary! Marion was saying everything was real great. He remembered her saying, "Turk is fine. He's real calm." Turk was five-three, pimples, and corduroy pants tight to his ankles. Of course, Harry Myrold reflected, he could possess a certain amount of calmness.

"Do you go out on dates?"

She looked at him strangely. "Sometimes. Why?"

"I was just curious," Harry Myrold said hurriedly. "I didn't mean to be inquisitive. My daughter is just reaching the dating age. I was just thinking about it, that's all."

"Oh."

"I suppose she'll be begging me for a lot of formals now." He smiled. "All kinds of parties, as you know. But I don't begrudge her a few party dresses."

The girl said nothing.

"I suppose you have a few formals yourself. Girls seem to have to have a new one for every dance."

"I never owned one."

"Oh."

They drove on in silence. A few miles out the traffic thinned considerably. The rain seemed to have stopped at the same time making the sky seem somewhat lighter. Soon Harry Myrold saw the traffic light ahead at Grand River.

"Do you go right to Grand River?"

"Ye-ah. I'll get out at the gas station if it's okay."

"No trouble at all. I can grab a right there."

The girl opened her purse again and put her hand into it. Harry Myrold glanced at her and then back to the road, but he could see that her hand stayed inside the purse. Not carfare. She was probably going to get something at the drugstore.

He eased into the right lane and braked slowly in front of the brightly lit Sunoco station. Two cars were parked by the pumps with attendants filling both with gas.

The girl opened the door and moved with it onto the street.

Harry Myrold said nothing, but her hand came out of the purse and he saw motion and a blur of white and the girl's hand was on the backrest of the front seat.

He looked at her and then to her hand. "What was that?"

"Take a look for yourself," she said, pointing a finger to the rear seat. "Take a good look."

It was on top of the brown box that said ROSE BROTHERS. It was white and flimsy, contrasting with the heavy brown box. A pair of women's panties. Ripped from one side to the other, across the front.

"Good God!"

"I'm the one's supposed to be yelling after what you've done," she said. "But I'm so scared, I can't yell. It's a horrible experience for a girl." Then she smiled. "Hand me your wallet or they'll hear rape all the way downtown and those two guys at the gas station will be all over you in two seconds."

"Good God!"

"Gimme the wallet. I don't want your papers, just the money."

He handed her his alligator billfold, staring. She dropped her books on the front seat and opened it, taking out the bills and throwing the billfold back to Harry Myrold. She flicked through the bills hurriedly.

"Six bucks!" She glared at him. "God, you're some big shot! Maybe you'd better turn that Buick in and go back to school." Then she smiled again. "What the hell. So long daddy-o."

He drove slowly the round-about way home. Thinking. And oddly enough, thinking about school. He still couldn't get past *aboris*.

His wife was waiting at the front door.

"How many did you have tonight?"

Harry Myrold looked very tired. Around the eyes especially.

"I didn't have any, Dorothy. I stopped to pick up my new . . ." He looked down at his hands in his pockets and saw the brown box on the rear seat with the white panties lying on top.

Dorothy turned without a word and walked out of the room. He waited until the bedroom door slammed, then he threw off his coat and walked into the kitchen and took the bottle of Manhattan mix out of the cupboard.

The next day, during his lunch hour, Harry Myrold walked over to a men's store on Washington Boulevard. He bought a double-breasted blue suit and wrote out a check for exactly $134.45.

Confession

1958

SOMEONE WOULD SAY "BUT, Father, over three thousand dollars. Who has that much to give?" And he would say, "Nuño." Because he would see it in his mind that way: the boy, Nuño, coming through the trees riding a broomstick, slapping his hip for speed but held back by the saddlebags that hung down from his shoulder and bounced against his legs; saddlebags heavy with $3,055 in U.S. currency.

They would say, "Nuño?" looking at him curiously, then begin to smile, because even though his face was serious they would realize he was kidding and even if he knew who gave the money he wasn't telling. It would be a mystery, something to talk about for a long time to come.

Unless, or until, whoever left the money became known.

All right, then they'd put up a plaque commemorating the cross-shaped church. *Built through the charity of—*

That's enough, Father Schwinn thought. *Be sure, find out a few things first.* He had had this money perhaps ten minutes and already it was spent. He took the saddlebags into his adobe and was out again before the boy had thought of something else to do.

"You're sure you didn't recognize him?"

"Father, he was almost gone when I saw him. I was sweeping in the church. I heard the horse and came out. The bags were by the door and he was already across the yard."

"Going what way?"

The boy waved his arm. "That way."

"You show me, eh?"

They moved through the pines, following the path to the church: the boy, Nuño, riding his broomstick sideways, close to the black cassock and now and then looking almost straight up to the priest's curled-brim straw and the bearded face beneath it that was the face of a stage driver or a mustanger or a man who knew the Apache and would be in charge of the Coyotero trackers at Fort Thomas.

The boy, Nuño, who worked for Father Schwinn but lived at Rindo's Station, remembered other priests he had seen in his life and they had looked like priests; at least not like stage drivers. He couldn't imagine standing in front of Rindo's when the Hatch & Hodges arrived and seeing one of those priests come down off the driver's boot. But he could picture Father Schwinn—not with a cassock on but with a coat that stuck out at the hip because of a Colt beneath it—walking the way they walked into Rindo's after hours up on the seat.

Like theirs, Father Schwinn's face had the look of a saddle or a pair of chaps that had turned dark brown and would always be the same. Or like the face in a picture you would never forget. Not like the face of St. Francis in a holy picture; Father Schwinn's beard was heavier and he didn't have that ring above his head. More like a picture the boy had seen of ex–President Grant; though Father Schwinn was not as heavy and he was probably taller. He was probably taller than anybody.

Now they were out of the pines and approaching the one-room adobe that was called St. Anthony's. It stood almost at the edge of the slope so that its pointed, mesquite-pole roof and white-painted cross were against the sky, sharply outlined in the morning sun.

"Show me where he was," the priest said.

The boy pointed. "There."

"Then he didn't go down the slope."

"No. When I was inside I heard him go around and I thought someone was passing, going down to Rindo's. But then he came back and when I got outside he was already across the open and the bags were—here. He was almost in the trees and all I saw was a man on a *trigueño*. Like Mr. Rindo's."

"Rindo's?"

"The horse. Like the *trigueño* he used to have. Father, *you* know."

"You didn't tell me that before."

"I just remembered."

"You're sure." He was watching the boy closely. "You have to be very sure about something like this."

The boy wasn't smiling now; his eyes open wide. "I'm sure."

"I mean, you say it was *like* Mr. Rindo's horse. You're not saying it *was* Mr. Rindo, or his horse."

"Father, how could it be? That horse was stolen."

"At the time of the holdup."

"Sure. When Eladio was shot."

There you are, Father Schwinn thought. *Do you want it plainer than that? A man takes money, but his conscience or fear or both make him return it. It happens, eh? Sometimes. But*—he thought then—*did it happen?*

"Father. Something the matter?"

"You said you heard him ride to the back of the church."

"I thought he was passing, going to Rindo's."

"But he didn't."

The boy was frowning, shaking his head slowly. "No."

Then why didn't he? the priest thought. *If it was stolen money and he was going to return it, why didn't he? If—and with the* if *hope returned, a little at a time; if it really was the stolen money. Who knew for sure? Money looked like money and* trigueño *horses were brown and the world was full of both.*

But he would have to be certain, getting all the picky irritating ifs out of the way, the good ifs and the bad ifs. And if the money belonged to Rindo, *even* if the money belonged to Rindo (though, God of all of us, it couldn't; you're much too just), then he would have to return it.

IT WAS ALMOST NOON as Father Schwinn walked down the slope from the church, covering the open thousand or so yards to the stage road and Rindo's Station with its low ramada-fronted adobe that was half saloon and half store, its outbuildings and horse pens, its windmill rising against the hot wash of sky. Rindo's was a way station on the Hatch & Hodges east-west line and would be for another nine months to a year, until the railroad came through from Willcox.

Then, they said, this place that you saw in a haze of dust and distance, and seemed forever to reach as the stage came down out of the Santa Catalinas, would become a rail stop, a cattle-loading point, and perhaps even a town. Rindo, Arizona. Some said that. Others, knowing Father Schwinn, said, "Uh-unh. St. Anthony, Arizona." And they would bet money on it.

The priest crossed the road to the station now, a square wooden sign under one arm. His eyes, shaded by the curled-brim straw, held on the ramada of the main house and a cigar was clamped in the corner of his mouth. He inhaled it, letting the smoke out slowly, studying the man who was half-sitting, half-lying on the porch bench with a boot heel hooked over the edge. A young man wearing range clothes and a revolver, his hat almost covering his eyes, but studying the black-cassocked figure, staring and not trying to conceal it.

To let you know he's not afraid of a priest, Father Schwinn thought. *All right. I believe you.* He mounted the three steps, bringing the sign from under his arm, and hooked it on a nail next to the screen door. The young man looked up, and his face, close now, seemed familiar.

That family over on the San Pedro? O'Malley. Matsey. Massey. *Massey*—that was it. He had seen the boy only two or three times in the past year, but he remembered the boy's mother talking about him, worrying about him. Mrs. Massey. He was sure of it now.

Another man, older, in his thirties, but with the same hipless look of a rider and also wearing a Colt revolver, appeared in the doorway. He was holding a glass of mescal and came out with it to look at the sign that read:

ST. ANTHONY'S
Confession Saturday 2 to 5
Masses Sunday 7 & 8:30

"Up there," Father Schwinn said, pointing to the church that was a small white mark on the rim of the slope. They both looked at him dully and he said to the older one, "Are you a Catholic?"

"Why?"

"Now why do you think?"

"Maybe I am," the Massey boy said. His face was raised, the pointed brim of his hat still low over his eyes.

Father Schwinn looked at him. "All right. Are you?"

"I don't see it's any of your business."

"You don't, eh? What do you think my business is?"

"Man walks around in a dress—I don't know."

Father Schwinn stared at him. "Your mother know you're here?"

The Massey boy hesitated. "Just leave her at home."

The older one moved closer to stand hip-cocked with the mescal glass in front of him. "Dick, you want to buy anything he's got to sell?"

"I didn't tell him to stop by."

"Sonny," Father Schwinn said, "a word of caution. You're too skinny to be talking like that."

He brushed past them and went inside, across the beamed, low-ceilinged room, toward Al Rindo leaning on the plank bar. Rindo, with his solemn, still-handsome face, his cavalry mustache and slicked-to-the-side haircomb, was watching him and had been watching since the priest stepped up on the porch.

"You bothering my customers again?"

Father Schwinn pushed up the straw, rubbing the red line that showed on his forehead. "I think what the church needs is a good persecution to weed out the weaklings and the fence sitters. Then you'd know where everyone stood."

Rindo's eyes rose. He remained leaning on his forearms, relaxed, his striped collarless shirt open at the neck. "Maybe I could start one. I'll call it Wipe Out Superstition."

"There's no money in it."

"Be something to do."

"No." Father Schwinn shook his head. "You think you're a pagan, but you wouldn't have the stomach for it." He moved the cigar from one side of his mouth to the other. "Who's the older one?"

Rindo straightened, looking past the priest. "Name is Frank Calder. He works some place over on the river."

"Near the Masseys'?"

"I think. I've only seen him a few times." His tone dropped. "Speaking of Frank Calder—" He reached behind him for the mescal bottle as Calder, with the slow chinging sound of his spurs, came up to the bar. He stood a few feet from the priest and nodded as

Rindo raised the mescal. Rindo poured, put the bottle back, and came around with an almost-full bottle of brandy.

"You ready for one?"

"Confession this afternoon. One sniff from the wrong party and the word's out I drink in the confessional."

"I thought that's what you came for."

"No, to put up my sign." He paused. "How's Eladio?"

"He'll be all right."

"No word about the holdup men?" He saw Rindo shake his head and asked then, "How many were there?"

"Eladio said two. By the time I got in from the pasture they were gone—with five thousand dollars."

The priest's dark eyebrows, that were as dark and thick-looking as his General Grant beard, rose inquiringly. "You're sure that much?"

"Add a few hundred."

"And one of your horses I think someone said."

"The *trigueño*."

"Yes." He looked at his cigar stub then put it in his mouth again, leaning closer to the bar as Rindo struck a match.

"I wondered"—he puffed, drawing deeply and exhaling the smoke—"what if someone found the money? Or, what if they were caught and Eladio identified them—"

"I don't think he could. Their faces were covered."

"But if they had the money. Could you identify *it*?"

"I don't know. Money's money."

The priest nodded in agreement. "Isn't that the truth?"

"Money's money," Rindo said again. "And there's always more wherever it came from."

"Why," Father Schwinn said, "does making money sound so easy when you say it?"

Rindo was looking directly at the priest. "Give people what they want and they'll pay for it."

"Like whiskey."

"Or brandy, or cigars." Rindo turned to the shelf again and came back opening a cigar box.

"Father?"

The priest smiled. "You can do better than that." He selected four cigars, putting them inside his cassock. "Now an honest-to-goodness devil—and I mean goodness from his point of view—would take me up on a high mountain and offer the whole world."

"I'm afraid," Rindo said, "you'd accept."

"Ah, but only a little at a time. Moderation, Mr. Rindo, in all things." Father Schwinn took the cigar from his mouth again. "I'm afraid I have to go."

Rindo nodded. "If I get too crowded with immoderates tonight, I'll send the overflow up the hill."

"You're a gentleman," Father Schwinn said. "And maybe I'll do for you sometime." He seemed about to go, but hesitated. "Like say a prayer your money's returned? How would you like St. Anthony doing a little interceding for you?"

"I understood he was dead."

"Yes, but he keeps active." The priest's tone lowered. " 'The sea obeys and fetters break and lifeless limbs thou dost restore, while treasures lost are found again when young or old'—or even Al Rindo—'thy aid implore.' "

Rindo nodded solemnly. "And then there's the one that goes—'Away, and mock the time with fairest show; false race must hide what the false heart doth know.' "

The cigar was back in Father Schwinn's beard. He bowed to Rindo. "Exeunt Macbeth."

THREE THOUSAND AND FIFTY-FIVE dollars would join three more adobes to the one that was St. Anthony's, forming a cross;

an adobe Greek-plan church, if there was such a thing, with the main altar in the center. Within a year they would need a larger church. The money would build a road that curved up invitingly from the growing town of St. Anthony, Arizona, to the church of St. Anthony On-the-Hill.

Three thousand and fifty-five dollars would buy new vestments, a baptismal font, stations of the cross.

Three thousand and fifty-five dollars would start a herd for the Aravaipa people up near Galiuro; a seed bull and some yearlings to keep peaceful Apaches from both starvation and the warpath. All around his circuit, which he traveled during the week, from Camp Gila south almost to Benson, from the foothills of the Santa Catalinas east, beyond the San Pedro, there was need for countless things that three thousand and fifty-five dollars would buy. A greater need than Al Rindo would ever have for the money.

All right, hold it right there, Father Schwinn thought.

He told himself again that if it was Al Rindo's money the church's need for it could not nullify Rindo's right to it. That much was certain. But *was* it Rindo's? Where was the proof? Rindo had admitted he couldn't identify the money. *And if you brought it to him to let him try,* the priest thought, *what would stop him from saying yes, that's the money? Why wouldn't he?*

"Bless me Father for I have sinned—" A woman's whispered voice in the darkness of the confessional. "It has been a month since my last confession." He listened, his head close to the basket-weave screen that separated them; and when she finished he spoke quietly, briefly to her, then closed his eyes and said the words of absolution as the whispered Act of Contrition came through the screen.

"Remember me in your prayers," he said.

There had been eleven people this afternoon: from families who had come to Rindo's for their Saturday buying; from riders in for a Saturday night. Eleven people in three hours. The woman was perhaps the last. It was almost five now and they knew the hours of confession.

Still he waited. The curtain of the confessional was partly open and he could see the cloth-covered altar and the crucifix on the wall behind it, their shapes dimly illuminated by the soft, red-glass-shielded glow of the sanctuary candle.

Would Rindo take the money if he showed it to him? No, the question was did he *have* to show it to him? And the answer to that was no. He had no obligation even to suppose, now, that the money belonged to anyone else.

Then why, he thought, *do you keep bringing Rindo into it?*

Where the red glow was now would be the center of the church. The crucifix—that could be suspended, hung from the ceiling, eh?

"Bless me Father for I have sinned." Again the whispered sound. A man's voice. Familiar? Yes; but he did not try to identify the voice. He listened. "It's been over two years since my last confession and since then I missed Mass about all the time and I stole things."

"What kind of things?"

"Money."

"Much money?"

"Over three thousand dollars."

Father Schwinn opened his eyes. His elbow was on the ledge of the basket-weave screen and as he looked up his hand moved from his forehead to his beard. "That's the total amount? From different places?"

"Nuh-uh. All from the same place."

"Did you cause physical harm to anyone?" He spoke slowly, quietly, knowing what the man would answer.

"We liked to killed one."

There you are, he thought. He felt disappointment, but relief at the same time. "This was at Rindo's, wasn't it?"

"That's right."

"Did you—" He stopped. "What are you going to do about it?"

"That's what I come to find out."

"You know you have to make restitution."

"What?"

"Give back what you stole. That's a matter of conscience. I can't force you; but if you don't make a sincere effort to return the money my absolving you means nothing."

"Well—that's the trouble. I don't have the money no more."

The silent, thoughtful gesture of Father Schwinn stroking his beard stopped. The voice. Dick Massey. Sprawled on the bench with his boot hooked on the edge. The priest saw him now as he had seen him and at once felt a tightening physical reaction. A warning.

He said carefully, "But you know where the money is?"

"Well—a couple days after the holdup this other one said he was going to give it back and I wasn't for it then. Not until he sneaked off with it and I realized he meant it. Then I decided maybe he was right and maybe I should be with him. You know? But when I went to Rindo's he wasn't there or hadn't even come."

"How many took part in the holdup?"

"I don't see that matters."

"I'll let you know what matters. Answer me."

The voice hesitated. "Three of us."

"Including the one with you a while ago?"

There was a silence. "Him too."

"Are you going to tell me he's coming in next?"

"I'll tell you how it is," the close, hushed voice said carefully. "This man was coming to give the money back. We know it because we followed him far enough to be sure. Then we lost him and cut fast to Rindo's to be there with him. But he never came. He would have passed your place this morning, but he never came to Rindo's. Instead you show up and start asking about the money was stolen."

"You're implying he left the money with me?"

"I'm saying it right out. All three thousand and something."

Father Schwinn paused, looking down, his right hand slowly tracing the purple ribbon-like stole that hung from his shoulders. "Rindo claims it was more."

"Then he was bragging. I know how much we took."

"This man—what made him want to return the money?"

"He shouldn't have been along in the first place."

"But now you say he's right. You should give it back."

"You told me yourself I had to."

"Which you knew I would, eh?"

"How would I know that?"

"And how do I know you're telling the truth?"

"You know whatever I tell you," the voice hissed. "But just you know it and you can't tell anybody not *any*body, because it's in confession. I can tell you anything I want and your mouth is shut tight."

"Because we're in a confessional—that means I have to believe you?"

"I'm telling you I want that money and you can't do a thing about it."

"You and your friend thought this up, eh? You think I have the money and I'll simply hand it over. With sealed lips, you might say."

"Listen, you don't have a thing to say about it."

"Boy, get out of here. You're talking about something you don't know anything about."

"What you hear in confession—what a priest hears, he can't tell. I know that much!"

"You're over your head, sonny." He said it calmly, his thoughts coming clearly now that he understood the boy's intention. "You go home and think seriously about what you've done. When you're sorry, and you know it, then come back."

"I'm not leaving without the money."

"Tell your friend it didn't work. Then stay away from him and look at yourself very closely. I'll give you that much advice."

The boy moved, bumping against the board partition. Then, close to the priest, the hammer of a Colt revolver clicked into a cocked position. "I said I'm not leaving without the money."

"Now you're going to shoot me, eh? Then what?"

"I'm telling you for the last time—"

"Boy, just get out of here, will you?"

"Listen—this is two inches from your head. Two inches. All I got to do is pull the trigger and you're dead." His words came strung together and he jabbed the gun barrel against the screen. "You hear me? Now get up and get the money . . . You think I'm kidding? Listen—you think I won't shoot you find out different. You hear? . . . You *hear* me!" His voice rose, sounding through the adobe room. "Father, I swear to God I don't want to do it, but you're *making* me!"

Father Schwinn had not moved. His head was close to the screen, one hand still at his beard. "Put the gun away," he said quietly. "Put it away and make a good Act of Contrition."

He waited. There was no sound, no movement, no breathing or stirring or creak of the straw screen with the gun pressed against it. Only the feeling of someone close to him. It was there with the seconds passing slowly, silently in his mind. It was there and abruptly, with sudden sounds, it wasn't there. With the swish of the curtain and quick steps in the empty church the Massey boy was gone.

Father Schwinn watched the sanctuary light flickering silently in the dimness, a small red glow that would be here through the night and through the days, unchanging.

He was tired and content to sit for a while without having to think, without supposing or doubting or half-believing or reasoning; but just knowing now and feeling the actual physical relief that accompanied it. The money was Rindo's. Perhaps he had known it all the time. No, he had felt it; which was not the same as honestly knowing.

Like with the Massey boy. Feeling there was hope for him; not honestly knowing it as you know something is objectively, unquestionably true, but being quite sure of it another way. The boy would need help, perhaps more kicks than kind words, and he would have to keep away from the older one, which was also part of the feeling; but the boy still had a conscience and because of it there was hope for him.

It had come close, he thought, thinking of the larger church then and the baptismal font and the new vestments and the cattle for the Aravaipa people and the countless things three thousand and fifty-five dollars would buy.

But not close enough. It could have happened but it didn't and after supper he would go to Rindo's again; this time with the money. *But wouldn't it have been good,* he thought (knowing it could never have happened but enjoying the thought momentarily), *to have used Rindo's money for the church.*

Off beyond the dark mass of the Santa Catalinas the sky would show the last red traces of daylight. But here it was dusk, with the cool, quiet feel of night coming. Father Schwinn had made sure no one waited in the pines, moving carefully through the trees until he was out on the open grade; and now, with the saddlebags over his shoulder, he was almost to the road. Light from the inside framed the screened doorway of Rindo's main house and a lantern near the end of the ramada showed horses hitched along the side of the house, keeping the front clear for the evening Hatch & Hodges arrival.

Someone came out the screen door and a cigarette glowed in the shadow of the ramada. Then to the left, a figure had emerged from the line of horses and was crossing the porch now. The cigarette glowed, brightening, then soared in a slow arc out toward the road.

Father Schwinn continued on, straining now to make out the

man standing by one of the support posts. It was the other one, though, Dick Massey, passing through the lantern light to stand by the steps, that he recognized first. Father Schwinn stopped, less than fifteen feet away from them.

"We were about to come see you about something," Frank Calder said. He spoke quietly, his words barely carrying to the priest. "But I declare if you didn't bring it with you."

Father Schwinn watched him. "You aren't easily discouraged, are you? Your friend here—he and I have been all through it."

"Well, maybe he didn't make our point clear."

"Not as convincingly as you might, eh?" Father Schwinn shrugged, one hand on the saddlebag that hung in front, over his right shoulder. "All right, you try it now."

"I'll tell you one time," Frank Calder said. "Drop the bags where you stand. Turn around and walk back the way you came."

Father Schwinn looked at Dick Massey. "You were that good. Not the same words, but the same meaning." He looked at Calder again. "And what happens if I don't?"

"You will."

"Ah—confidence." The priest's gaze went to Massey. "You hear the way he said that? Very calm. Very sure of himself. He poses better too. You notice? Hip out—so I don't miss the gun—relaxed, thumbs in the belt. Very good. Now you—you look all arms, and you keep shifting from one foot—"

"That's enough talk," Calder said.

"Cold and commanding." Father Schwinn nodded approvingly. "And without raising his voice. That comes of practice."

"I told you what to do," Calder said.

"Yes, I know you did."

"You've got until Dick brings the horses around."

Father Schwinn glanced at the boy. "Did you know you were getting the horses? Or anything he tells you, eh?" He was looking at

Calder again. "Then what?" Calder stared at the priest; he said nothing. "Then you draw your gun?"

"If I pull it, you're dead."

"Another lesson," Father Schwinn said to the boy. "Don't draw your gun unless you intend to kill. Even if it's in church."

The screen door swung open. The Massey boy half-turned to face the man coming out, but Calder kept his eyes on the priest. The man held the door, steadying himself, then let go and moved purposefully toward the line of horses. They waited in silence: the boy glancing over his shoulder, Frank Calder not moving or taking his eyes from Father Schwinn, not until the man swung out past them and the sound of his horse stretched into the night.

"Life," the priest said, "has its anxious moments, eh?"

"Get the horses," Calder said.

"Get the horses," the priest repeated. "That's an order, boy. It's also a sign your friend's had enough. Standing there not knowing who might come out next. A roomful of people behind him." Father Schwinn paused, his gaze shifting to Frank Calder and holding there. "He has to do something, eh? But what?"

"I told you once," Calder said, "to drop the bags."

"Now you've told me twice."

Calder's head jerked to the side. "I SAID GET THE HORSES!"

Father Schwinn's smile was in his beard and he let his gaze linger on Calder as he said, "He told you that time. But," he said carefully, "if you leave now you might miss the main lesson." He saw the boy staring at him; confused or uncertain or afraid. Or fascinated? *Don't flatter yourself,* the priest thought; but he felt the boy closer to him now, not out somewhere in the middle, and he said, "Your friend has to do something sooner or later. But what? Shoot me? Threaten me again. Or"—the priest shrugged—"what, just take the money? We go through the same things, over and over, until—"

"Until," Calder said tonelessly, "I get sick to my stomach hearing you talk." He came down the steps carefully, his hands sliding away from his gun belt, his eyes not leaving the priest as he walked directly up to him.

"All that talk for nothing," Calder said. He seemed calm again, sure of himself. "You didn't truly expect I'd back down, did you?"

"My friend," Father Schwinn said, just as carefully, "you don't have it yet."

Frank Calder hesitated. In that moment, standing close to the black cassock, close to the distracting movement of the priest's right hand going to the strap of the saddlebags, sensing that he should do something—yell or draw or push or fall back—it was too late. Father Schwinn's left hand hooked into Calder's face. The saddlebags were off the priest's shoulder and his right fist followed through, taking Calder in the stomach, doubling him as he fell back. Instinctively Calder's hand was on his revolver and it was free of the holster, barely free of it, as Father Schwinn's left fist slammed into him again. He went down, still holding the Colt, and the priest's boot came down on Calder's wrist, pinning it to the ground.

"The lesson," Father Schwinn said, looking up at the boy, who was staring at him and hadn't moved. "If you can't convert them, confuse them. Now get out of here." He heard steps on the wood floor inside and saw shapes at the screen door, pushing it open. "But we'll talk some other time, uh?"

THEY WERE IN RINDO'S office with the door closed, Rindo standing, facing the priest who sat holding a brandy and a fresh cigar.

"I was curious," Rindo said guardedly, "if you thought your prayer had anything to do with it." He saw Father Schwinn frown. "You said something about, I think, St. Anthony?"

"Oh—" Father Schwinn nodded, remembering. "To tell you the truth I forgot to say it." He took a sip of the brandy. "You don't want to call on him too often. Only when the situation seems impossible—eh?"

"Uh-huh." Rindo watched him suspiciously. "There are still a few things I haven't got clear in my mind."

"Like how much reward to give me?"

"Well, you're not too proud to admit what you want."

"Mr. Rindo, if I refuse your offer it would be a gentlemanly gesture. It would have nothing to do with my pride."

Rindo watched him closely. "The more I see of you the more I believe you're even more of a realist than I am."

Father Schwinn blew a thin, slow stream of smoke toward the ceiling. He watched it thoughtfully. "Yes, a church shaped like a cross is real. Even made out of adobe. And vestments are real." He looked at Rindo again, holding him with his gaze. "Mr. Rindo, let me tell you about a few real things, eh? Like these Aravaipa people up near Galiuro . . ."

Evenings Away From Home

1959

LEAVING A DISMAL MARCH afternoon in Detroit and landing that evening among Arizona palm trees and illuminated swimming pools will tend to mellow anyone's outlook. The fact that it's a business trip makes little difference. The fact that you've brought along a miserable sinus-aching Detroit-type cold is an impediment only so long.

I'm not saying this to excuse what happened. A guy with a wife and three children is obliged to keep his moral fiber in one piece even when he's two thousand miles away from home and even when a girl like Terry McLean is involved.

But I am saying that moral fiber tends to lose some of its stuff by the time you've checked into the Desert Sands, noticed the candle-lit dining room serving midnight supper, heard the cool combo music coming from the cocktail lounge, and walked out past the swimming pool set among palms and flowering shrubs to C-unit and up to room 36 on the balcony level—getting a picture window view of the whole scene before taking nose drops, aspirin, and going to bed. Boy.

Then (I'm not finished) learning the next morning that along with its atmosphere the Desert Sands was also resting and suntanning headquarters for all the Westway Airlines stewardesses who didn't have homes of their own. What a coincidence, uh? No, I didn't plan it that way. Don Franklyn did.

Don Franklyn, Los Angeles freelance sometime fashion photographer: like two girls out in the middle of a wheat field modeling strapless formals; or up in an apple tree with polka-dot flannel nightgowns on. Next time in *Life* maybe with a picture story of Sebring or some European Grand Prix, catching the color of all the people and the cars, especially the girls in slacks and sunglasses around the red Ferraris.

The ad agency I worked for had used Franklyn before. But I was fairly new then on the Sirocco account and this was the first time he and I did anything together. It may seem strange that a thousand-a-day photographer would be taking cues from a thousand-a-month art director (me), but that's the way it is. The art director designs the ads, in this case a magazine campaign to sell $6,000 Sirocco sports cars, and if picture-taking is involved he's responsible for that too. In case anyone is wondering why I was there in the first place.

Franklyn arrived the same evening I did. But evidently while I was taking nose drops he was listening to the cool combo and downing stingers.

I might as well tell you now, Don Franklyn liked to play any time before or after work, and when Franklyn played he put all of his heart, soul, and credit cards into it. I guess you would classify him as a free thinker; he said and did just about whatever he wanted. Still, he was nice about it.

That first morning in the Desert Sands coffee shop, for example, we had just met and were talking over the job and what we expected to get, Franklyn fortifying himself with a large tomato juice and black coffee while I tried not to blow my nose. He nodded to a table where four girls were sitting, brown and poised and very Westway Airlines-looking, and said, "What do you think of that one?"

He didn't say which one; you just knew he meant the dark-haired girl in the white jersey turtleneck who was facing our way.

"How would you like her?" Franklyn said.

"Man."

Franklyn went over to their table. He stood talking to the dark-haired girl and to her only, one hand on the table, the other on the back of her chair, the girl staring up at him, nodding carefully, studying and judging this big, calm, confident guy with the gray crew cut.

An hour and a half later Terry McLean was out on location with us. Franklyn had rented a station wagon for his equipment. I drove the white top-down Sirocco we borrowed from the local dealer. Terry McLean took one look at it and rode with me.

Nothing happened on the way out; I would just like everyone to realize that driving ten miles out into the desert with a girl like Terry McLean—now in a straw sailor, tan-and-blue-striped Italian sweater and white shorts—a guy is not likely to be thinking about home fires or car payments or even the mortgage. All that is off somewhere beyond a distant shore. The here and now is an ultraresponsive motorcar doing seventy through high-desert country and an extremely handsome dark-haired girl in the next bucket seat, no more than the width of a gearbox away.

For ten minutes the guy can be an international something or other streaking across southern Spain with the "papers" and the girl. That is, if the guy doesn't have a runny nose. I'll tell you it is very hard to play Cary Grant when you're blowing your nose.

Our location was an empty one-street movie set that was used by a number of television westerns. There we shot Terry McLean in, on, and around the white Sirocco against a backdrop of crumbling adobe.

We had all day to get what we wanted. Franklyn wandered around setting up likely shots, asking me what I thought, and eventually getting around to taking pictures. He photographed Terry sitting cross-legged on the car's rear deck, her head lowered, but her eyes looking right at you over the top of her sunglasses, the straw sailor straight on her head.

He took pictures of Terry taking pictures, Terry standing in the Sirocco and aiming at the saloon and sheriff's office, Franklyn shooting the car from all angles, but almost always getting an interesting profile of Terry McLean's white shorts.

He would shoot with his eight-by-ten view camera on a tripod and then click some with the 35 mm that hung from his neck, getting black and white as well as color, then ambling over to the station wagon and taking his time to load the cameras again.

I felt obliged to keep Miss McLean company when Franklyn wasn't shooting. Really—I mean it about feeling obliged. We'd walk over to the ramada shade and stand in front of one of the stores while I—the great conversationalist—blew my nose and tried to keep things humming with questions like Where are you from? How long have you been with Westway? And how do you like it?

Dallas. Two years. And just fine. While she watched Franklyn across the street at the station wagon.

"Maybe you should be a model," I said, which sounded at the time like "How would you like to be in the movies?"

She looked at me, taking off her sunglasses. "Do you think I'm all right?"

"Like a pro."

"There's not much to it, is there?"

"Not when you have what's needed to start with."

"Thank you." She put her sunglasses back on. "You should do something for that cold."

"I'm taking nose drops."

She was watching Franklyn again. "Is he satisfied? I told him I'd never modeled before or anything."

"I think he'd tell you if he wasn't."

"I've been trying to decide if he's married, but I can't tell." Terry McLean had a way of changing conversation courses abruptly.

"Can you ordinarily tell?" I asked.

"Most of the time."

"Am I?"

"Definitely. With kiddies."

"Oh . . ."

"You don't have to wear a ring," Terry McLean said. "It's just a look."

"Good or bad?"

She shrugged. "Not bad . . . just a look."

"Definitely for me," I said, "but you don't know about him."

"He may have been married once," she said, watching Franklyn. "But that doesn't mean still."

"I think he is." I said it and I was glad.

That brought her around again. "You *think* he is."

"I'm pretty sure then."

It was her turn to say, "Oh . . ."

We had lunch on the board sidewalk at the edge of the shade. Franklyn, the arranger, had brought Desert Sands field rations: chicken sandwiches, celery, olives and stuff, apples, cheese, and a bottle of Johannesburger Riesling in a scotch cooler. He did forget wineglasses, but it didn't bother anyone but me. Because of my cold I felt obliged to use a thermos cup, while Franklyn and Terry McLean passed the bottle back and forth taking swigs.

She loved it. "Who'd ever have thought," she said, "that I would someday be a girl model seen in millions of magazines."

"If the client buys the ad," I said.

She ignored this. "Suddenly the most sought-after girl-model in New York."

"Rocketed to fame," Franklyn said, "in a three-liter flat-six Sirocco. Why not?"

She looked at him. "This is kind of fun, isn't it?"

Franklyn took the wine bottle from her. "We call it our champagne flight."

"Westway doesn't have one," Terry McLean murmured. "We serve coffee to Salt Lake City. Coffee and sandwiches to Seattle."

"A job can be its own reward," Franklyn said. "If you remember to bring the booze."

By that time I think she was more than ready to chuck her two years with Westway and go full-time into modeling. She asked Franklyn a lot of leading questions about the business, getting around to the kind of jobs he did and the places they took him.

Franklyn never once really encouraged her; he let Terry draw her own pictures and conclusions, carefully playing out line, and never giving a hint about his marital status.

We worked some more that afternoon, getting the gimmicky along with the straight, and finally knocked off about five.

Back at the Desert Sands, Franklyn and I had a couple of bourbons together in his room with our shoes off and I learned a little more about him. He lived in Pallas Verdes with a view of Catalina on a clear day, bought a new station wagon every year, owned a forty-two-foot cruiser, was married to a girl who had once been a movie extra, the father of a seven-year-old daughter called Pammy and was not forty-five as I had suspected. Don Franklyn was thirty-four. Three years older than I was.

He liked his work. He liked staying at the Desert Sands (this was his fourth time). He liked working for my agency because their art directors knew what they were doing. He liked bourbon before a shower. He liked four-to-one martinis and stingers and some classical music, two or three of the TV westerns, San Francisco, Cal Tjader, Julie Harris, *Shane,* Key Clubs, credit cards, and evenings away from home after a full day of shooting.

By then it was about that time. We got cleaned up and met Terry McLean, in a yellow sunback and earrings and pumps and looking even better than she did in the sweater and shorts, for dinner. Candlelight, martinis, turtle soup, rare filets, a very good salad and Stingers after.

And through all the courses and all the bright conversation, I kept hoping I wouldn't have to blow my nose, tried to sniffle without anyone hearing, but blew regularly, resignedly, as gentlemanly as I could about every five minutes. Which even done softly is not sweet music at the table.

As we were getting ready to leave, Franklyn said, "You ought to do something for that cold."

"I'm taking nose drops," I said.

"Rest is the best thing. Remember you're flying home."

"What's that got to do with it?"

He looked at Terry. "I've heard flying can do something to a cold. Produce complications."

She nodded doubtfully, then seemed to catch on and said, "It's the altitude."

"Not the coffee and sandwiches, uh?"

She kept her expression neutral. "I think the pressure and all."

"So," I said to Franklyn, "you think I should go to bed."

"Buddy—" Like I'd wounded him. "You're coming with us. I in*sist*."

He insisted for all of fifteen seconds. I told him I was going to bed anyway—bought a paperback, went up to C-36 overlooking the lit-up pool and the palms and layin bed wide awake for the next three hours wondering all the things you wonder in a situation like that.

Can a guy with a wife and three children back home be jealous of another guy who runs off in a $6,000 sports car with a slick babe and unlimited credit?

Yes.

Yes. Whether it makes sense or he has a right to or what. Yes.

Especially with Don Franklyn doing the running off. He made

it look so effortless, and at the same time made you feel so square.

I remember wondering how I would feel being with the two of them again the next day. Would they have private jokes? Words with secret meanings?

That turned out to be a waste of anguish. Don Franklyn appeared the next morning in the coffee shop with a ponytailed ash blonde by the name of Nancy Hayes. Also a Westway girl. Also a dish. Also everything you would expect Franklyn to pick. She was to be our model.

But what about Terry? I asked him that the first chance I had.

"Terry McLean?" Franklyn said, as if he and I knew all kinds of Terrys. "Oh, she had a hop to Salt Lake City today. Didn't I tell you?" Like who needs her?

Well, out we went into the desert again, this time with Nancy Hayes in pale blue Capri pants and a black sweater, eager to please and with a special smile that said she too, already, would rather be a girl-model than anything else in the world.

We got action shots that day, working mostly during the late afternoon when the light did good things to the saguaro cactus and brought out the shadowed contours of the mountains.

We moved around quite a bit to vary the background and when Franklyn and I weren't with Nancy Hayes, he was up on some ridge setting up a shot. That's why I had trouble finding out what happened the night before. Naturally I was curious. I mean did they go to a show or what?

I'd say, "Did you have fun?"

"When?"

"Last night."

"Oh . . . yeah."

Then he'd be looking through the view camera and the next minute the white Sirocco would come slicing through a curve, its dust rising into the high-desert background.

"She told you last night she had this flight today?"

"That's right."

"I'll bet it's her last one. I think she's going to quit."

Franklyn glanced over. "Why?"

"Take up modeling."

He shrugged. "They get married."

"Her? I mean is she going with someone?"

"A Westway pilot."

"She didn't mention him to me."

"Their flight plans only cross about once a week."

"They're not too serious then."

"You're never sure," Franklyn said. "Only careful."

The Sirocco came flat out from the other direction, Nancy Hayes smiling and her ponytail blowing in the windstream.

"Tell her to slow down," Franklyn said, "and to follow me."

By the time I got back he had moved to get the car coming straight up a steep grade.

"You go to a show?"

"What?"

"Last night."

"No, we just fooled around."

"Watched haircuts?"

The Sirocco was climbing straight on with the road S-ing down below it.

"That was good," Franklyn said.

So the Sirocco went back and came up again, roared past and left its dust hanging in stillness.

"I don't know if I'd want to drive these roads at night."

Franklyn, loading his camera, didn't react.

"What'd you do, stay right at the Sands?"

"We drove to a place in town for a couple."

"That's not too far. Then came back, uh?"

"Uh-huh."

"I suppose you were pretty tired by then."

"Kinda. We took a swim."

"You went for a *swim*?"

"Just in and out. You know."

"At the Sands?"

"Yeah."

"It wasn't too cold?"

"Fine."

"Not many girls'd go swimming that time of night."

He didn't say anything.

"You think?"

"I don't know. It was her idea."

"Really?"

He kept looking at me. "Talk again."

"What do you mean talk again?"

"I think you got rid of your cold," Franklyn said. "I don't hear it anymore."

It was gone, or practically gone; probably dried out by the thin desert air the day before. The strange thing was, I hadn't noticed it. I'd gone all day without blowing my nose more than four times and I didn't even realize it until just then.

"The rest did it," Franklyn said. He probably believed it too.

The action shots wrapped it up. The work was over, and right away, putting his equipment in the station wagon, Franklyn started making plans for the evening. Cocktails, dinner—maybe Nancy even knew another girl who wasn't busy. Huh?

Nancy Hayes's ponytail bobbed up and down. She knew loads.

Except, I told them, I was planning on getting an evening flight out if we finished early enough.

This news, I'm sure, didn't affect Franklyn's plans one way or the other. But it did postpone them and keep him hopping for a time.

While I changed and packed Franklyn took care of the flight reservation and also checked me out of the Desert Sands. We got to the airport with about fifteen minutes to spare. Franklyn said I'll come in with you. I said no need to. He said well, it was a pleasure working with you. I said let's do it again sometime. He said you name it. I said well, thanks for the ride and all. He said you better step on it.

Franklyn took off like an A-class dragster. I ran into the terminal, got in line at the ticket desk, kept watching the clock and the reservation clerk on the telephone, finally, finally getting to the desk—to find out that flight 457 would be delayed at least an hour.

But I'd miss my connection in Denver.

Let's see what we can do, the clerk said, and started leafing through schedules. Anyway—there wasn't one combination of flights that would get me to Detroit before the next day, and all included a few hours layover somewhere. So why not stay and take the through flight in the morning?

Why not.

I had a bourbon in the terminal bar deciding whether or not to call Franklyn. Tell him what happened. There'd be a pause and he'd say gee, that's great. Another pause. You want me to pick you up? With half a bourbon on the dresser, lather on his face, and the ponytail over in some other unit at that moment being combed into a neat slick shining bun.

I couldn't do it.

I had another bourbon and relaxed, the whole evening, the whole night before me; already it was dark and the bar was about three-quarters filled, with the sound of people together and ice in glasses and soft Cole Porter–type music in the background. One more bourbon. A Westway girl I recognized from the Sands walked by with some guy; she smiled and I nodded, wondering if the smile meant anything more than a smile.

I got a cab and went back to the Sands.

Probably I should have checked in first, but I didn't; I had a steak and more soft music and another bourbon—no sign of Franklyn or his new friend—so by the time I went to the desk to register it was about ten o'clock. And there wasn't a vacancy in the place.

Fortunately there was still Franklyn. The management knew we had been working together, so there was no objection to putting me up in his room. My bag was taken over, but I didn't follow it until about an hour later.

No, I went into the cocktail lounge where the cool combo played and sat at the bar being good, only nodding to the Westway girls I recognized and only as they were going by. One of them, I felt, would sit next to me any minute and say Hi. Hi. Can I buy you a drink? Fine. Lighting her cigarette then, the girl saying I heard you were here taking pictures. It must be fascinating. It's all right. Another drink. The girl: we could go to my place and talk. It's quieter.

We could also go goofy thinking things like that. *Be a good boy to the bitter end,* I thought, *and go to bed.*

That got me to Franklyn's room and in the sack reading by a little after eleven. At eleven-forty-five the phone rang.

"Hi"—a girl's voice; breathless—"I just got back."

"Terry?"

"You were expecting Mamie Van Doren?"

"Not even Charles."

"You sound different."

"I was in bed."

"Would a swim and a shaker of stingers get you out?"

"Wow."

"Why not?"

"I said wow."

"In about ten minutes?"

"All right." Very casually.

"See you at the pool then."

About fifteen seconds. That's all it took.

The room was quiet. Probably the quietest a room has ever been. So quiet you could hear bare feet on the carpet, and the suitcase fasteners snapping open were like pistol shots.

You're going swimming, I said; not out loud, but I heard it loud.

She's a friend. You worked with her and she's a friend and you're going swimming. At places like the Sands people go swimming at night.

Even not at places like the Sands people go swimming at night. Night or any time.

If you want a swim you go swimming. Right?

Besides, it was for fun. I mean like a joke. She thought she was meeting Don Franklyn; there was no question about that. But I'd show up instead. So it was for laughs. A swim and laughs.

Both were even good for a person.

My trunks were on.

A terry cloth beachcoat, trimmed in the blue plaid of the trunks, remained folded in the suitcase. If you want to know why I didn't put it on I'll tell you. Which has nothing to do with my wife, Pat, insisting I take it because they wear outfits like that at places like the Desert Sands. I said but I don't like *outfits*. And she said she was sorry she ever bought it for me, packing it anyway.

That's the reason I didn't wear it—because it *looked* like an outfit you'd wear at the Desert Sands. It said look at me in my resort outfit. Anyway, not wearing it had nothing to do with my wife.

I put on a sweater and a towel around my neck, then changed the towel to just over one shoulder, then to just carrying it, picked up cigarettes and the door key and went out along the balcony and down to the yard where it was quieter than ever and dark before you got to the pink lanterns that glowed in the shrubs around the pool.

A swim would be all right.

And one stinger. No more than two.

She'd probably be all wrapped up in a big heavy beach towel.

I passed through an archway in the shrubs and saw her down at the deep end, standing by a table in a white suit with brown, brown arms and legs and a shaker on the table and not a big heavy beach towel in sight. She was lighting a cigarette, looking up, looking funny—surprised. No, scared. That was all the warning I had.

The shrubs moved. There were four or five quick steps on the cement. I started to turn and he hit me. He hit me smack solid on the side of the head and I stumbled, seeing a blue-gray uniform and dark blue stripes on the sleeve that was swinging at me again. My shoulder took the punch, but it moved me nevertheless and I went into the pool headfirst with my towel and key and cigarettes—choking then and coming up quick for air.

The airlines pilot was waiting at the edge of the pool, his big hands on his knees, his pale, dead-serious eyes square on me.

"Boy," he drawled. "You want to come up and take my picture? I'll wait for you."

I stood in only chest-high water. "Listen—"

"I'm all ears, boy."

Which wasn't true. He was at least half muscle.

"Never mind."

He walked off, heading for Terry McLean. She stood waiting like a little girl who was about to catch hell from her dad; and when he took her hand she went along good as gold.

Again, the next morning, we had to rush to make my plane. Franklyn was pleasant, whistling most of the way to the airport. He even went in with me and waited patiently while I got my ticket squared away. There were about two minutes to spare then.

Franklyn said, "Well, it was a pleasure working with you."

"Maybe we'll do it again sometime," I said.

"You name it."

"I appreciate the ride."

He kept looking at me. "Talk again."

"I know," I said. "I've got another cold."

"You ought to take better care of yourself," Franklyn said. "Get more rest."

I shook hands with him quickly and ran.

For Something to Do

1955

PAST HOWELL, HE KEPT the speedometer needle at seventy for almost six miles, until he was in sight of the mailbox. Then he eased his foot from the accelerator, braked, and turned off the highway onto the road that cut back through the trees. The road was little wider than his car, a dim, rutted passageway that twice climbed into small clearings, but through most of its quarter of a mile kept to tree-covered dimness until it opened onto the yard and the one-story white farmhouse. He left the car in the gravel drive and went in the side door. It was almost seven o'clock in the evening.

"Ev?"

He heard Julie's voice and passed through the kitchen to see his wife at the end of the hall coming out of the bedroom. She went to him quickly, kissing him and holding herself against him for a moment before looking up.

"I was starting to worry—"

"They haven't been here?" Evan asked.

His wife's hair, smooth dark, parted on the side and clipped with a silver barrette, hung almost to her shoulders where it turned up softly and moved as she shook her head. She was twenty-three with a slight, boyish figure, a perhaps too-thin face, though her features were delicately small and even, and with freckles she did not try to conceal because her husband liked them.

"Did they call?" asked Evan.

"Not a word since Cal telephoned this morning."

"If they left Detroit at two—" Evan paused. "Isn't that what Cal said?"

Julie nodded. "He was picking up Ray at two o'clock and coming right on."

"They would've been here three hours ago if he did."

She started to smile as she said, "Maybe they were in an accident." In the dimness, but with light coming from the kitchen doorway, her teeth were small and white against the warm brown of her face.

Evan smiled, too, looking at his wife and feeling her close to him. "Thank God for small blessings."

"Or Cal forgot the way," she said.

"Or they stopped at a bar."

Her smile faded. "That's all we'd need." She followed Evan into the kitchen and leaned against the white-painted, oilcloth-covered table as he washed his hands at the sink. She liked to watch him as he lathered his hands vigorously then rinsed them until the calloused palms glistened yellow-pink and fresh-looking. She liked what she called his "honest farmer tan": face and arms a deep brown with a line across his forehead and upper arms where the color ended abruptly. She even liked his "farmer haircut" with too much thinned out from the sides—just as he liked her freckles and the way her hair moved when she shook her head. They had been married less than a year and noticing and liking these things about one another were as important as anything they shared.

"I was beginning to worry about you," she said.

"It took longer than I thought it would."

"A reluctant calf?"

Evan nodded, drying his hands.

"Did he pay you?"

"Not yet."

"He didn't pay for the brucellosis shots either."

"He will, when he gets his wheat check."

"Eight miles both ways and I'll bet he didn't even thank you."

"He mumbled something."

"Ev, that's a sixteen-mile round-trip . . . and a messy afternoon in his barn. For what? Eight or nine dollars."

He looked at her curiously. "That wasn't a child I delivered, it was a calf."

"Four years of veterinary medicine to charge eight dollars—"

"Twenty-five. I had to cut."

"It's still too little, with the attention you give."

"Do you expect him to pay more than the calf's worth?"

She shook her head faintly. "Good Sam."

He frowned moving toward her. "Julie, what's the matter with you?"

"I'm sorry."

"You sound like Cal, talking about money like that."

"I said I was sorry."

For a moment Evan was silent. "You're upset about them coming, aren't you?" He was standing close to her now and he drew her against him gently. "All of a sudden you sound like a different person. Listen, don't let him get you down like that."

She closed her eyes, her arms going around his waist. "I was afraid they'd come while you were gone. Then I hoped they would because I didn't want you to be here."

"The worrier."

"Ev, this isn't like the little worries. First I thought: *it's better if you and Ray don't meet.* Then I thought: *no, I don't want to be here alone.* And I wasn't sure which would be worse."

"Julie, Ray knows you're married."

"That's just it."

"But you went with the guy for two years. He can't be that bad."

"He was hard to get along with and conceited and . . . I don't know. I can't even think of one thing in his favor."

"Well, maybe he's grown up."

"I think that would be asking too much," Julie said.

They spoke little during supper.

Julie thought of Ray Perris. She had gone with him during her senior year in high school and off and on during her first two years at Michigan State, whenever she came home to Detroit and Ray bothered to call her. Then, in her third year, shortly after Ray was called into the army, she met Evan. There was no formal breakup with Ray, no ring to return, no good-bye. Ray never wrote, only once called her when he was home on furlough; and as far as Julie knew, Ray was still unaware that she was married. Until now. Not long ago she'd heard that Ray was out of the army and had become a professional fighter. This didn't surprise her. He had entered the Golden Gloves in high school; but, it seemed to Julie, more for the sake of wanting to be known as a fighter than for the actual boxing. Since meeting Evan, the only time she thought of Ray was to wonder how she could have ever gone with him. Perhaps only because she had been seventeen.

Then the phone call this morning from Cal, her cousin. Ray was in Detroit and he was bringing him out. And from that moment, suddenly realizing she was going to see Ray again and not wanting to see him, she was afraid.

Evan thought about Cal. How he would pull up into the drive unexpectedly, uninvited, and sit in the living room with them until all the beer was gone. Cal was twenty-three, Julie's age, four years younger than Evan; but aside from that they had almost nothing in common.

The first few times he came, Evan tried hard to like him. He offered to show him around the farm; but Cal wasn't interested. For conversation he brought up the Detroit Tigers, Lions, and Red Wings, in that order, going from baseball to football to hockey. But Cal was a fight fan and Evan was familiar with few names, none of them current, in the boxing world.

Cal did talk. After a few cans of beer he carried the conversation and invariably his remarks were directed to Julie.

Why would anybody who knew better want to live in the sticks? I mean what do you do for kicks, sit and look at each other? Nothing to do, you work your francis off and all you got to show for it is a one-story house and a four-year-old car. If Ev wants to be a vet—I mean it takes all kinds of people, believe me—why don't he get one of those dog and cat deals? Plenty of them in Detroit and those guys are making *dough.*

Evan argued with him mildly the first few times; but when he realized his anger was rising he would stop. It wasn't worth it. Cal had more success with Julie. She was easily drawn into an argument, as if she were obligated to talk some sense into Cal, to make him see that living on a farm and not making much money didn't necessarily mean you weren't happy. And when she became angry, Evan would see Cal smile. A number of times he had to restrain himself from throwing Cal out bodily.

Evan would tell himself, *The next time he opens his mouth, out he goes. Even if he is her cousin.* But he sat quietly and put up with Cal, because he couldn't help feeling a little sorry for him.

But it's not the same now, Evan thought. *It's nice to be nice, but you can carry it too far.*

He thought then, *You're feeling sorry for yourself.*

But that wasn't it, for he was almost always completely honest with himself. He was thinking that he and Julie had been married for almost a year and everything was going smoothly, but for one moment this afternoon his wife had sounded like Cal and she had not even been aware of it.

You did not let a man ruin your marriage or even try to or begin to or even have it remotely in mind. That, you did something about.

They had eaten supper and were doing the dishes when the two-tone ivory and green station wagon swung onto the drive and came to a sudden, gravel-skidding, nose-down stop behind Evan's car. The horn blew, and kept blowing until Julie and Evan came out on the front porch.

They heard Cal's voice as he got out of the station wagon, almost stumbling, slamming the door, and Julie closed her eyes. When she opened them he was coming toward the porch. "We were starting to worry about you."

Cal winked at Evan as if they were old friends. "That's the day."

"What happened to you?" Julie's gaze went to the station wagon as she spoke. The curved windshield was green-tinted and she could not make out the figure behind the wheel, though she was certain it was Ray Perris.

"We stopped for some hunting," Cal answered. "Ray figured if we're going out in the woods let's have some fun. So you know what the punchy guy does? He stops at a hardware store and buys two .30-30's." Cal snapped his fingers. "Just like that. The guy's loaded."

"You stopped for more than that," Julie said.

"So we picked up a case of beer."

Evan watched him. Cal stood with his hands on his hips, one blunt-toed Cordovan shoe in front of and almost perpendicular to the other in a fencing-like pose. "You're a little early for the hunting season," Evan said.

Cal looked up at him. "Is that right, Doctor?"

"What were you hunting?"

"I don't know. What lives in the woods?"

Don't let him get you, Evan thought and he said, nodding to the station wagon, "What about your friend?"

"He's a shy guy." Cal grinned. "Waits to be invited." His eyes went to Julie. "Ask your old boyfriend in for a beer."

"I think you've already had enough."

"Is that right?"

"You could hardly get out of the car."

"Is that right?" Cal turned to the station wagon. "Ray, we're going to get a drunkometer test!"

"Cal, act right today, *please*!"

They heard the car door open and slam closed. Cal said, "There's a real bomb. Two hundred and thirty horses. Digs out from zero to sixty in ten flat. Something?"

Neither Julie nor Evan answered. They were watching Ray Perris rounding the back end of the station wagon, taking his time, his hands in the back pockets of his khaki pants.

He wore a tight-fitting short-sleeved yellow and white sport shirt and both of his forearms bore tattoos: a tombstone with the inscription IN MEMORY OF MOTHER on the right arm, and on the left, a dagger with RAY in ornate, serifed letters on the hilt. Air corps-type sunglasses covered his eyes (though the sun was off behind the trees and it was almost dark) and his dark hair, curling low on his forehead, was thick and combed straight back on the sides. At the nape of his neck his hair ended abruptly in a straight line.

Cal scratched idly about his shirtfront. He was hatless with light-colored hair that was crew cut on top and long on the sides and his entire face, pale and angular, seemed creased as he smiled.

"Ray's next fight's in Saginaw," Cal said. "So he figured, hell, train at home for a change."

Perris nodded. "Besides wanting to see Julie." He was staring at her, ignoring Evan.

She tried to smile. "It's nice to see you, Ray. I don't believe you've met my husband—"

It was Evan's turn to smile, but his mouth was set firmly and his expression didn't change as he extended his hand and almost drew it back before Perris eased his from his back pocket.

"Cal said you were hunting," Julie said to him.

"We shot sixteen beer cans."

"You should've had Ev with you." Julie stopped. "I mean if it was the season. Ev was practically born in the woods; hunts every year, sets traps in the winter." She watched them shake hands briefly.

As they did, Cal said, "Like in the ring, huh, man?"

Perris's hands went to his back pockets again and he stood hip-cocked looking at Julie. "This cousin of yours, all he wants to talk about is fights."

"He's already notched twenty-three wins," Cal said. "Only lost four and drawed one. Another year and he's in line for a shot at the middleweight title. How about that?" Cal paused. "You know what they call him around the gym? Tony."

"Tony?" Julie said.

"Tony Curtis! You don't see it?"

Julie nodded, not sure if he was serious. "There's some resemblance."

"*Some*—hell, he looks like his twin!"

Perris was studying the house. His gaze moved to the chicken house and beyond that the barn. His eyes returned to Julie as he said, "How much land you got?"

"Eighty-five acres, most of it wheat. Some corn. Of course Ev doesn't have time to work it all now, with his practice. A neighbor sharecrops it for us."

"How much money does this Ev make?"

The question startled her and she hesitated before saying, "We get along fine."

"He makes about four thousand a year," Cal said. "Tops."

Perris grinned. "I can lose and make that in one night. Honey, if all you got out of school was him, you should've stayed home."

She glanced at Evan and away from him quickly. "You can't help whom you fall in love with." She smiled as if carrying on a joke.

Cal said, "While Ray is off in the Arm Service."

"Ev and I would've gotten married even if Ray had stayed home!"

Cal shrugged. "That's not the way I see it. Ray turns his back and the horse doctor comes along."

"I don't care how you see it! All you want to do is argue. You've nothing better to do than that."

"Nobody's asking me," Perris said. "I don't think you'd of married him either. What do you think of that?"

Julie hesitated to control her voice. "I think you've had too much to drink."

"And what's Ev think about it?" Perris turned, his expression cold and partly concealed by the sunglasses. "What's old Ev the horse doctor think about it?"

Evan met his gaze squarely. He stood with his feet apart, unmoving, and said, "You better get out of here right now. That's what I think."

"Ray," Julie said quickly. "There was never anything between us. That's what makes this whole thing so silly." She stopped. Perris was not paying any attention to her.

"What was that, Ev?"

"You heard what I said."

"Something about getting out."

"I can't say it any plainer."

Cal grinned. "Man, he's talking now."

"Asking for it," Perris said.

"Sure." Cal nodded. "Why don't you deck him and get it over with."

"I'm waiting for him."

"You got a long wait."

"Stop it!" Julie stared at Ray Perris, her face flushed and tight with anger. "What are you some kind of an animal that you fight over nothing? Ray, I swear if you even make a fist I'll call the state police!"

Perris glanced at Cal. "Take her inside and open the beers. I'll be right in."

"Ray, I swear—" Cal's hand closed on her arm and pulled her off balance. "Let go of me!" She saw Evan rushing at Cal and then she screamed.

Ray Perris took a half step and drove his fist into Evan's body stopping him in his stride and as he doubled over, Perris's left stung against the side of his jaw and he went to his knees.

Perris stood close to him, waiting. Beyond, past his legs, he saw Cal forcing Julie up to the porch. Cal stopped to watch and called out, "Ray, be careful of those hands!"

Evan breathed in and out getting his breath, then lunged at Perris, swinging his right with everything he could put behind it.

Perris came inside, taking the roundhouse of his shoulder, and threw four jabs piston-like into Evan's body. Even went back, staggered by the force of the short punches and Perris came after him. Even tried to bring up his guard, but Perris feinted him high and drove his left in; and when Evan's guard dropped, Perris threw the right that had been cocked waiting. It chopped into Evan's face and he felt the ground slam the back of his head and jolt through his whole body.

He felt himself being dragged by his legs, heard his wife's voice but wasn't sure of it. Then he was lying, half leaning against a tree. He felt his shoes being pulled off and he opened his eyes.

Perris was walking away from him toward the station wagon. He saw him look at it, then open it again and take out the two .30-30's. He held both under one arm, the shoes in the other hand,

and called to Evan, "You touch that car and I'll break your jaw!"

He turned and walked to the house. On the porch he said something to Cal, who was standing in the doorway holding Julie. Cal came outside. He went to Evan's car and let the air out of both rear tires, then returned to the house. The door closed and there was no sound in the yard.

He was perhaps sixty feet from the porch, not straight out from it but off toward the side where the cars were parked; and as he lay propped against the tree staring at the house, at the lighted living room windows, not believing that this had actually happened, his lips parted with a thick throbbing half numbness, he tried to assemble the thoughts that raced through his mind.

He thought of Julie, forcing himself to remain calm as he did. He pictured himself getting a pitchfork from the barn and breaking down the door. Then he remembered the .30-30's.

They wouldn't shoot. No? You think they're not capable of it? And they're drunk—beyond what little reason they have. This doesn't happen, does it?

He could run for help. Even without shoes he could run down to the highway and stop a car, get to the state police at Brighton.

He pictured the blue and gold police car pulling up and two troopers going into the house and Cal and Ray looking up, surprised; and one of the troopers saying, "Don't give your pals so much to drink and they won't get out of hand." He saw Cal wink at Ray, waiting for the troopers to leave.

He was aware of the night sounds: an owl far off; crickets in the yard close to the house and in the full darkness of the woods behind him.

No, he thought. *You do it yourself. You have to get them out. You have to do it so that it's once and for all, or else they'll come back again. They're not afraid of you, but they have to be made afraid. Do you understand that?*

He heard the owl again and he could feel the deep woods behind him.

The woods . . .

For perhaps a quarter of an hour more he remained in the shadows, thinking, asking himself questions and groping for the answers and finally he knew what he would do.

His hand went up the rough bark of the tree to steady him as he got to his feet. He moved along the edge of shadow until the station wagon was between him and the house, then stooped slightly, instinctively and ran across the yard to his car.

With his hand on the door handle he noticed the ventipane partly open. He pulled it out to a right angle then put his arm in, pressing his right side against the car door, rolled down the window, brought out his veterinary kit, and stooped to the ground with it.

The inside pocket, he thought, remembering putting his instruments away after delivering the calf that afternoon. His hand went in, came out with a three-ounce bottle of chloroform; went in again, felt the mouth speculum—*no, too heavy*—then his fingers closed on the steel handle of a hoof knife and he drew it out, a thin-bladed knife curved to a sharpened hook.

The rifles, he thought then. *No, they won't follow you without the rifles. Just bring them out.*

From the edge of the drive he picked up a rock twice the size of his fist, walked to within six feet of the station wagon, and hurled it through the windshield. He waited until the front door swung suddenly open, then ran for the trees, hearing Cal's voice, then Ray's, hearing them on the steps—

"There he is!"

"Get the guns!" Ray's voice as he ran to the station wagon.

Cal came out of the house with the rifles and Ray said, "Come on!"

"Where'd he go?"

"Not far without shoes."

From the shadows again, but deeper into the trees, Evan watched them for a moment. They stood close together, Perris talking, describing something with his hands, then taking a rifle from Cal, the two of them separating and coming toward the trees. Evan moved back carefully, working his way over to where Cal would enter. Perris was nearer the road, perhaps thirty yards away.

Evan crouched, waiting, hearing the rustling, twig-snapping sound of them moving through the scrub growth and fallen leaves. Cal was coming almost directly toward him.

He let Cal pass—one step, another—then rose without a sound and was on him, one hand clamping Cal's mouth, the other pressing the hoof knife against his side hard enough that he would feel the blade. He felt Cal go rigid and he pushed against him, turning him to make him walk to the left now, broadening the distance between them and Perris.

About twenty yards farther on Evan stopped. His hand came away from Cal's mouth, went to his shirt pocket, and brought out the chloroform.

Cal didn't move, but he said, "Rays going to beat you blue."

Even said nothing, putting the hoof knife under his arm. He drew his handkerchief and saturated it with chloroform then retuned the bottle to his pocket. "How is Julie?"

"She locked herself in the bedroom."

"Did he touch her?"

"Ask him."

"All right, Cal. Call him over."

"What?"

"Go ahead, call him."

Cal hesitated. Suddenly he screamed, "Ray, he's over here!"

The sound of his voice cut the stillness, rang through the darkness of the trees and was loud in Evan's ear as he clamped the handkerchief against Cal's face and dragged him as he struggled into dense brush. In a moment Cal was on the ground unconscious. Evan picked up the rifle and started running. He heard Ray's voice and the sound of him hurrying through the foliage and he called back over his shoulder, "Come on!"

He kept running, driving through the brush, feeling sharp stabs of pain in his stockinged feet and twice again he called back to Perris, making sure he was following. Within a hundred yards he reached the end of the woods.

The first quarter moon showed an expanse of plowed field and far off on the other side, a shapeless mass of trees against the night sky. He turned right along the edge of the field for a few yards then moved silently back into the woods. Not far in he crouched down to wait.

There was little time to spare. In less than a minute Perris reached the field and stopped. He scanned it, his eyes open wide in the darkness.

"Cal?"

There was a dead stillness now without even the small, hidden night sounds in the background.

"Cal, where are you?"

Perris turned from the field uncertain, he hesitated, then started into the trees again.

Now, Evan thought. He flipped the lever of the .30-30 down and up and a sharp metallic sound, unmistakable in the stillness, reached Ray Perris.

He stopped. Then edged back to the field.

"Cal?"

Evan waited. Through the trees Perris was silhouetted against the field. Watching him, Evan thought, *Now add it up, Ray.*

He saw Perris turn to the field again and without warning break into a run. Evan brought the rifle to his shoulder and fired. Dirt kicked up somewhere close in front of Perris and he stopped abruptly, turned stumbling and went down as he reached the trees again.

Then— "Ev, what's the matter with you!"

Silence.

"Ev, we were just clownin' around! Cal says, 'Come on out and see Julie.' I said, 'Fine.' On the way out he says, 'We'll throw a scare into Evan.' You know, for something to do, that's all. We'd had some beers and that sounded OK with me. What the hell, the way Cal talked I figured you for a real hayseed. Then we come here and you get on the muscle. Get mean about it. What am I supposed to do, let you throw me out? I'm not built that way."

He was quiet for a moment.

"Ev, I'll forget about the car. You were burned up—OK, I'll let it go. What the hell, it's insured."

Silence.

"You hear? Answer me!"

Just like that, Evan thought. *Forget all about it. No, Ray, you're not scared enough yet. You might want to come back.* He raised the rifle, aiming high, and fired again and the sound rocked out over the field.

"Ev, you're a crazy man! They lock up guys like you!"

Now you're talking, Ray.

Minutes passed before Perris spoke again.

"Ev, listen to me, I'm walking back to my car and if you shoot it's murder. You understand that? Murder!"

Suddenly Perris stood up. "Answer me!" He screamed it. "You hear what I said? I'm coming out and if you shoot it's murder! . . . You go to Jackson for life!"

"I'm coming now, Ev." He started into the trees. "Listen, man, just hold on to yourself. You're burned up, sure; but it isn't worth it. I mean not Jackson the rest of your life. You got to think of it that way."

Perris started to run.

Evan was waiting. He gauged the distance, crawled to the next brush clump, and came up swinging the rifle as Perris tried to run past. The barrel slashed down against the .30-30 in his hands and he went back, dropping it, trying to cover, but was too late. Evan's fist whapped against his face and he stumbled. He tried to rush, bringing his hands up suddenly as the rifle was thrown at him, deflected it, ducking to the side, and looked up in time to receive the full impact of a right that was swung wide and hard and with every pound that could be put behind it. Evan kneeled over him and pressed the chloroformed handkerchief to Ray's face before carrying him back to the yard.

Julie was on the porch. She screamed his name when she saw Evan, but he talked to her for a moment and after that she was calm. He went back for Cal then loaded both of them into the station wagon and drove down to the highway, turned left toward Detroit, and went about a mile before parking the station wagon off on the side of the road.

They would come out of the chloroform in fifteen or twenty minutes. If the state police found them first, let Perris tell whatever he liked. Even the truth if he didn't mind the publicity that might result. It didn't matter to Evan what he did. It was over.

He crossed the plowed field and passed again through the woods, picking up his hoof knife on the way back to the house.

Julie held open the door. "Ev, what if they come back?"

"I doubt if they will."

"Then we won't think about it," she said.

They sat in the living room for a few minutes then went out to the kitchen to finish the dishes.

The Italian Cut

1954

AT FIVE O'CLOCK THERE was still no sign of Roy. Elaine stood at the dinette window looking down three stories into the darkening court of the apartment building. If she pressed her left cheek to the pane she could see a short stretch of sidewalk and beyond it, the NO PARKING BUILDING ENTRANCE signs, the street pavement glistening in the October rain. From the living room window she could see only one of the signs, and only half as much of the pavement.

She was thinking, and was almost completely sure of it, that Roy had stopped for a beer. There wasn't anything wrong with that, but at least he could call. Roy's shift was out at three-thirty and usually he was home by four-ten, the latest. Except on bowling night and softball night and, it occurred to her now, almost every time it rained that Grady didn't have the car.

That was it. She wasn't sure whether Grady had taken the car. Roy rode with him when he did; when he didn't, they took the bus together.

She had seen Inez, Grady's wife, come in just before three-thirty pushing the stroller with little Grady in it and her other arm loaded down with groceries. Elaine would have called, but the rain started just then and Inez had hurried through the court. It was lucky she and Grady had a first-floor apartment—with the stroller and all.

I forgot about that, Elaine thought. *I'll be climbing three flights.* She smiled, turning from the window. The first six weeks Roy would be carrying her up and down.

She glanced at the mirror over the buffet then stopped, her fingers lightly touching the short hair at the nape of her neck and she studied the dark curl that clung close to the soft curve of her cheek. She had had it cut that morning. Roy'll die! She went on then to the wall telephone and dialed.

"Inez? Hi . . . Listen, did Grady drive today? . . . Oh . . . No, he's not home either. They're probably in some bar . . . Uh-huh . . . Every time it rains. We should be used to it by now . . . No, I was just anxious for him to get home . . . I wasn't sure if Grady drove . . . Uh-huh . . . Inez, listen, why don't you and Grady come up after a while? . . . No, we've been to your place too many times. Get a sitter and come up . . . Uh-huh, it's on I think . . . No, I've just seen it once or twice. Roy likes to watch the fights. They come on at the same time . . . you can miss it this once. I've got something to show you . . . No! It's a surprise! . . . You sort of buy it, but not like you're thinking."

Elaine moved the length of the telephone cord then leaned to the side until she could see herself in the buffet mirror. She smiled, turning her head from side to side.

"Uh-huh, you wear it . . . That's right, but you don't buy it at a store." Elaine giggled. "Inez, I've got something to tell you, too . . . Ohhhhhh, you wrecked it! How'd you know? . . . Uh-huh . . . No my mother used to say you could tell by the eyes." . . . She shook her head. "They look the same to me . . . Just two weeks . . . Uh-huh . . .

No, I haven't told him yet . . . Because he gets so excited. He'll run out and get a baseball mitt and it'll turn out to be a false alarm . . . What? I know." Elaine laughed into the phone . . . "I'm just kidding. I'm going to tell him as soon as he gets home . . . OK . . . About eight-thirty or nine, if they're still standing up . . . OK, good-bye." She hung up the receiver and stepped into the kitchen.

It was a quarter past five by the electric clock above the refrigerator as she took out the hamburger. Not really late, but he still could have called.

Tonight of all nights, Elaine thought. All morning she had planned how she would tell him. She would wait for him to sit down with the paper. (She could picture him turning to the sports section. Wednesday night: he'd be studying next Saturday's football schedule, picking out four or five teams to play on the odds card.) She would bring him a bottle of beer then lean close to him so he'd be looking right into her eyes. "Roy, do you notice anything?" He'd make a funny crack and then she would tell him. "Roy, I'm pregnant. I'm sure of it this time!"

No, she thought now. *Say it some other way.* She had been sure three times before. Three times in the seven years of their marriage and nothing had happened. But this time she *was* sure. She had only thought she was those other times. "Roy, I was *sick* this morning!" Telling him in the sound of her voice what a wonderful feeling it was to be sick that way—after seven years. "That's why I'm really sure. I never was sick those other times!"

But the haircut—

Well, he would see it right away. There was no getting around that. *But he'll get used to it,* she thought. *And then he'll love it.* Telling him about the baby, almost at the same time, she considered perfect timing.

It was ten minutes to six when Roy came in, and he did notice her hair right away.

"What happened to you?" He peeled off his jacket and dropped it over the arm of a chair. He was wearing a red and white jersey with FALCONS lettered across the front of it. He was of medium build, but not more than five foot seven and sometimes, when he walked, he held his arms out as if he were conscious of the muscles in them.

Elaine came to him from the dinette. She was smiling. "Like it?" She turned her face to let him see both profiles.

He looked at her sullenly. "You look like you got your head caught in a fan."

"It's the Italian cut."

"That makes it all right?"

"It's the latest thing."

"There's a guy on a drill press at work got hair just like that. He'll be glad to know it."

Elaine shrugged. "All right, you don't like it."

"For seven years your hair's long, like a woman's supposed to be; then one day I come home and find you looking like a guy and I'm supposed to like it."

"Roy, all summer it was so hot—"

"So when it starts to get winter you have it cut off."

"You might as well get used to it."

"Just like that."

"Well, they can't glue it back on."

"How much did it cost?"

"Six dollars."

"Six bucks for that!"

"Roy, he had to do more than just cut it. It had to be styled, and set—"

"Was this guy an Eyetalian that cut it?"

"I don't know. He said my hair was perfect for it."

"What'd you expect him to say?"

"Roy, why don't we just forget it?"

"You'd have to keep your hat on."

Elaine turned and walked to the kitchen.

"Get me a beer," Roy called after her. He sat down in the big chair across from the televison set and picked up the evening paper, glancing at the headline (something about a pact OK'd), and turned immediately to the sports section.

"Here's your beer," Elaine said.

He dropped one side of the paper and took the bottle from her, raised it, and drank it down to the top of the label before lowering it. Then he looked at Elaine, who was still standing in front of him. "Thanks."

"How many does that make?" she asked.

"How many what?"

"Beers."

"What're you talking about?"

"You weren't working overtime."

"So I must've stopped by a tavern."

"Well, didn't you?"

"No." He took another gulp of beer, set the bottle down, and picked up the newspaper from his lap.

"All right, then you didn't have a drink," Elaine said. She turned to the kitchen.

Roy lowered the newspaper. "You gotta know, don't you?"

She looked back at him, but did not speak.

"I told you I was going to be late. I told you we were having election of officers right after work."

Elaine frowned. "I don't remember. Officers for what?"

"The bowling league!"

Elaine shook her head. "I don't remember you telling me that."

"But you remembered to get an Eyetalian haircut."

She was thinking: *there's no sense driving it into the ground.* She walked out to the kitchen, hearing him get up and follow her.

He stood in the doorway as she put the hamburgers under the broiler.

"I got nominated for president."

She glanced at him. "Then what do you look so glum about?"

"I got nominated, not elected."

"When do they vote?"

"Tomorrow after work. We didn't have time today."

"Well, you'll be elected tomorrow then."

"I got nominated the last one," he said bitterly. "On a fluke!"

"What do you mean?"

"Grady's name was in for it. Him an' another guy. But Grady got up and said he didn't want the job. He said he wanted to nominate me instead."

"Well?"

"I don't want no charity."

"That's not charity."

"What do you call it? I organized the league. Five years ago I organized the whole deal and got it going. And not once—not one damn time am I the president! Grady feels like a big shot and puts my name in. I'm a substitute for a guy who don't even want to be president!"

Elaine rinsed her hands and dried them on a dish towel. "I think that was pretty nice of him."

"You don't know anything about it."

"Somebody must've seconded it."

"After Grady made a speech."

"Well, Roy"—she smiled—"maybe you just weren't cut out to be a politician."

"I *organized* the league!"

"You've been a team captain. Roy's Boys."

"Team captain isn't president."

"Why don't you wait and see?"

During dinner, Elaine turned on the television when she saw

Roy was not going to talk and she watched a panel show while they ate. But when they were finishing their coffee she said, "Grady and Inez are coming up after a while."

Roy looked up. "What for?"

"Just to be sociable."

"I don't feel like being sociable."

"You can watch the fights. I felt like talking to Inez."

"You want to show her your hair?"

"That's part of it." She watched Roy get up and go into the living room. He sat down and picked up the sports section, not looking at her.

Grady and Inez came up at five minutes to nine. Inez thought Elaine's hair was perfect. Should have been short a long time ago! Elaine was watching Roy. She saw him look at Inez disgustedly, then he turned to the television and switched channels.

"Who's fighting?" Grady said.

Roy shrugged. "A couple of clowns."

"It might be a good one," Grady said.

"You want a beer?" Roy asked him.

"What do you think I came up for?"

"I asked you if you wanted a beer."

Grady's face sobered. "Yeah, I want one." He was a heavyset pleasant-faced man nearing forty and losing his hair. "What's the matter with you?" he said to Roy.

Roy ignored him, looking at Inez and Elaine. "What about you?"

Elaine nodded and Inez said, "Fine." She added, laughing, that the beer commercials on the fights made her thirsty, but Roy walked out as she was saying it.

When he came back in with the bottles of beer between his fingers Grady was looking at the sports section.

"Roy, you pick your teams yet?"

"Not yet."

"You can't beat those bookies. They hit the point odds right on the nose—then take ties. They can't lose."

"You got to know how to play them," Roy said.

"Who do you like, for instance?" Grady said.

"State and thirteen."

Grady shook his head. "They got no quarterback."

"What're you talking about! What's his name, Buddy—"

"He's too small," Grady said.

"Small!" Roy was standing looking down at Grady. "I played quarter at a hunnert and thirty-two pounds!"

"Roy, that was in high school."

"So what!"

"They didn't use a T then," Grady said mildly. "A quarterback today's got to be big enough to throw the ball over his linemen."

Elaine saw the color rise in Roy's face and she felt relief when Inez called his name and he stopped whatever he was about to say and looked at her.

"Grady," Inez said, smiling, "told me you're up for president of the bowling league."

Roy was staring at her now. "Is that how he said it?"

Inez laughed. "I don't know if those were the exact words."

"That's what I want to hear: the exact words."

Inez tried to smile. "You sound like a lawyer."

"And you sound like you're changing the subject," Roy said. He was standing in front of the television set. Behind him the first round had already started. "I want to know how he really said it," Roy insisted.

"That's what he said. He said you were up for president." She glanced at Elaine saying it.

"Roy," Elaine said. "Your fight's going on."

"Didn't he say," Roy went on, still looking at Inez, " 'I threw Roy a bone this afternoon. He looked like a hungry dog, so I threw him a bone.' "

Grady stared at him in astonishment. "Roy, what's the matter with you?"

"Isn't that what you said, Grady? Maybe not in those words, but something like it." He tried to mimic Grady's voice; he was not close to imitating it, but they knew that's what he was doing, saying, " 'Inez, Roy means well, even if he don't have too much between the ears. So I thought I'd make him feel good and put his name up. Had a hell of a time getting somebody to second it. Had to make a speech. He won't get it, but it'll make the little runt feel good.' "

Grady said, "Roy, you think you're being funny?"

Roy glared at him. "Isn't that how you meant it?"

Grady rose, looking at his wife. "I think we better be going."

Roy said curtly, "I think so too. We don't need any charity tonight. When we do I'll call either you or the Goodwill."

Elaine did not move. She watched Roy, even as Grady and Inez went by her to the door, Inez saying something half-whispered which she did not hear clearly. Her eyes rose as Roy passed her following them to the door. She heard the door open, and then slam. Suddenly she was aware of the crowd at the boxing arena screaming and whistling. The camera showed a close-up of the ring and she saw that one of the fighters was down, the referee bending over swinging his arm, counting. Counting to ten. It was all over in the first round.

Roy passed her again. He sat down on the edge of his chair and leaned forward as if engrossed in the ring announcer's description of the judges' scoring the fight. He took a swallow of beer and lit a cigarette, not taking his eyes from the television screen.

Elaine sat still. She felt uncomfortably self-conscious, and now, without reason, she pictured her hair looking almost ridiculous and she wished she had not had it cut. At least not today. There were things she wanted to say to Roy, feeling her anger grow as she looked at him, but they were obvious things and would only make him madder. She wanted to say something sarcastic, but the right words wouldn't form in her mind.

Roy stood up, switching off the television, and turned to her abruptly. "Now I get the silent act."

Elaine raised her eyes. "What do you want me to say?"

"You'll think of something."

Damn him! "Well"—she kept her voice calm—"do you think you behaved like a normal human being?" Oddly, then, she could not help thinking: he must feel silly standing there with FALCONS written across his chest.

"When I get a deal like that I act how I feel!"

She felt the anger again and said, unexpectedly, "Roy, why don't you grow up!"

His face colored. "You sit there with that screwball haircut and tell me why don't I grow up!"

"Now why would you take it out on my hair?"

"Where do you get off telling me to grow up—that's what I want to know! You're perfect—never do nothing wrong. I come home after I get a rough deal—I got something important on my mind—and all you talk about is that stupid-lookin' haircut!"

Elaine was standing now, almost stiffly. "Why do you keep bringing up my hair?" she said, not keeping her voice calm any longer. "You know why? I'll tell you why. Because when something goes against you you're not man enough to face the facts. You have to blame something else, like my hair, that doesn't have a damn thing to do with it. You have to hear yourself yell so you'll still think you're a big shot. The great athlete! You've been out of high school for twelve years, but nobody'd ever know it. You're still a hundred-and-thirty-two-pound quarterback. You're still a flashy shortstop because you know how to crease a baseball cap the right way. You're the great bowler—all form and no score! You know how to outfigure the football bookies—but you always lose! You know how to do everything—but nothing right! You know why they don't want you for a president? Because your lousing everything up wouldn't be bad enough—all season they'd have to listen to you blowing off about being president!"

Roy stood with his hands on his hips, his face drawn and tensed. There was a silence, and then he said, "You through?"

Elaine hesitated. "One last thing," she said. She leaned forward slightly, as if for emphasis. "Grow up!"

Roy stared at her for a moment. Then he walked past her, picking up his jacket as he went out.

The door slammed. She closed her eyes and seemed to relax then, her breath coming out in a slow sigh. That was that.

Now he'll go out and get plastered, she thought. *That's supposed to solve everything.* Perhaps she shouldn't have said the things she did. Well, it was done now. And strangely enough she felt a little better for it. Let him go out and get drunk. If he thinks he's got something on his mind now, wait till he wakes up tomorrow with a hangover.

She took the beer bottles and glasses to the kitchen, and returning, she caught her reflection in the dinette mirror. She stopped and looked at her hair. There was nothing the least bit ridiculous about it. She saw her eyes then. She leaned closer to study them—as she had been doing for almost two weeks—and it dawned on her that she had not told Roy about the baby.

It was ten when she went to bed.

It was almost two in the morning when she finally heard Roy come in. She could hear him in the living room. Then the light went on in the bathroom and without raising her head from the pillow she saw him momentarily in the bedroom doorway. The water ran in the bathroom for a long time before he came out, switching off the light. He stumbled against the foot of the bed, swearing under his breath. She could feel the mattress sink on his side as he sat down, and a moment later, she heard his shoes hit the floor. He stood up, taking off his pants, then flopped down again, the bedsprings squeaking. He didn't bother to remove the jersey but lay back with a long moaning sigh, and a moment later, he was breathing evenly, sound asleep.

Elaine was on her right side, her back to him, and her eyes were open in the darkness. She could picture him lying on his back, his mouth slightly open. Now, and until the alarm went off, with nothing to worry him. Lying peacefully, with FALCONS written across his chest.

Feeling him close behind her, it went through her mind: *you made your bed, now lie in it.* But she was immediately sorry she thought this, even coming to her mind as it did; because now, picturing Roy, she felt sorry for him. He wants to be somebody, she thought. That's all it is. He wants a little recognition. There's nothing wrong with that. But he doesn't have as much patience as most people. He's not so easily satisfied. My gosh, you can't blame the guy for wanting to win. She started to think: but that's no excuse for being a poor loser— And she put it out of her mind, picturing him again.

He was good-looking—not overly tall and his hair was starting to go back—but better-looking than most men. So what if he did like to flex his muscles. At least he had them to flex.

He brought home over ninety dollars a week, and he liked his work. ("Honey . . . you see the castings come off this automation station and I drop her into load position . . . transfer her down . . . drop her into the tank . . . then I got fifteen seconds to spot a leak and mark it . . .")

Most men came home, buried their faces in the paper and didn't say anything. Inez was always complaining: "Grady never talks. He sits down with one of these pocket books and I don't hear from him all evening."

You couldn't say Roy didn't talk.

Still, she thought, *there was no excuse for the way he acted.* And she became angry again thinking about it. Let him get his own breakfast tomorrow!

She thought of something else after that, so she would be able to fall asleep.

She was awake before Roy, before the alarm went off, but she remained in bed pretending to be asleep until he dressed and left the apartment, not bothering about breakfast.

Elaine got up thinking: *You can't even force the guy to do penance. He'll get a better cup of coffee at the plant than I make.* And she thought now: *but please, God, at least make him be hungover.*

Roy got home that evening at five-thirty. Elaine came out of the kitchen hearing the front door. She stood across the room from him as he took off his jacket and dropped it on the arm of the chair.

Roy looked at her unconcernedly. "Hi."

"Hi. How do you feel?"

"Pretty good."

She had decided not to ask about the election, but she didn't know what to say and she felt suddenly uncomfortable in the silence.

"How was it?"

Roy looked up. He was lighting a cigarette. "What?"

"Your election."

"Oh. I didn't go.

"You didn't go!"

"Naw." Roy hesitated, and started to grin. "Listen, you might not believe this, but remember last night you said I was all form and no score? Well, I was thinking about it today. I never averaged over one-thirty-six in my life, so I figured why waste all that time trying to bowl if you'll never be any good anyway."

Elaine's lips parted in surprise.

"So," Roy went on, "I figured the hell with it. Let the other guy be president. He bowls about one-seventy and gets a big bang out of it."

Elaine was taken off guard. She was completely unprepared for this. "Roy," she said hesitantly, "you're not kidding me?"

"Why should I kid you?"

"It just doesn't sound like you."

"I told you you might not believe me."

Elaine relaxed, smiling at him. She felt like going to him and putting her arms around his neck and she thought at that moment about the baby and she smiled all the more. But something else occurred to her then.

"Roy, if you didn't go to the meeting, where have you been?"

Roy grinned. "I ran into this guy after work. He asked me if I was interested in playing basketball and I told him maybe, it depended. So we had a couple of beers and he told me about it. A Wednesday-night league at the Y—sounds like a pretty good deal—so I told him OK."

For a moment Elaine was silent. She stared at him, seeing him smiling at her. "Roy," she said then, "with your experience they might even make you captain."

His face brightened. "I never thought about that."

"Come on," Elaine said, half turning to the kitchen, "you can tell me about it during dinner."

The Only Good Syrian Foot Soldier Is a Dead One

THAT MORNING HE WAS trampled to death during the retreat of the Syrian cavalry. Immediately after lunch he was brought down by a Roman lance and now he lay in the sun among the dead and wounded, his eyes open, his head resting on his arm, while thirty yards away the Ultra-Panavision camera moved slowly, left to right, over the scene.

He watched the camera boom lower and the cameraman climb off to stand with the director. They lighted cigarettes and now Howard Keating, the centurion and star of Sidney Aaronson's production of *The Centurion,* his helmet off, his dark hair pressed to his forehead, joined them and accepted a cigarette and light from the director. A girl in tight toreadors and sunglasses handed him a towel, which he pressed to his face and tossed back to her.

Don't think about us, Allen Garfield, the dead Syrian foot soldier, thought. *Stand around. Smoke cigarettes. Call the script girl over with the camera log and fool around with her awhile. Now the production manager, get him over. And the casting guy. Everybody act casual. Now laugh at something dumb the director says. Now stand there and shuffle your feet and look up at the sun and step on cigarettes and have a few more laughs while we lie out here in the goddamn sun.*

Near him he heard two of the extras who had been stabbed, hacked, lanced, or shot with arrows, talking to each other in Spanish. For three hundred pesetas a day they would lie here as long as the director, the centurion, and the cameraman wanted to smoke cigarettes. For three hundred pesetas they would lie here all day in sun or rain or snow and live very well at night in Madrid. Most of the dead and wounded were Spanish; there was only a handful of English and Americans, perhaps a dozen.

During the two and a half years Allen Garfield had been in Spain, *The Centurion* was the fourth Sidney Aaronson spectacular he had worked in as an extra. Without speaking a word or releasing a scream that had been recorded, he was killed on the average of twice per picture, and had acquired something of a reputation in the casting office as a good dier.

In *Lepanto,* as a Moorish pirate, he had leaped to the Spanish galleon, chopped three times at the Duke of Valencia, then hesitated just long enough on the next down swing to let the Duke run him through. In *The Sack of Rome,* with a black ponytail pinned to his hair and a fur piece over one shoulder, he was dragging a virgin from the temple of Vestus when a javelin fixed him to the temple door. He was killed four times in *The Gods Smiled,* Sidney Aaronson's four-and-a-half-hour entertainment on the futility of war. He was killed as a Persian, a Saracen, a German lance corporal, and a G.I. frozen to his machine gun on the Chosin Reservoir. While in the same picture Howard Keating, tightening his jaw muscle as a Spartan, a Crusader, a Spad fighter pilot, and a Marine Corps combat officer, was wounded twice and wondered aloud, through 2,500 years of war, if it was all worth it.

THE GOLDEN SNAKE, TWISTED into a Syrian armband, cut into Allen Garfield's cheek, and he raised his head a few inches from his arm, his gaze holding on the scene thirty yards beyond the dead and wounded: the camp of the director, who had put on his straw cowboy hat and was still talking to the centurion, who was now wearing sunglasses.

The rest of the crew were small tan figures, some shirtless with handkerchiefs knotted on their heads, some standing among the cables and camera boom and lights and generator equipment, some sitting under the tarp awning and some in the shade of the truck where two legs extended from the open cab and silver square sun reflectors leaned against the paneled side.

They don't know what they're doing, Allen Garfield thought. *So they stand around until the director has one of his great ideas. You have to have truly great ideas to make a twelve-million-dollar motion picture look like a high school pageant.*

Once, during the filming of *The Gods Smiled,* Allen Garfield was standing near the director. They were between takes of the Crusades sequence. At this time he had still believed the director, Ray Heidke, to be a savvy, sensitive, dedicated craftsman; somewhat colorful, a bit eccentric perhaps; but basically one of the good guys.

It was mid July, ninety-five degrees in the sun and they were on the Mohammedan village set. The director wore shorts, sandals, no shirt, and his trademark, the willowroot straw cowboy hat, the crown funneled down over his eyes like a beak.

"Billy," the director said to the cameraman. "First you get your establishing shot of the square. Then I want you to truck in. You're the eyes. You're what the Crusaders see as they enter the town. Nothing's happened, right? The place's deserted. We get the reverses later, the Crusaders looking up, their reaction, their feeling goosey about the whole thing. I just want you to see this. So you come to the end of your truck. Fifteen feet from that doorway in the wall. You're aimed at eye level. We cut from a reverse to you. *Bang*, the doors bust open and these mothers come screaming out. I mean they come with those curved swords like *nothing* can stop them. You see it?"

The cameraman nodded thoughtfully and the director turned to Allen Garfield and the group of Saracens, almost all of whom were Spanish.

"Ramon," the director said to his production manager. "Tell them to come out yelling like Franco just outlawed poon."

Allen Garfield, leaning on his spear, grinned. "You mean you want us to look sore."

"Hey, we've got an American Mohammedan," the director said. "Where are you from, son?"

"Royal Oak, Michigan."

"You worked for me before?"

"In *Sack*. I was a barbarian, Mr. Heidke."

"Well, you're coming up, aren't you?"

Allen Garfield grinned. He felt good. "Sir, I was wondering . . . you're shooting everything down in the street . . . what if you went up high for some down shots of the Crusaders? You know, as they'd appear to the Mohammedans waiting to ambush? You don't see the Mohammedans, but you see what they see, you know, and you build suspense."

The director's gaze stared calmly from the shadow of his hat brim holding on Allen Garfield. "You build suspense, uh?"

"Like in *Gunga Din*. Remember when they came into that village?"

"No," the director said, "I don't believe I remember that. Did you see this *Gunga Din* in Royal Oak, Michigan?"

Oh, God, Allen Garfield thought and said, "It's just a suggestion. I don't mean a *suggestion* really. I just mean the scenes are like, similar."

The director nodded. "Like similar. You know, I'd like to see this *Gunga Din*." He said then, "Do you think if I went to Royal Oak, Michigan, they'd show it to me?"

Throughout the rest of the day, the rest of the week, and almost whenever he saw or thought of the director after that, Allen Garfield pictured himself standing in the Saracen costume holding the spear and imagined the replies he could have made.

Very calmly, looking right at him, "I think if you ever went to Royal Oak, Michigan, they'd . . ." Then something right between the eyes.

"They'd string you up in front of the theater."

"They'd tie you to a front-row seat out of revenge and make you watch all your pictures."

Or, how about, you just stare at him very calmly and say, "That remark is about as intelligent as the pictures you make." Or . . .

"Gee, Mr. Heidke, how does it feel to know everything?" Very humbly.

"How does it feel to be as smart as you are?"

"How does it feel to be a smart-ass?"

No, the best thing would be to shake your head like, This is too much. Hand him the goddamn spear and walk off. Walk off right in front of the whole cast and crew, because you don't have to take that jazz from anybody. Not any*body.*

But Allen Garfield had grinned. He had stood before the director in his Saracen robes holding his Saracen spear and had grinned.

WHAT IS IT? SOMETHING the better part of valor? Live to fight another day. The trouble was you couldn't fight them. You smile and act nice or you don't work. Or, the dead Syrian foot soldier thought then, you turn the camera around. You shoot them and show what fantastic jerks they are. Exposeville. Only with taste.

Shoot that, Allen Garfield thought. *Write a script about all the waiting and standing around smoking cigarettes and the absolute disregard for anybody else. Write about the director who doesn't know what to do next and covers up practicing his golf swing with a sword.*

Write about the star leaving the cigarette in his mouth while the makeup girl tries to powder his face and he runs his hand up her side and can't believe it when she clamps her arm down. The next day there's a new makeup girl to powder the small muscle that moves in the jaw of the star who receives 1,500 letters a week, on the average, but who has his secretary read him "only the dirty ones."

And how he drinks German beer, only German beer in Spain, out of a Roman goblet, all day yelling for his goblet between takes and sometimes stopping in the middle of a take to go off to the bathroom while dead Syrians lie waiting in the sun.

Let's get some contrast in it, Allen Garfield thought.

Like standing in the rain in the commissary line for forty-five minutes listening to everybody talking Spanish and seeing the station wagon go by with the half dozen or so catered lunches from the Hilton.

Another line late in the afternoon, two thousand extras queued up for the bus ride back to Madrid and the Rolls going by with Keating and the girl in tight pants, just the two of them in the backseat with a thermos of martinis.

Later, Keating and the girl will be in the group at Aaronson's villa. They would watch a newly released film on the wide screen that came down out of the ceiling, no one even whispering during the film because Mr. Aaronson demanded absolute attention. After, they would speculate on whether or not the film would make money. And after that the Rolls would return Keating and his protégée to the Castellana Hilton, passing the bar on the Avenida de José Antonio where Allen Garfield sat with the two English actors, also Syrian foot soldiers, drinking Scotch that had been distilled in North Africa.

That would be a good contrast: the in group talking about box office and residuals and Aston Martins and Marbella; while he and his friends talked about films: tore them open, probed their content, and quoted inane anachronistic lines (MARCELLUS *haughtily ignoring his chains:* "That will be the day, when a Roman bows before a Syrian dog"), shaking their heads at the Roman westerns Mr. Sidney Aaronson passed off as motion pictures.

Another one. Keating stopping at the desk to see if there was a letter or call from his wife; the girl waiting by the elevator; Allen Garfield crossing the Plaza Major toward his pension, the street dark, wet, cafés closed, chairs and sidewalk tables stacked, a cab going by with dim yellow lights. Mood stuff.

Now he rested his head on his forearm, closing his eyes and feeling the sun on his face. *Go to sleep. Let them screw around all they want. Take the rotten three hundred pesetas a day, the rotten five whole bucks a day, and be happy. No worries, no problems. Think of all the jerks would trade places with you.*

Be a good boy and go to sleep.

Or get up and walk off.

He opened his eyes.

Get up. Walk off right in front of them and don't say a goddamn word or look at anybody and if you have to walk all the way to Madrid then walk all the way to Madrid.

And if you could walk on water, he thought then, closing his eyes again, *you could walk all the way home.*

In a scrapbook under the coffee table in his parents' home was a photographic history of Allen Garfield.

Allen Garfield, five, posing with one hand inside his coat front. Allen Garfield in striped blazer and straw hat for his appearance on *Stars of Tomorrow.* Allen Garfield, fourth from left, Royal Oak High School Players. Allen Garfield in a scene from *The Second Mrs. Tanqueray.* Allen Garfield's graduation picture; long hair, horn-rimmed glasses, spread collar, Windsor knot. Allen Garfield in a dozen or more Kwick-Pix dime-store photographs with trench coat collar up, with and without pipe. Allen Garfield in MG with girl in front of Wayne State University. Allen Garfield with cigarette in mouth, tie pulled down, holding script. Allen Garfield in model-agency photograph, his hair combed to the side now so that it curved down over his high forehead, with the caption: Fashion Model . . . Narrator . . . Actor. Born, 1930. Eyes, Brown. Hair, Dark Brown. 5'8-3/4", 161 lbs. 39 Regular.

The model agency photograph, reduced to a two-column newspaper width, was also in a clipping from the weekly *South Oakland Press* headed "This 'n' That" with the byline Helen Howard. The column read:

Watch for a favorite son to become a celebrity. A '48 R.O. High grad remembered as the class wit. Actor and model before going with JBK as a Disc Jockey. Of course, Allen Garfield!

Only it's Gare Garfield now and he's a MOVIE STAR!

Gare will appear on *The Outriders* Wednesday night, Channel 7. He's one of the bad guys in this one and admits—according to his mother, Mrs. Allen J. Garfield, Sr., of 483 Emily Court—to having only a few lines. But what a start!

Gare was invited to Hollywood three years ago with a whole slew of D.J.s for a motion-picture premiere. Me thinks stars got in Gare's eyes, for he stayed!

Breaking into pictures hasn't been easy. Between calls from the casting office Gare has kept busy as a lifeguard, dance instructor, and director of a Little Theater group. But from here on it looks like an open field to stardom for Gare Garfield, one of the nicest people we know.

In Hollywood he had changed his name from Allen to Gare and thought of himself as lean, silent, sensitive, and intelligent. His break would come. He would get a small part with good lines and he would make it look easy. A little methody, but not too much. From then on the roles would be better. He would be sought after as a seasoned feature player; a pro who, if he felt like it, could upstage the socks off the star just by scratching himself.

There would be picture spreads in movie magazines and Sunday supplements. But he would insist, no phony stuff. No three hundred sweaters and all that crap. If they wanted shots the shots would have to be real: Gare Garfield wearing glasses, reading. Gare Garfield in coveralls working on his Mercedes. Gare Garfield in New York going into P. J. Clarke's, suit coat open, thin tie, nice thin build. He would be with a fairly well-known fashion model and there would be stories that they lived together when he was in New York.

That, he decided, was the image he wanted; and so there would be no hint of phoniness, he changed his name back to Allen.

He was in another episode of *The Outriders;* appeared several times in *Bourbon Street Beat* and *Surfside 6.* Once, in a feature film he was the man coming out of the revolving door as Doris Day hurried in. Nine times, in street scenes, he walked in front of, behind, or stood in the immediate vicinity of the star of the picture. But in six years, on and off, as a professional actor in Hollywood, he spoke only one line: "Let me stomp him, Frank." A line eventually cut when the scene was shortened to allow for commercial time.

All right, he had told himself. *That's the way it is. They don't want talent. They line up these vacant-faced, stoop-shouldered clowns and say you, you, and you, give them Flash Gordon names, put them in tight pants, show them how to twitch their jaw muscles and throw them into scenes with perky little fanny swingers who have been taught to stick out their chest, cock their head, and act surprised.*

All right, if that's all Hollywood was, if all they wanted was the same old ap-cray, he'd go somewhere else.

A friend in properties at Fox told him about the big one Zanuck was planning in France. Allen Garfield had roughly one hundred and fifty dollars. It would take about four-fifty to get to Paris. So he wrote to his mother asking her if she would bet six hundred dollars on the greatest opportunity of his career. His mother spoke to his father, who was used-car sales manager at Woodward Chevrolet; they withdrew a third of their savings and sent it to their son.

Allen Garfield reached France in time for the filming of *The Longest Day.* As a German artilleryman defending Utah Beach he was killed coming out of a bunker by Paul Anka.

The question is, Allen Garfield, the Syrian foot soldier, thought, *why do you always get killed? Why does this one now in his centurion's armor and sunglasses have a Rolls and a girl in tight pants while you still wear a rotten sport coat with wide lapels and rotten flannels that have never been cleaned since you've been in Spain? Why does he have forty-dollar Italian loafers and you have to knot your toes to keep the rotten toes of your rotten shoes from curling up? You are as smart as he is. Smarter. God, yes, smarter. You have more basic, honest talent. Your speaking voice is every bit as good. Better. But he has the Rolls and the girl and the suite at the Hilton. Why? Those are simple questions,* Allen Garfield decided. *So there must be simple answers.*

THE ANNOUNCEMENT CAME THROUGH a hand amplifier in Spanish first: "That is all for today. Return weapons and costumes to the properties building. Buses leave in forty minutes for Madrid."

The dead and wounded rose, collecting swords, spears, and shields as the announcement was repeated in English.

It takes them an hour, Allen Garfield thought. An hour to decide to quit. He moved off with the others slowly, his eyes on the group by the camera boom. *Let's have a truck shot now of director and actor wondering what to do tonight. Do we get drunk at my villa or yours? But maybe Keating won't make it with all the beer.*

He saw the casting assistant watching the Syrians file past. He saw the casting assistant's gaze hold on him. Then move away. Then move back again, past him, out to the field.

"You want somebody for close-ups?"

The casting assistant squinted at him. "You're?"

"Garfield. You've used me—"

"Yeah, I remember." The casting assistant nodded. "Come on."

"Give me a cigarette and I will."

The idea was to act relaxed. The pro. *You can take it or leave it,* Allen Garfield told himself. He accepted the cigarette from the casting assistant and said, "I need a light." But the casting assistant was already moving toward the group by the camera boom. Allen Garfield followed.

"I got one, Ray," the casting assistant said.

The director, Ray Heidke, and the centurion, Howard Keating, looked at Allen Garfield. They did not nod or speak or acknowledge his presence. They looked at him.

"You worked for me before," the director said.

"Yes, sir, Mr. Heidke. This is the fourth time."

"You were in *Gods*."

"Yes, sir."

"I never forget a face."

"He has great expression when he gets it," the casting assistant said. "That's why I thought in this one—"

"He's too short," Howard Keating said.

"With the helmet and all . . ." the casting assistant began.

"He's too short," Howard Keating said.

The casting assistant shrugged. "We got plenty where he came from."

"Howard," the director said. "Let me do it, all right?"

"Certainly, you do it. Only you build up the centurion, then you show somebody like this guy giving him a hard time."

"Howard," the director said patiently, "he doesn't give you a hard time. He surprised you, right? You're holding your shoulder where you just got nicked. Your sword's on the ground. You *feel* or *sense* this mother coming at you from behind. Over your shoulder, Christ here he comes. You hesitate. Think. He rushes, sword raised. You let him come, one, two, *three* counts. You stoop, pick up your sword. The guy coming chops down to take your head off. You sidestep, lunge. Unngh! You stick him right in the navel.

"Now, Billy," the director said to the cameraman, but looking at the sky, "let's move. We get the guy up in the rocks first and I think we put a Brute on him the way the light's going. Where's the guy? Get up there. You don't need the shield. Billy, I want you to tilt up from Howard to the guy. Then back off and we get it all. Look, just put the goddamn shield down anywhere, all right?"

Allen Garfield made his way up the gulley that rose between the rocks to an opening eight feet above the ground. He turned and stood poised. It seemed higher up here.

"All right," the director called. "I want to see you jump."

Allen Garfield looked down, adjusted his footing and waited.

"You going to jump?"

"I thought you'd give me a signal."

"Just jump, all right?"

He jumped; he felt the shock on the bottom of his feet and fell forward in the sand, losing his sword.

"Somebody," Howard Keating called out, "get me my goblet."

The director lifted the funneled brim of his hat and pulled it down loosely, his eyes on Allen Garfield. "One more time. Understand me?"

Allen Garfield jumped again, jumping out farther this time with his feet wider apart; he felt the shock but was moving toward Howard Keating as he landed and this time stayed on his feet.

"Let's do it," the director said.

They shot the empty defile. Then they shot the defile with Allen Garfield standing in it, crouched, as if he had just appeared. "Come on," the director said. "You're a shifty Syrian. You see this wounded Roman. You think: *I got me one.* Ten points for a centurion and he doesn't even know you're there."

Allen Garfield jumped. As he hit the ground the director called, "Cut! . . . Howard, let's keep the beer out of the shot, all right?"

"He came too soon."

"Let's all be ready this time."

Allen Garfield jumped again and ran toward Howard Keating.

"Cut! . . . Howard you have to come around to stick him, right?"

"I got too many moves. Look around, stoop, wait, pick up the sword."

"All right then," the director said. 'It's in your hand. But you're down on one knee. You still don't know the guy's coming at you . . ."

Allen Garfield jumped, ran for Keating, held back, giving the centurion time to come around.

"Cut! . . . Howard, what are you doing?"

"He's coming too fast. I hear him land. I don't have time to turn around he's on top of me."

"Hesitate after you land," the director said.

Allen Garfield jumped, almost went down, hesitated, raised his sword and went for Keating.

"Look at him! How can I turn when he's right on top of me? Tell him to slow the hell up!"

"You land," the director said, "give it a three count. One, two, three."

Allen Garfield jumped, landed, hesitated. One, two, three, he counted, waited another moment to be sure, then ran at Howard Keating, holding back somewhat, raising his sword, raising it higher and seeing the exposed curve of Keating's neck.

"Cut!"

"Ray, get this idiot out of here!"

The director lit a cigarette going over. He placed it between Howard Keating's lips. "Howard, we're close to it, aren't we?"

Howard Keating didn't answer.

"Howard, aren't we close to it? We've got the moves down. It's only the timing. Howard, one more take, what do you say?"

He drew on the cigarette and didn't answer.

"Just one, that's all."

The centurion took his time. He flicked the cigarette away and watched it arch to the ground before looking at the director. "You tell me it makes sense. I have to wait around while you teach a five-dollar-a-day idiot his timing?"

"Howard, one more take?"

"It won't do any good."

"Howard . . ."

"All right, one. But one means *one*."

For the eighth time Allen Garfield pulled himself up the defile. He turned, adjusting his footing and stood looking down, tightening and untightening his grip on the sword. He felt the heat still on his face and was aware of his heart beating.

He watched the assistant with the slate that bore the scene number move quickly from in front of the camera. He watched the camera hold on Howard Keating, then begin to pan and tilt up toward him. He kept his eyes on Howard Keating and when the director said "Now!" he jumped.

He landed on the balls of his feet, hesitated, counted *one . . . two,* and ran at Howard Keating, ran at him raising the sword higher, judging the distance to Keating's neck, aiming and at the point of hacking down with all his strength when Howard Keating suddenly turned, stumbled, lunged forward trying to recover his balance and drove his sword into Allen Garfield's stomach.

Someone screamed. Someone said, "Oh, my God!" Someone

was kneeling close to him, lifting his hands from his stomach. The face moved away and a blanket was spread over him and tucked gently under his chin.

The director's voice said, "Son, we're fixing up a bed in the panel. You'll be all right . . . just fifteen twenty minutes you'll be at the hospital and everything'll be fine."

But he knew, holding his stomach and lying very still, he would never reach Madrid.

God, the breaks, he thought. *The rotten, cheap breaks.*

The Line Rider

1954

"LISTEN," ACE SAID. "I want to tell you something."

"Now what?"

"If you can't handle the women then don't fool with them."

Chick said, "What do you mean *handle* them?"

Ace shook his head. "It ain't somethin' you learn by gettin' it explained to you.

Chick's eyes went to the lean man riding next to him. Ace had about the pointiest Adam's apple he'd ever seen. In fact he seemed all points: his chin, his hawk nose, even his hat brim the way it was curled and funneled in front, everything pointing forward and nodding gently with the easy walking motion of his horse.

"I can take care of myself," Chick said.

"Then I won't worry about you."

"Hell, no."

"Just remember what I said about the women."

"You'd think I was just a kid."

"How old are you?"

"Twenty."

Ace grinned. "If you're a day over seventeen I'll buy all the mescal you can drink."

"Well, get your money out."

"I'm not even sure you're that old."

Chick did not say anything and they rode on in silence, coming out of scattered pine, then down a gravelly slope that dipped into an aspen stand and over the tops of the slender trees, another hundred yards or so beyond, they could see the village of La Noria.

"See it?" said Ace.

"Course I do."

"That gray thing in the middle's the bandstand."

"I got eyes."

"I didn't know you'd ever seen one."

" 'Course I have," Chick said. "You see one pueblo you seen 'em all."

Ace smiled to himself and he did not speak, not until they were through the aspen and approaching the square, passing down a street between the first adobes. "The cantina's over there on the right," he said then.

Chick did not reply and he was thinking: *listen to him you'd think I'd been livin' in a cave all my life.* He was pretty sure he did not like Ace. Last night he'd been glad to see him, when Ace rode up to the line shack after being away for four days. But the good feeling of seeing him didn't last.

Ace talked too much. He talked and talked tryin' to make you think he was a big shot, reminding you he'd put in a lot more years than you and had seen some sights in his time. Hell, he wasn't any more than twenty-nine or thirty and if he was such a big shot know-it-all why didn't he have a better job than a forty-a-month line rider?

You don't have to take no ten-cent advice off him, Chick thought.

You got the same job he has and you're old enough to figure out a few things for yourself.

They dismounted, half-hitching their reins to the rail that ran almost the full width of the cantina. "Looks like we got it all to ourselves," Ace said.

Chick frowned. "It don't look like such a swell place to me."

"I imagine you seen a lot of places in your *twenty* years."

"Enough," Chick said.

"Usually there's boys here from other spreads . . . from both sides of the line." Ace motioned toward the far end of the square. "The border ain't a quarter mile off that way."

"It don't matter to me," Chick said. He followed Ace into the cantina.

Behind the bar, a Mexican, middle-aged and wearing a full mustache, straightened slightly, taking his elbow from the edge of the bar, and said, "Good afternoon," nodding his head and smiling.

Ace nodded. "Where is everybody?"

"It's early," the man behind the bar said.

"Give us some mescal."

"Clear or colored?"

"Clear," Ace told him. "I don't want no damn chicken scraps in mine." He placed a dollar piece on the bar and motioned to Chick to do the same. "You tell us when we've drunk that up. We got to leave early."

"Sure," the man behind the bar said, and placed a label-less half-filled bottle and two glasses on the bar. He was filling the glasses when the two Mexican girls came in.

Ace rolled sideways against the bar to look at them. "There's everybody," he said, grinning. He raised his glass and sipped the mescal then held it belt high as he continued to stare at the girls.

"Alicia and Luz," the man behind the bar said.

"Alice and me are old friends," Ace said. He remained leaning against the bar and did not move as Alicia, the first girl, came up to him. Ace gulped down his mescal then straightened, putting his arm around her waist, and pulled her against him. The girl laughed and said something to him in Spanish.

They're old friends all right, Chick thought. *My gosh.*

He was behind Ace at the bar, his hand on his drink, but he had not tasted it and now he felt self-conscious even though no one was looking at him. He saw the girl who was with Alicia move over to a table and suddenly he had a funny feeling in his stomach as she glanced at him. She smiled momentarily and looked away.

Chick raised the glass of mescal. He put it to his lips, not fully conscious of what he was doing, and the unexpected sweet taste of it almost made him spit it out. *My gosh!* He could feel the heat of it in his stomach almost immediately.

The girl at the table was looking at him again: a soft, almost shy smile; it was in her eyes and touching the corners of her mouth. *Boy,* Chick thought. He looked at Ace still holding Alicia, then back to the girl at the table. He picked up his drink and walked over to her.

"Are you waitin' for somebody?"

The girl looked up at him. "Not now."

"Can I sit down?"

"Of course."

He pulled his chair closer to her as he sat down. "What'd that man say your name was?"

"Luz."

"That's right. Mine's Chick."

She said, "Chick?" sounding like Cheek the way she said it. She smiled. "*Chico.*"

"What's that mean?"

"It means boy," she said. "*Chiquito,* little boy."

"You sure got a crazy language."

She nodded her head, still smiling at him.

He did not know what to say and he tasted his drink, making a face, not believing anything could be so sweet.

"Don't you like that?" the girl asked.

"It's all right."

Her eyes went to Ace, then came back, smiling, to Chick. "I've seen your friend here before, but not you."

"This is the first time for me."

"You work together?"

Chick nodded. "For the biggest spread in the valley. Me and Ace are ridin' the south line seein' everything's under control. See, I just come down to work with him a few weeks ago. He told me about comin' here and said, 'Why don't we both ride over sometime?' . . . and here we are."

She said, almost shyly, "I'm glad you did."

Chick grinned. "You're funny."

She was looking at his glass. "Why don't you have another drink?"

"I believe I will."

"It's good for a man to have a drink after he's been working hard."

"Say, do you work here?"

She looked at him quickly. "Are you angry?"

"Why should I be angry?"

"Some people don't believe a girl should do this work."

"What kind of work is it?"

"What I'm doing. I sit with you as I drink."

"Oh." There was a silence and he said, "I don't see anything wrong."

"Some do." She rose from her chair. "Give me the money and I'll get you another drink."

"It's already paid for."

"Oh." She took his glass to the bar and came back with mescal in it and placed it in front of him.

"I don't see why you can't do whatever you want," he said.

"Well, all people aren't as kind as you."

He had no reply to this and he drank some of the mescal. It seemed to taste better. Not as sweet. He raised the glass again, finishing. "That's pretty good."

"I've never tasted it," the girl said. She rose and he watched her go to the bar again. *My gosh, she's pretty! Such a little thing . . . big eyes, and that smile. Bet she couldn't be more'n fifteen.*

As she sat down again, he said, 'What're you, about fifteen?"

She nodded. "I think so."

He leaned back, raising the glass, and looked at the clear liquor against the light, then drank it down. "I'm seventeen."

"Oh."

"I've only been workin' for this outfit a year. I was a *caverango*—you know, mindin' the horses—until I was sent on this line ridin' job."

She nodded. "I see."

"It's a lonely job and that Ace ain't fit company, but it's one of the steps you got to take if you're goin' to stay in the cattle business. I want my own place someday."

"That will be nice," the girl said.

"It can be done, too."

"I believe it."

He said then, frowning, "What're you workin' here for?"

"I have to work somewhere."

"Don't you have kin?"

"Not here." The girl shook her head. "And they are very poor."

"You ought to get married."

She smiled softly. "That would be nice."

"Aren't there any men around?"

"None that I care for."

"Really?"

"I'm telling you the truth."

"You know," he said seriously, "it takes a while to build good stock, but it's worth the hard work cuz you can be rich from it."

"How long does it take?" she asked.

"Years."

"Oh—"

"But it's worth it. The waitin' is worth it." Their eyes held and after a moment she lowered hers. She looked at his empty glass, then picked it up and went to the bar. He took the glass from her when she came back, touching her hand. She sat down, pulling her chair closer to his.

"I never met a girl like you before."

"What do you mean?"

"I mean a girl I could talk to like this."

She smiled. "I'm happy."

"I feel like I've known you a long time."

"That's the way it is sometimes with two people."

"You think it's fate?"

"God can do whatever he pleases," the girl said.

"Maybe that's it," Chick said. "I feel like I've known you ever since I was born."

"Perhaps," the girl said, "we met in heaven."

Chick grinned. "Hangin' from a tree by our navels." His face reddened. "I'm sorry."

"That's all right."

"See, other girls'd get mad, but you understand."

She touched his hand and said, "*Chiquito*," softly.

He felt a sudden tenderness and he wanted to put his arms around her and just hold her. But his eyes lowered and he drank his mescal quickly. As he looked at her again, Ace called to him. He glanced at Ace, then to the girl again. "We got to go."

"So soon?" She seemed disappointed.

"We got to work for our pay."

As he rose he saw her lips form an O and a soft kissing sound came with it.

He could feel his face flush and he said, hurriedly, "I'll come back tomorrow."

All the way back to the line shack Ace sang "The Hog-Eye Man"—three verses and the chorus over and over again, singing loud in the dim stillness of the hills. It was not a pleasing sound, but Chick was glad that he was singing. They wouldn't have to talk then and he could think about Luz.

That night, for a long time before going to sleep, he thought about her; and the next morning it was the same, seeing her as soon as he opened his eyes, though now her face was not so clear in his mind. He would close his eyes and concentrate hard to make her reappear. He could hear her voice and throughout the morning he went over and over again the parts of their conversation he could remember—

Telling him she was glad he had come. Touching his hand and saying *Chiquito* in that soft voice of hers—soft and warm and with a faint huskiness.

That's funny how you can meet a person and *know* that you and that person were bound to meet. And when you see her it's like you're the only two people in the world.

That would be somethin', wouldn't it? You and her the only two people in the world.

We could pick out whatever house we wanted . . . even one up in Tucson, and all day we'd sit out in front in the shade, lookin' around. Then we'd eat. And after that we'd get us a buggy and go for a ride—

No . . . have one other person alive. Some old man. He'd be sittin' in front of his house and when we go by he'd say, "There goes Chick Williams and his little Mex gal."

Ride out a ways, then stop the buggy.

He'd put his arms around her. "Honey, that red thing over there's our sun goin' down. Sure it's ours; we're the only people outside that old man and he's too old to appreciate it."

Maybe you could give that old man a job. Somethin' where he wouldn't have to move around any.

"Honey, why don't we just stay right here till the moon comes up?"

She'll turn her head to nod all right and that's when you kiss her. Take her face in your hands and kiss her lightly the first one. Maybe two that way. Then put your arms around her and really kiss her good.

Boy!

He looked over at Ace currycombing his horse.

"Ace, why don't we go to La Noria later on?"

"Suits me," Ace said, not even looking at him.

Chick relaxed. That was easier than he'd expected.

But in the early afternoon a wagon pulled up loaded with salt chunks wrapped in gunny sacks and they spent the rest of the afternoon dropping the salt licks for the herd scattered all over the meadows. After that they had to eat, wash up, and Ace had to shave before they were ready to leave.

Ace sang "The Hog-Eye Man" most of the way there, but this time he was singing more to himself, not shouting the chorus, and it was just something to pass the time and fill the stillness. He made up his own verses when he was tired of the ones he knew: obscene ones that didn't rhyme and he sang these over and over again.

Chick felt good. Even with the sharp little knot inside of him. He'd breathe in and out slowly to make it go away, but it stayed where it was halfway between his stomach and his chest, right in the middle. It would've been good to tell somebody how he felt, but not Ace, and especially not when he was singing that song.

Coming out of the aspen, approaching the pueblo, the knot was even tighter and taking big gulps of air didn't relieve it a bit. He thought: *What's there to be so nervous about? You'd think you were goin' to ask somebody for a job.*

"You're awful quiet," Ace said.

"How could I say anything with you singin' that dirty song?"

"You can sing with me on the way home."

"Maybe I will. Maybe I'll even drown you right out."

They passed between the first adobes entering the square, reining in the direction of the cantina. "Big night tonight," Ace said. In the dimness they could see a line of horses standing at the rail. Light showed in the windows of the cantina and they could hear faint sounds of laughter.

"How come?" Chick asked.

"Saturday night, boy."

"I lost track of the days."

"That's what line ridin' does," Ace stated. They dismounted and tied up at the end of the rail.

Chick saw her the moment they entered the cantina. She was sitting at a table between two men, looking at one of them and smiling at something he was saying. He watched her as he followed Ace to the bar, but she did not look up.

"Have to stand tonight," Ace said, his eyes roaming over the crowded room. The oil lamps hanging from the beamed ceiling were up to full brightness and a haze of tobacco smoke hung motionless over the table area. Most of the men were Mexican vaqueros; the others, like the two sitting with Luz, were riders from the American side, from any one of a half dozen spreads located in this southern stretch of the San Rafael valley.

"You want mescal?" asked Ace. He made room for himself at the bar.

"All right with me," Chick said. He glanced over his shoulder. Still the girl had not seen him.

"You look disappointed," Ace said.

"What do you mean?"

"I mean you look disappointed."

"You're seein' things."

"Not yet I'm not," Ace said. He picked up both of the drinks the man behind the bar had poured and handed one to Chick. "I know what's botherin' you." Ace grinned. "That little chilipicker over there."

"You're crazy," Chick told him.

Ace's grin broadened as he looked down the length of the bar. Alicia was standing near the end talking to a vaquero. "I got somethin' botherin' me, too," Ace said, and started toward them.

Chick watched him: Ace putting his hand on the vaquero's shoulder, the vaquero turning, looking at him sullenly, then smiling as Ace said something: Alicia smiling too, then laughing, a high shrill laugh; Ace raising his drink to her—

He can sure be friendly when he wants, Chick thought. He looked at Luz again just as she was rising, picking up the two glasses from the table. A few feet from him she squeezed in next to the bar.

"Luz?"

Her head turned and at first she seemed not to recognize him. "Oh . . . how are you?"

"Fine. How're you?"

"Good." She turned back to the bar and said something in Spanish to the bartender who raised a bottle and filled the two glasses. She handed him a coin.

"Luz, I said I'd be back today and I am."

"What?"

"Don't you remember, I said—"

"Oh . . . yes."

"I thought tonight we could go out for a walk instead of stayin' in this smoky place." He grinned at her. "Take a look at the moon."

She was picking up change the bartender had placed on the bar and suddenly she was talking to him again, snapping the words, and her eyes blazed angrily. The bartender handed her another coin.

As she picked up the glasses, Chick said, "I thought we could go for a walk."

She glanced at him irritably. "Can't you see I'm busy?"

"Later on, then?" His hand touched her arm.

"Do you want me to spill these!"

"I thought—"

"Listen, find a girl who isn't busy."

She turned from him and went to the table. He watched her sit down between the two men and then he walked out of the cantina. He moved slowly, hearing the cantina sounds behind him, as he took his horse from the rail and led it across the square and between the adobes.

You really got a way with women, haven't you?

He thought of something Ace had said the day before. Something about if you can't handle the women then don't fool with them.

You know what he meant now, huh? Now you know it takes more'n a high opinion of yourself.

But it won't happen again, will it?

Riding back he sang "The Hog-Eye Man" and by the time he reached the line shack the glimpses of her in his mind were less frequent.

Perhaps a little bit of her would always remain in his mind, but for some reason he felt pretty good. Freer.

And at the same time he felt every bit of at least twenty years old.

The Trespassers

1958

CHRIS WAS ON THE back porch, a loden coat thrown over her shoulders, when the sound of rifle fire reached her again. This time there were three moment-spaced reports coming sharply, clearly from beyond the barn and tractor shed, echoing over the orchard and the open pasture, the reports stretching thinly out of the woods that were perhaps five hundred yards from the house.

She was certain now that someone was shooting on their property; someone who had no business being there. Deer season or not, the fence should tell them it was private property.

Unless the hunters were friends of Evan's.

Waiting, listening, her gaze still fixed on the far slope of the pasture, Chris worked her arms into the coat and fastened the wooden toggles. The hood remained folded away from her dark hair that was parted on the side and held in place by a plain silver clasp. A gray skirt showed below the coat; she wore matching kneesocks and black snow boots that were comfortably well worn.

That could be it, she thought. *A neighbor, or someone from Howell.* She could picture Evan talking to one of the store clerks in town, to a man he hardly knew, telling him to come around anytime, the woods were always there waiting. That could very well be it. Easy Ev being friendly, inviting everybody in town to tramp all over their property and shoot or scare away whatever game might be there. He would have forgotten about her father coming up in the morning.

Tomorrow would have to be as near perfect as possible. Ideally, Evan and her father would shoot a buck in the morning; in the afternoon they'd relax, mix drinks, and let the talk come naturally. That was the way Chris pictured it. Both of them in a good mood, feeling something in common now with the drinks on the table between them and the buck hanging in the tractor shed. When her father would finally bring the conversation around to his business, Evan would be in a receptive mood and listen without letting his gaze drift out the window to the barn and the orchard standing dark and silent in the November dusk.

It was her father's idea that Evan come to work for him. It was his problem, too—to convince a twenty-four-year-old easygoing ex–basketball star, one year out of Michigan State and only six months married, that he would be happier and make considerably more money as a manufacturer's rep than he could as a seventy-two-acre farmer with six cows and a sizable mortgage.

It wasn't a recent idea. Her father had talked to Evan about it before, but seldom with any hope of success. Evan would turn him down politely, mildly, saying that he'd just always wanted to farm and feeling the way he did about it, at least he ought to try it.

But tomorrow's session could be different. Now, for the first time, Chris would side with her father; not arguing it with Evan, but letting him know, gently, that her father's idea was at least reasonable. Evan could be an asset to any sales organization. He was calm, not likely to panic under pressure; he made friends easily, looked exceptionally presentable with a suit on, and still had a name in Detroit as a Michigan State basketball star. But—

There was a tricky part to it. Chris realized it first in a personal way, feeling that the quality she loved most about Evan was the very thing that sometimes made her angry. Her father translated it into practical terms. The quality that marked Evan as a good potential salesman, his easygoing friendliness, could also be his biggest liability. "Right now," her father had said, "he doesn't know where to draw the line. You're too friendly, too patient, and people take advantage of you." But with direction, guided by her father's experience, Evan's friendliness could be developed into a valuable asset instead of a rug people were likely to walk over anytime they felt like it.

Sure, keep the farm. Her father was for that. Ideal for weekend hunting; fine for during the summer. But why break a full-time pick on a project that couldn't gross more than four thousand its best year? What was the assurance Evan could handle it on his own and make it pay even that much?

This uncertainty raised doubts in Chris's mind. The doubts banded together into a conviction that her father was right and that tomorrow was the day Evan would give in. If for no other reason, she decided now, than for her sake.

Evan's pickup came past the corner of the house, rolled slowly over the gravel drive to stop in front of the garage. He waved getting out. Chris raised a red-mittened hand. She watched him reach over the side panel and lift out a box of groceries. He smiled coming toward the porch, then frowned, gritting his teeth and hurrying, as if the box was too heavy for him. Chris pushed the door open and stepped aside.

"Did you hear the shooting?"

"It's hunting season." He paused to kiss her on the cheek before going in.

"This shooting was on our land," Chris said when he appeared in the doorway again.

"I wondered," Evan said. "There's an old yellow convertible parked on the road in from the highway." He was already moving down the steps. "I almost went in the ditch getting around it."

"Evan—"

"I'll be right back." He went to the pickup, this time lifted out a case of beer and came back holding it close to his chest. "I hope your dad'll settle for beer."

"He's been known to." Chris watched him anxiously but waited until Evan was putting the case down on the porch. "Then you don't know who's in our woods."

He straightened, moving the case against the wall with his foot. "How do you know they're in ours?"

"I was standing right here. You could tell."

"Well, there aren't any signs posted. I mean you can't really blame them."

"Evan, they had to climb a fence to get in."

He had turned and now his gaze hung on the horizon of the pasture slope, as if picturing the trees that were thick down beyond it. His hand came out of his coat pocket with a tobacco plug and he bit off a corner of it, still staring at the slope that was bare except for snow patches and dark tree-stump dots.

Waiting now, wondering what he was thinking, she watched the slow movement of his jaw as he worked the tobacco into his cheek. He looked more like a professional athlete than a farmer, a Major League baseball player, though he had taken up plug tobacco because it was a farmer thing to do. Chris was sure of that. At least he handled it well, as if he'd been chewing tobacco all of his life.

Right now, though, the thoughtful, slow movement of his jaw was exasperating.

"Evan, don't you think you should tell them to leave?"

"Why?"

"Why? Because they're trespassing on your land! And if they haven't killed a deer already, they've probably scared them all away."

"So why bother?" He pulled work gloves out of his pockets.

"And if there are no deer there," Chris said, spacing the words, "where will you take Dad tomorrow?"

Evan seemed to smile. "You know all rich girls, even ex-ones, call their fathers Dad. They say, 'Dad did something.' Like he was the only one the world with that name. They never say, 'My dad.' You ever notice that?"

"You're changing the subject."

"I just happened to think of that."

"All right, my father is looking forward to hunting with you tomorrow. But if someone's in the woods today, there won't be anything to hunt tomorrow. Now does that make sense?"

"You always worry about little piddlin' things."

"Evan, are you going to tell them to leave or shall I?"

"They might even be gone already."

"Are you going to find out?"

"I don't see why we should. What if it's somebody who drove all the way up from Detroit to hunt. He works in a plant, looks forward to it all year. Then we go out and ruin his day."

She stared at him, and at the end of the silence her voice seemed more quiet. "Evan, don't you ever get tired of being a nice guy?"

"I just don't think it's important enough to have to tramp all the way out there."

He's afraid: it came to her all at once and in one brief moment seemed to explain everything about Evan. He was really afraid of people—for some reason unnaturally worried about what people thought of him. So he was always friendly, overly friendly. Did that make sense? Thinking about it, she became self-conscious and made her mind see something else. Her father. All right, her father.

Abruptly she said, "I know what Dad would do."

"I guess he would," Evan said.

"Well, he doesn't let people walk all over him!"

"No, you can't say he does that."

"If it's a question of standing up for your rights . . . if it's something you've paid for, something you're entitled to, why should you care what other people think?"

Evan frowned. "Who are we talking about?"

Don't go into it now, she thought and said, "Just tell me what you intend to do."

"I'm going to do the chores, if it's all right with you."

That was it. Chris brushed past him; she was down the steps in two strides and walking across the yard. Let him call. Just let him call. She'd keep right on walking and not look back, not even when he came running after her.

But Evan didn't call. And by the time she had passed the barn she knew he wasn't going to.

All right, then he's not, she thought, passing the feedlot now that extended out from the barn. She felt awkward, picturing herself as he would see her from the porch, and she concentrated on maintaining a natural, unhurried stride, her hands deep in the pockets of the loden coat. *Just don't look back*, she told herself. *Or stumble.*

Once through the orchard, following the trace of road that curved into the pasture gate, she felt more sure of herself. She could trip on the deep, frozen ruts and it wouldn't matter; he couldn't see her now, not until she reached the high ground of the pasture.

Now you're worrying about what somebody thinks of you, she thought. Then told herself it was natural; Evan, after all, was her husband. But to be afraid of what everybody thought—to use friendliness as a defense—perhaps being even physically afraid of people, that was something else.

And now you're stretching it all out of proportion, she told herself. Still, she continued to think of Evan, remembering first the things she liked to remember, seeing him again in a basketball game: tall and long-legged with his relaxed, deft ball-handling and a slow-motion way of going and following through when he took a shot. But after the game they would go out to eat—and there it was.

They could sit in a restaurant for almost an hour waiting to be served or waiting for the check. Evan never complained about the service; and even after sitting there so long, he would still be polite to the waitress and thank her when they left.

Her father's presence seemed to assure good service. (She couldn't help thinking of him in contrast to Evan.) He would no more than raise his eyes and a waiter would be at their table. Just as he could pick up a telephone and there would be last-minute good seats for a Detroit Lions football game. Comparing them now, remembering little things about each one, she was more sure than ever that her father was right about Evan.

To Chris, thinking as she moved carefully over the uneven ground, circling the low places that were filled with water and thinly frozen over, the open pasture sloped gradually, almost imperceptibly. Looking up, she was surprised to see the trees so near. They formed a dark, solid expanse between the snow of the pasture and the dull, overcast sky.

Chris stopped at the edge of the trees. Finding whoever was here could be a problem. She hadn't thought of that before. There was no sound in the trees; no tracks either, she noticed, moving into the dimness. She walked slowly, listening, hearing only her own steps in the dead leaves that almost completely covered the ground.

Evan had mentioned seeing a car. Remembering this, Chris moved in the general direction of the side road that led in from the highway. Less than fifty feet farther on, as she came to a clearing, Chris saw the spot of color, a yellow shape barely visible through the saplings and beyond the wire fence marking their property line. That would be it. Evan had said a yellow convertible.

Nothing to it, Chris thought. *Now—*

She glanced to the side and stopped. Two men stood watching her from the near end of the clearing: one facing her, a rifle cradled in his arm; the other half turned, looking over his shoulder. Not until he came around did Chris see the whiskey bottle held at his side. He was perhaps nineteen or twenty, bareheaded, with a brush cut that was growing out and needed trimming. He smiled, a thin, vaporous trace of his breath forming in the crisp air.

"Well now—" His gaze seemed dulled, clouded by too much to drink, though he stared at Chris calmly, openly appraising her and obviously liking what he saw.

The man with the rifle was at least thirty: a tall, narrow-shouldered, thin-faced man, his cap cocked on one side of his head and the peak turned up. He nodded to Chris politely, touching his cap with one finger; but with the gesture was the trace of a relaxed, amused smile.

He said, "Can we be of some help to you?"

"Maybe she's lost," the younger one said. "Or she come looking for somebody."

Chris stood still, her hands deep in the pockets of the loden coat. "I'm looking for you if you've been doing the shooting."

"A lot of people shooting," the one with the rifle said, "during the hunting season." He spoke slowly, with a relaxed confidence and an unmistakable Deep South drawl.

Just tell them, Chris thought, feeling a sudden irritation. She hesitated, though, and said, almost apologetically, "I'm afraid you're hunting on private property."

"Well, you don't have to be afraid of that," the one with the rifle said. "Maybe the owner doesn't mind us hunting his land."

"If I didn't make myself clear," Chris said, quietly, "I'm telling you you'll have to leave."

"You're saying you *own* those woods?" the younger one asked.

Chris looked at him. "I hope you're not trying to be funny."

"I ask a simple question—"

"Of course we *own* these woods."

"You say so and that proves it." The younger one glanced at his friend. "Just take her word for it."

"I don't think you're in a position to question it," Chris said coldly.

"You don't, huh—why not?"

"You're trespassing and you know it."

He shrugged, shifting his weight to stand hip-cocked, one hand parting the open coat and the thumb hooking into his belt. The other hand still held the whiskey bottle at his side. Noticing it again, Chris saw another rifle leaning against a stump.

"You prove you own this place," he said, "then we're trespassing. How's that?"

"Vince," the tall one said, swinging his rifle down-pointed under one arm and working his hands into his pockets. "She said *we* own it." His eyes remained on Chris. "Who's we, you and your daddy?"

"My husband and I."

"He must be off somewhere."

"He's at home."

"Then how come he didn't come out here himself?"

"What difference does it make whether I tell you or my husband does!" Her voice rose. Chris knew that her face was flushed. She paused. "I think this has gone far enough."

"Maybe she doesn't even have a husband." Vince, the younger one, kept his eyes on Chris. "I mean maybe she's just saying it . . . you know?"

The other man stood with his narrow shoulders drawn up. He seemed rigid, feeling the cold, though his voice was soft and relaxed. "I wouldn't put it past her having a husband," he drawled. "I just don't picture him home and her coming out here by herself. I was thinking, maybe she thought it was her husband doing the shooting. She comes out to fetch him and finds us instead."

"Crazy," Vince said, grinning. He raised the bottle, studying it in the fading light, then took a long drink, one hand around the neck of the bottle. Lowering it his eyes were on Chris again.

"You want some?"

"No, thank you."

"I mean it'll relax you."

"Look," Chris said, "either you leave right now or I call the state police."

Vince shook his head. "I mean she needs relaxin'."

"I was thinking," the older one said mildly, "how come if her husband's home she'd go to all the trouble of calling the police? Why not just get him?"

Vince raised his arms, gesturing lazily. "All the talk. Why don't we just have a drink?" He extended the bottle toward Chris. "What do we need all the talk for?"

Chris half turned to walk away. "I'm warning you. As soon as I get home, I'm calling the state police. If you're still here . . . if they arrest you, I promise we'll make a charge."

"Vince," the older one drawled. "What she's saying is she doesn't want to drink with you." He saw Chris moving away. "Wait a minute now." When she stopped, hesitantly, he moved a few steps toward her. "You scared of Vince?"

Chris said nothing at first, thinking, *Just leave. Quick.* But still she waited, watching the older one now. "I don't think there's anything more to be said."

"Don't mind Vince any," the older one went on easily. "Hose him off and slick his hair down he's a pretty clean-cut boy. But"—the man paused, his eyes not leaving Chris—"he's still just a boy."

"You skinny hillbilly," Vince muttered. "I'm all the boy she can handle."

The older one shrugged, the hint of a smile softening his bony face. "I was thinking though," he said, "maybe what she's looking for is a man." He moved toward her again. "I bet that's it. A grown man you can appreciate and trust not to tell things."

You waited too long! Chris knew it, feeling the need to run, to be away from them. She had been uncertain, only sensing a danger at first, feeling the tension inside her growing, warning her. But the gall of them—their posing, play-acting, self-confident gall had been too much, had sparked the irritation, had touched off the outright anger that had compelled her to stand up to them. But now—

She didn't run. Deliberately she made herself walk, though not hesitating now, or stopping or glancing back when one of them called. His voice came sharply. The younger one. Vince. Or James Dean or whoever he thinks he is. She was aware of this in her mind, in and out of her mind as she pictured them coming after her, as she tried to hear their steps but could hear only the crisp, leaf-sweeping sound of her own boots. She didn't stop to listen, to make sure, not while she was still in the trees, not even when she had reached the meadow and found herself in the open, feeling the cold wind and the frozen, humped ground beneath her.

She heard the sound of an engine then, a car starting, and she wanted to stop, to make sure they were leaving. But Chris went on, straining to keep up the same long-strided pace, until she reached the high point of the meadow, until she paused, breathing heavily, finally looking back.

One of them stood at the edge of the trees watching her and she knew instantly that it was the older one.

But the car sound—it couldn't have been anyone else.

The figure at the edge of the trees started across the meadow: a thin, dark shape against a white expanse of snow.

Chris ran the rest of the way—stumbling once while she was still in the meadow, breaking the thin ice of a low place and falling full-length in the shallow water, sobbing as she fumbled with the gate latch, running through the orchard, then in the open again, almost to the yard, and now she screamed, calling Evan, not seeing him on the porch, but screaming his name as she ran across the yard.

Inside the barn, the sound seemed faint, faraway. Evan listened. He stood near the hay bales that were stacked high against the dividing, lengthwise wall of the barn. He wasn't sure of the sound at first, not until it came again, then there was no doubt what it was or who was calling him.

By the time Evan got to the double doors and pushed out to the cement ramp, Chris was even with the barn—running when he first saw her, but now stopping suddenly, looking toward the house.

"Hey, Chris—"

He saw the car then, the yellow convertible swinging past the corner of the house, cutting sharply and barely missing the back end of the pickup. The car braked, almost coming to a complete stop. Then it was moving again. Moving as Chris whirled and ran for the barn, the car crossing the yard in a straight, deliberate line toward them.

"Evan—" She was on the ramp now, out of breath, reaching for Evan.

"What's going on? . . . Hey, you're all wet!" He saw the car swerve to line itself up with the low ramp and Chris was pushing him inside, pulling the heavy door behind them. Abruptly they were in semidarkness and for a moment there was silence, as if the engine sound had been shut off with the daylight.

But it came again, an idling rumble, the guttural, gradual rising sound of dual exhausts. Evan moved instinctively, pulling Chris out of the way, turning with her to shield her as both doors burst open—the near one swinging toward them on its ripped hinges, raking the cement floor with a scraping, splintering shriek before the bottom of the door jammed against the cement. With it was the engine sound a yellow shape hurtling past them. The other door was sheared off cleanly, lifted, and bounced aside as the yellow shape rammed into the hay bales. The engine sound rose and died and the top bales came down on the car, covering the hood and rolling off the canvas top.

The outside light that streaked in now was filled with fine dust. It swirled soundlessly over the car, rising to the peaked ceiling of the barn. Chris stood rigid. She could feel Evan and hear him say something, a whispered, urgent sound close to her, but her gaze was fixed on the car.

Then the whisper again, more clearly. "Chris . . . who is he?"

"They were in the woods, two of them. I told them to leave—" She could see Vince in the car sitting hunched over the steering wheel, his hands close together on it and his head almost touching his arms, not unconscious, for she had seen him move; no, more like he was resting, waiting. Her words ran together as she tried to tell Evan everything at once, quickly, before Vince looked up or got out or did whatever he was going to do.

Evan's hand moved over her shoulder gently, calming her, and her eyes rose to his face: to the weathered, angular, warm-looking face that she wanted to touch, that showed a small bulge of tobacco as he shifted it from one cheek to the other, staring at the car, studying it with intense interest, yet impassively. He could have been looking at a new tractor, deciding whether or not to buy it.

The decision was made. Chris felt his hand slip away. He started for the convertible and immediately Vince sat up. Vince moved away from the wheel and a rifle barrel came through the open window.

"If you got any ideas—"

Evan walked toward him. "I thought you might need some help."

"Hold it there!"

"You looked for a minute like you were hurt."

"You hear me!" The barrel moved, a short, threatening jab, and Evan stopped. He stood five or six feet from the car door.

"I think you better give me the rifle," Evan said.

"Move again I'll give it to you."

Evan frowned. "Are you serious?"

"Try something."

"You've been watching television too much."

Vince's eyes shifted to Chris. "Tell her to come up where I can see her."

"What'll you do, shoot me if I don't?"

"I'm telling you one time."

"You're absolutely nuts. Do you know that?"

"You get to the count of three," Vince said.

"Then what?"

"Tell her!" He screamed it, jabbing the rifle again.

Evan glanced over his shoulder at Chris. "You want to hand over the rifle, Vince? Then we'll talk about what you're going to do about my doors."

Vince stared, his pose showing no more expression than if he were asleep with his eyes open. "I'm going to teach you a lesson, man." He barely moved his mouth saying it, yet the words came out clearly.

Evan stared back at him. "Sitting in the car?"

"I'm coming out."

"Today?"

Vince pulled himself toward the door, the rifle barrel coming out farther. "You just keep asking for it, don't you?"

"And you keep sitting there," Evan said mildly.

The door latch clicked free. Evan waited. He waited until the door started to open, until the rifle barrel angled away and he saw one of Vince's feet beneath the door, Vince stooped and momentarily off balance, just beginning to straighten up—

Evan moved then, pivoting as he lunged, and threw his hip solidly against the car door, slamming it into Vince's legs and stomach.

The door swung open as Evan bounced off and now he let it come, stepping in and around it, hooking his fists into Vince's body, hitting him twice, then a third time, before Vince could cover himself and turn away. Evan pulled the rifle out of his hand, stepping back with it, and Vince slumped against the car door as a boxer hangs on the ropes of a prize ring.

From where she was standing, Chris saw only Evan's back and the barrel of the rifle almost touching the ground at his side. She heard him say something to Vince, not the words, only the sound of his voice that seemed softer, more gentle, now that it was over and she was aware of the dimness again and the hay dust still hanging in the shaft of light.

But the other one, Chris thought.

And that suddenly she knew it wasn't over, that this was no more than a lull, a moment's rest that ended abruptly as her gaze moved from Evan and she saw the other man in the doorway, his tall, hunch-shouldered frame sharply silhouetted in the outside light.

He was watching Evan, though not facing him directly, his rifle held in both hands across his body, holding it as he might have carried it walking to the barn, holding it lightly, but with the barrel almost squarely on Evan.

She saw the man look at her quickly, then back to Evan, edging one foot out as if to stand more firmly. Evan was looking at him now—Chris was sure of that—though he hadn't moved and the rifle he'd taken from Vince remained at his side.

She watched them, feeling the silence like a tight string between them, waiting to be broken by a word or a movement or whatever it would take. It could happen. It wasn't a dream. She was standing here watching them, feeling it, not knowing what to do, but knowing it could happen.

Until Evan spoke, the sound of his voice coming quietly out of the silence.

"What are you and I supposed to do, shoot it out?"

She saw the man's face begin to relax, a smile forming slowly. "That would be something, wouldn't it?"

"Chris." Evan glanced toward her. "You better get out of those wet clothes." When she hesitated Evan moved toward the man in the doorway.

"I think your wife got the wrong idea about us," the man said. He stepped back. "Seems to've put her in a state of nerves."

"Maybe that's it," Evan said mildly. He looked at Chris again, offering his hand. "Come on, you don't want to catch cold." And when she came to him he put his hand on her shoulder, moving her past them. "I'll be just a minute."

Chris stopped on the ramp. "Evan, I'm calling the state police."

Evan looked at the man, close to him now. "Do you think we need the police?"

"What for?" The man frowned thoughtfully, then glanced at Vince still leaning on the car door. "Because of him? Vince didn't mean anything. I mean it's nothing we can't settle among ourselves, is it?"

"No police," Evan said, looking at Chris again.

"Evan, these men—"

"Go on. You're just afraid you're going to miss something." He smiled, motioning her gently to leave. "Go on now."

All the way across the yard, every few steps, Chris would glance back at them. Evan watched her until she reached the house. But once inside, looking out through the door window, she saw him turn again to the man with the rifle. They walked into the barn together.

Call the police. She knew it was the safest thing to do, what her father would do, and right away, without wasting a moment. It was foolish to take a chance, to assume the whole thing settled while both of them were still with Evan. Still, Chris waited.

She waited until the yellow convertible backed out of the barn and rolled down the ramp. She waited until it came around with its rumbling engine sound and she saw Evan between the two men in the front seat. Chris backed away from the door. When the car stopped by the porch she moved quickly through the living room to the front hall and picked up the telephone receiver.

There were footsteps on the back porch. But no sound of the door opening.

Then they were taking him! He tried to get in the house, but they caught him, pulled him back to the car.

But there was no car sound.

Chris waited as long as there was something to imagine, until all the possibilities began crisscrossing through her mind in confusion and she couldn't wait a moment longer. She jammed the receiver down on the hook and ran back to the kitchen.

Evan and the tall, hunch-shouldered one stood at the foot of the steps, both of them holding an open bottle of beer. Vince was in the car looking straight ahead. Evan was pointing beyond the car, and when his hand came down the other man nodded. They talked for at least five minutes, shifting their weight, nodding, Evan shaking his head when the man offered a cigarette. Finally they finished their beers. The man said something else to Evan, got in the car, and a moment later the yellow convertible was gone.

Chris opened the door as Evan came up the steps.

"After what they did, you end up drinking beer with them."

"Well, I offered—I don't know why—he said OK. I don't know, it just happened."

"I might never understand you," Chris said. Her shoulders rose as she inhaled, then dropped as she let her breath out slowly. "But at least they're gone."

"They'll be back Saturday," Evan said. "To fix the door."

Chris stared at him. "You took their word they'd be back?"

"And their license number."

"But . . . they could deny ever being here."

"Not with yellow paint marks on the door and a headlight rim somewhere under the hay. I pointed that out to Frank."

"Frank?"

"The skinny one. He wasn't such a bad guy. The other one was feeling sick to his stomach. I didn't talk much to him."

Chris stepped out on the porch. "Evan, answer me one question. Were you afraid?"

He was stooping, putting the empty beer bottles into the case. "Sure I was. In the barn."

"But you wouldn't let me call the police."

"It was over by then."

"You make it sound so easy. Like it was nothing at all."

"I don't know." Evan stood up. "There was no reason to get excited when it was all over."

Chris shook her head wonderingly. "What a salesman you'd make."

"You sound like your dad."

"You don't even realize you would, do you?"

Evan shrugged. "I might make a good bartender, but I don't think I'd want to be one."

"Easy Ev." She said it thoughtfully, watching him pick up the beer case and push the door open with his hip. He was inside for a few minutes, then was standing in the doorway again.

"Aren't you coming in?"

"Evan, do you know something? I think Dad could take a few lessons from you."

"What made you say that?"

"I don't know. I was thinking, too," Chris said. "What if I called him not to come tomorrow?"

"You said he was looking forward to it."

"Well, I was thinking, what if just you and I went out? And you could teach me all about hunting and things."

Evan nodded. "That'd be fine."

"After all," Chris said, "if we're going to be living out here . . ."

The Bull Ring at Blisston

1959

WHERE ELADIO MONTOYA CROSSED the ditch, leaving the tomato field for the gravel road, three men stood watching the yellow station wagon coming toward them. It had turned off the highway a moment before and now came trailing a swirling cloud of fine dust and with a rattling sound of stones striking the underbody. The three men stood at the edge of the road waiting for the vehicle to pass. But when it seemed almost to be going by, its front end dipped suddenly and it came to a skidding stop in the gravel.

Eladio saw Sherman David at the wheel, sitting low in the seat but with his elbow on the window ledge. A girl in a tan sunback dress sat next to him. She was holding a highball glass, which she passed to Sherman David as he raised his right hand. He glanced down at a clipboard propped against the steering wheel, then up, and said, "I'm looking for Eladio Montoya."

The man nearest David muttered something in Spanish, shaking his head. He looked around, as did the two with him, and when he saw Eladio standing close by, his eyebrows went up and he said, "You're right here!" And to Sherman David, "That's him, right here."

"You're Eladio Montoya?" David asked, studying him sullenly.

"That's right."

"Then get in."

Eladio hesitated. "Did I do something wrong?"

"It's plain to see they've all got a guilty conscience," David said to the girl. He wedged the clipboard up over the sun visor and said to Eladio, "Come on, you even get a ride out of it."

Eladio opened the rear door, stooped, stepped in. He saw the girl's face close to his as he looked up, but her gaze shifted as he slammed the door and the station wagon moved off. It picked up speed for perhaps two hundred feet. Then it braked suddenly, turned in, and backed out of a side lane. A moment later it passed the three men, who were still standing at the edge of the road.

Before reaching the highway they passed more of the migrant workers returning from the tomato fields. All of them would stop and turn to watch the station wagon go by.

"Can you imagine," David said, "crossing the country to get a job picking tomatoes?"

"I could imagine going to California or Florida," the girl said. She looked at the empty highball glass in her hand, then extended it out the window. Her hand came back empty and went to her dark hair, smoothing it at the part and holding it lightly against the wind blowing in through the window.

"I couldn't imagine living in Michigan," she said, "unless you had to."

"Wait'll you spend a winter here," David said.

"I hope you're kidding."

"We'll go up north and ski."

"We'll go to Florida and swim." She half-turned on the seat, placing her arm on the backrest, and looked at Eladio. "What do you do in the winter, go back to Mexico?"

"I don't live in Mexico," Eladio said.

"Most of them are from Texas," David said. "About May they get in their junk heaps and drive up to Traverse City to pick cherries. Then August they come down here around Blisston for tomatoes."

He came not quite to a full stop at the highway, then turned right, glancing at the girl. "Wait till you see how they live."

"I saw," the girl said. She looked at Eladio again. "You must have lived in Mexico, though, to become a bullfighter."

He looked at her with open surprise and wanted to ask how she knew. But he said only, "Yes, during that time I lived there."

"I saw a corrida in Mexico City the year before last," the girl said. "Perhaps you were in it."

Eladio shook his head. "Last season was my first—at Juárez."

"Then you weren't a bullfighter very long."

"No."

"How did you get into it? If you don't mind my asking."

"Well, for a few years I placed the banderillas"—he raised his hands and brought them thumbs down to indicate placing the barbed sticks in a bull's neck muscles—"for a matador named Luis Fortuna. Then he was injured badly and before I took my alternative—you know, graduated to the big bulls—he quit and became my manager."

The girl listened politely. "I should think there would be more money in bullfighting than picking tomatoes. What made you quit?"

Just like that, Eladio thought. *What made you quit?*

"Because I got tired of it," he told her.

He looked out as they turned off the highway to follow a gravel road bordering a field of full-grown corn. Within a quarter of a mile they were in view of a weathered barn and machinery shed and, beyond these, showing clean gray and dull-shining against a background of trees, was a group of Quonset buildings.

As they approached the barn, David said, "That's where they live. Believe it or not."

"I know," the girl said patiently.

"Nine families in the barn," David explained. "Another in that chicken house there. Three or four more families in the machine shed and a bunch of them in the old house. Look at that"—he extended one finger from the steering wheel—"you ever see so many kids?"

In front of the barn a dozen children stopped playing to watch the station wagon. In the sunlight a woman stood half-turned, her arms raised to a clothesline of faded denim and khaki. The gaze of the women followed the yellow movement of the vehicle, watching the children now running into the dust that hung in the air behind it.

Eladio could hear the children and he could feel the women watching, but he kept his eyes on the windshield, looking past the soft wave of the girl's hair, looking over the curve of her deeply tanned bare shoulder.

"A good picker can make fifty or sixty dollars a week, with any luck." The words were those of Eladio's brother, Tomás Montoya, whose wife and six children lived with him in the chicken house, and whose 1947 sedan needed a secondhand engine before it would take them back to El Paso.

These things were in and out of his mind as he looked at the girl who threw highball glasses out of the window.

No, he thought. *Maybe that was the first one in her life she has ever thrown. Maybe she has always wanted to do it, so she did. One night in Juarez? I threw an empty Manzanilla bottle at a brick wall, driving along in a car, and throwing it up and over the top of the car. But I was dog-tired and it was late.*

She's perhaps twenty-one or two, he thought. *Ten, eleven, say twelve years younger than this one with the flat, unpleasant face and the hair like rusted wire. This one with the fine shoulders but soft-appearing stomach who has money. Is that what it is between them?*

She acts older than her years. Even sitting and not talking she acts older. Older than you, though you know she isn't."

DAVID LOOKED UP AT the rearview mirror. "Here's where you get off." He came to a stop next to the tubular, cast-iron fence which extended out from one of the Quonset buildings and formed a pen that was approximately thirty by fifty feet in area. As the girl opened her door he glanced at her. "Where're you going?"

"I'll wait here while you get the others," she told him. "I need air more than I do a ride."

"Okay." David looked over his shoulder at Eladio who had gotten out. "And you start limbering up."

"I'm not sure I understand," said Eladio. "For what?"

"Megan," David asked. "What did you call it?"

"A corrida," the girl answered. "Only this won't have all the parts, so it won't be a corrida. Not unless you can find a picador and a banderillero up at the house."

"I'll ask," David said.

"Just be sure to bring something for a cape," the girl said.

"Wait a minute!" The words came out of Eladio suddenly. But he hesitated then and said more calmly, "Let me understand this. You want me to go in that pen and cape a bull? Is that it?"

"*The* bull," David said. "My red Jersey."

"Listen," Eladio said, still keeping his voice calm, "you don't just go in and play with an animal like that."

"Sure you do," David said. "If you're a bullfighter."

"Okay. Then I don't need a job that bad."

"You're not married, are you?"

"No."

"Pretty independent guy."

"I said I don't need the job."

David took the clipboard down from the sun visor. He studied a sheet of paper that was attached to it before looking up again. "I'm ready for that one, smart guy. You got a brother working for me. He's got a wife and six kids. Right?"

Eladio nodded, watching David carefully.

"That's all there is to it," David said.

Megan standing on the other side of the car, looked in the window. "Sherm, if you have to do that, let's forget about it."

"Now wait a minute," David said. "This is supposed to be a brave guy. Playing with bulls is his business. All right, I ask him to play with mine. We have people up at the house expecting this, waiting to see him perform, and if I have to hold a club over his head to make him do it, I will."

"I don't think it's worth it," the girl said.

"It was your idea. You brought it up in the first place!"

"We were talking about bullfighting," Megan said patiently. "Yes, I might have brought it up. Then we talked about your bull; and you remembered someone telling you Eladio had been a bullfighter. But you didn't promise them a bullfight."

"Listen—the guy who keeps his coat on, he's a two-hundred-thousand-dollar die contract if I entertain him right." He glanced at Eladio. "You're fighting the bull." The station wagon shot forward leaving Eladio and Megan standing facing each other.

After a moment Eladio said, "Is he crazy or something?"

"Hardheaded and also a little drunk," the girl replied.

"He's serious about firing my brother, if I don't do it?"

"I'm sure he is."

"He reminds me of Luis Fortuna."

"The man you worked for?"

Eladio nodded. "Maybe all bosses come from the same tree."

The way he said it made her ask, "Why, what did Luis do to you?"

"That's a long story."

"We've got time."

"Well, I told you I was his banderillero before he quit. He never placed his own. Sometimes he tried, but he did it poorly; so I placed them and sometimes the crowd liked the way I did it. You know, they'd start *olé*-ing. Well, that made Luis mad. He was jealous of me, but I didn't know it then. I learned it after he became my manager, after he'd signed me to a no-good contract and picked the worst bulls for me and . . . no, it's too long a story.

He looked at the enclosure thoughtfully and after a moment asked, "How does a man get like that? You know, with a mean streak."

"I don't know about Luis; Sherm seems to work at it," Megan said. "He was left this place along with a tool and die plant in Detroit. Both practically run themselves, so Sherm runs loose."

"And you run with him?"

She hesitated. "We're going to be married next month."

"You don't seem very sure about it."

"And all of a sudden you don't seem very nervous."

"Before walking into the arena," Eladio said, "you never intentionally worry about the bull. You talk or pray or try to think of other things. But the worry, which is a poor word, is always there."

"I'm sorry."

"That's all right." He asked then, unexpectedly, "Have you known him long?"

"Sherm? I met him in Florida last winter. Why?"

"I just wondered. You seem . . . like on your own."

"I suppose I am."

"It makes a difference, doesn't it?"

"I'm not sure I know what you mean?"

"I mean you grow up faster when you're on your own. Sometimes too fast."

"Oh." Megan watched his gaze go to the bull enclosure and she asked, "What are you thinking?"

"I'm thinking that a Jersey isn't a Miura or a La Punta or any name of bull bred for the arena, and that makes a difference too."

"You could cape him once or twice," the girl said, "and if he doesn't respond, call it off."

"Just like that."

Abruptly she asked, "Why did you quit bullfighting?"

"I told you," he said, still not looking at her.

"You said you got tired of it. Which isn't true."

"No, but it took only a few words to tell." He turned to her as he spoke. "The truth takes more words. You want to count them and see?"

She stared at him, not answering, and he said, "At Juárez on January seventh, a bull named Isidro who weighed twelve hundred pounds and favored his right horn and who refused to charge unless it was on his ground put three inches of this same right horn into my hip, which in turn put me into a hospital for seven weeks."

He repudiated her look of sudden sympathy and understanding by going on relentlessly. "Listen, my hip healed in seven weeks, but something else didn't heal, the fear I had of the bull that afternoon. You understand that? In one afternoon my nerve vanished. In one afternoon I went from matador to migrant worker, from killer of bulls to picker of tomatoes. Because I was afraid, not because I got gored. You tell that to this Sherm and see what he says."

"Perhaps you'd better tell him."

"No, I'm through talking."

"Then you're going to do it?"

"I don't see that I have a choice," Eladio said.

Less than a quarter of an hour later he was standing in the bull ring of the farm near Blisston, Michigan. In his right hand he held a square of red blanket that had been cut to the approximate size of a muleta. The blanket reached to the ground in folds, though it was spread open by means of a short stick rolled into the end of the blanket that he held.

"Now we'll see how good you are," Sherman David said. He stood at the fence with a highball in his hand, his arms resting on the iron rail, which passed him belt high. His head was pressed lightly against the top rail.

A man in his mid-fifties, wearing a Black Watch–plaid sport coat and also holding a highball, stood next to David. His other guests, a man and two women, were farther along the fence. All were holding drinks. Megan stood behind them, but she moved to the fence as David called across the enclosure, "Send him out!"

The door of the Quonset rose with the grinding sound of metal rollers and in its place was a dim, empty square. But only for a moment. The bull came out cautiously, dull brown at first, then rust-colored as it moved into the bright sunlight. Seeing Eladio, the bull stopped. Its head rose, then lowered slowly and the animal moved forward again.

Eladio stood with his feet slightly apart, the blanket muleta limp in his right hand. Then, abruptly, he switched the blanket to his left hand. The instant he did so the bull's head jerked, following the movement.

Now you see it, Eladio thought in Spanish, speaking to the bull. *This thing in my hand. See if you can take it. See if you can tear it away with your black-tipped devil's horns.*

Sherman David yelled, "Come on, get started!"

Megan glanced at him irritably and as she looked back at Eladio, the bull charged. Its horns dipped low as it rushed the limp square of blanket, then hooked up as the blanket was withdrawn.

The bull reared, following the blanket high, its forelegs extended stiffly, and as it came down, twisting, throwing its head, Eladio pivoted on one foot and moved back a few yards before planting his feet again. He stood with his head cocked, his left hand extended and holding the blanket.

Megan drew in her breath as the bull charged again, as it rushed with its head lowered at Eladio. He did not move his feet—only his head, following the charge of the bull, and his arm as it drew the blanket up and away in a *pase natural*. The abrupt maneuver again fixed the bull in the air with its forelegs extended and off the ground.

Suddenly the bull turned. Its head went down, and as it began its third charge, Eladio pivoted, passing the blanket across his body to the right, and his back was to the rage-inflamed animal as it grazed past him, hooking at the rising blanket. He had taken the bull with a *pase de pecho* and now, having turned, he stood facing the people lined along the fence. He glanced at the bull circling to the left near the far corner, then looked up hearing David.

"Do something fancy. You handle that thing like it was a blanket." Both David and the man next to him laughed. Eladio saw them raise their glasses, then he heard the bull and he looked in that direction.

The bull came straight on with its head down and horns pointing. Eladio extended the blanket, made his knees and body stiff and now looked again at Sherman David. He held David's gaze, not moving his eyes, and only when the pounding sound was on top of him did he sweep back the blanket muleta and the bull brushed him, half turning him as it rushed past.

He heard David say to the man next to him, "Maybe the cape's too small. He can't seem to do much with it."

Eladio stared at him before unrolling the stick from the blanket and letting it fall. He held the blanket in his left hand, his right side exposed to the bull, but now the blanket, unopened, hung in folds close in front of him, and again his eyes went to Sherman David.

He stood this way, his body arched stiffly and his feet almost together as the pounding sound of the enraged beast returned and grew louder and was near him and was with him. He was still seeing Sherman David, now across the bull's back, now with the smell and heat of it, then half stumbling against the rushing flank as the blanket was torn from his hand.

The bull circled toward the Quonset, hooking at the blanket caught on its right horn. But Eladio did not look at the bull again. He walked to the fence, went through the rails, and came up next to Sherman David.

"Now my money," Eladio said.

"For that?" David sipped his highball. "You got to put on a show to get paid."

Eladio stared at him as he raised the highball again, saw his eyes over the rim of the glass, and then his face, half smiling, as the glass came down.

"I told you to do something fancy. Hell, all you did was hold it at your side." Again David almost smiled. "I can see why you didn't last. No showmanship." He glanced at the man in the sport coat. "Right, Mr. Thornhill?"

Mr. Thornhill did smile. "Well, I don't know anything about the sport, but what he did looked rather basic."

"Basic!" Megan came from behind David. "Sherm, those were *naturals*. He did them without looking at the bull. Don't you realize that?"

David winked at Mr. Thornhill. "Megan's a reader."

"Sherm, you've never in your life seen a man that close to death. He actually played with it!"

"Sure, honey." David grinned at her. He turned, extended his arms to herd his guests toward the station wagon.

Megan's eyes went to Eladio. He was looking past her, his chest rising and falling with the deepness of his breathing. "You had that bull," she said. "Do you realize that? You had that bull from the moment it came out."

"I don't know." Eladio lowered his gaze tiredly. "It was the moment."

"Of course it was the moment. Every time you walk into an arena it will be the moment. You don't look into the future!" She said then, more calmly, "There was only one thing wrong. You fought the wrong bull."

His eyes moved to hers, but he said nothing.

"Do you know what I mean? . . . Answer me!"

"I'm not sure of anything."

From the car David called, "You coming?"

Megan ignored him. "That one. That's the one you have to face. You do well with a bull—you're sure of that now. But you're mixed up with these Luis Fortunas and Sherman Davids. They make you feel that everything's against you. Too much for one man to fight. They make you lose confidence in yourself, and because of it you think you have a fear of the bulls.

"Fortuna cheated you and gave you unpredictable bulls. But one almost killed you because you felt defeated, because you were thinking of Fortuna instead of the bull. Sherm gave you a bull: but you took this one."

Eladio looked at her intently. "Why? Why this one?"

"Because I was watching. It's true, isn't it? I was for you and you could feel it. Through the fence and across the fence you could feel it."

"But you're engaged to him. You're not on my side—"

"It's not a question of *sides*. If you had felt alone in that pen your lack of confidence might have killed you. That's the point."

"Megan!" David called from the car.

Eladio said, "How do you know all this?"

"What difference does it make. It's true. You're a man," she said earnestly. "More man than he'll ever be. But you have to convince yourself of it."

"Just like that."

She nodded emphatically. "Yes, just like that. And since there's only one way to do it, there's no problem, is there?"

He watched her walk to the station wagon and get in. He watched the car U-turn and drive off through the trees and already it was in his mind what to do.

But don't think about it, he thought. *If you think about it it will become a problem and you'll make excuses for yourself. Which is what you've been doing since Juárez.*

Take Sherman David; take him just as he had taken the bull. Fight him? Perhaps. If it came to that. But at least stand up to him. That was what the girl meant. Whatever followed would be something else. Another matter.

And then what?

Then go back to Juárez and buy Luis Fortuna a drink and tell him you feel sorry for him. He smiled openly and almost laughed out loud.

IN THE CENTER OF the patio, a round table was set with silverware, glasses, and lighted candles. Sherman David and the sport-coated Mr. Thornhill stood here. To the right of the candlelighted table were Megan, standing, and the other guests, two of them seated near the right-angled brick wall of the patio.

This scene was before Eladio as he approached the house. More than an hour had passed and the sun had set beyond the far trees, though there was still light in the sky. Eladio, wearing a shirt with a tie and carrying his coat and suitcase, was almost to the rock garden that rimmed the patio before Sherman David saw him.

"What do you want?" he demanded.

"My money," said Eladio.

"Get out of here."

"I charge one hundred dollars for exhibitions."

"That's fine. Now get off my property."

"Not before you pay me," Eladio said. He put his suitcase down, folded his coat over it, and stepped to the flagstone patio. He started around the table, watching Sherman David through the soft candlelight.

David half-turned to the serving table. He put his glass down, reached toward the tray holding the ham, and when he turned back to Eladio a carving knife was in his right hand.

David's wrist moved and the knife blade made small circles in the air. "All right, you want your money. Let's see you get it."

Mr. Thornhill, standing a few feet from David, put his glass down carefully. "Sherm, I don't think you're in any condition to be playing with a carving knife."

David glanced at him. "Just stay out of it." He saw Thornhill's face tighten and he looked at Eladio again. "This guy's my business. He's like all the rest of them. They come up here thinking they're doing you a big favor. They mess up your place, let their kids run wild, and you're supposed to pay for it." He stared at Eladio. "Is that the way you guys figure it?"

Eladio said nothing.

"I charge one hundred dollars for exhibitions," David said, imitating Eladio's slight accent. "Boy, that kills me. Real big talker till you call his bluff. Then he shuts up. Come on, I'm talking your language now."

His hand rose and again the blade flashed in small circles. "You guys are famous for the knife routine. Let's see you do something about it. Come on, put up or shut up."

Eladio stood motionless, feeling his empty hands and the awkwardness of the silence. He said nothing because his mind told him nothing to say. He saw Megan pick up two forks, holding one in each hand.

"A man who has placed banderillas in a bull," she said mildly, "could hardly be bothered by a carving knife." She looked from Eladio to David. "Sherm, the way it's done—you wait for the bull with just the barbed sticks in your hand. You've no cape to distract the bull; and when it charges, you go up over the horns and place the sticks in its back."

David stared at her. He was about to speak, but his gaze shifted as he saw Eladio pick up two forks from the table and start toward him, raising them, one in each hand, as he came.

"Or you can go after the bull and not wait for it to charge," Eladio said. He raised the forks higher as David lowered his shoulders and shifted his weight to the balls of his feet.

"Come on," David said. "I'll play it your way."

"Sherm!" It was Thornhill's voice. "You drunken idiot! Put that knife down!"

Eladio's eyes went to Thornhill. He saw his face pale and drawn with anger, but at the same moment, knowing suddenly that he was off guard, sensing David's lunge even before it came, he pivoted instinctively, sucking in his stomach, and brought the forks down.

David slammed against the table, sprawled over it with his outstretched arms smashing glasses, sending the candlesticks off the table, and in the sudden dimness he felt the forks press against his shoulder blades.

"You place them about here," Eladio said. "It weakens the neck muscles, so the bull will come for the final act with his head down." He tightened the forks against David's back. "Do you want a final act, Mr. David?"

"I think Mr. David's had enough," Megan said. "Pay him, Sherm, and consider yourself lucky."

"No," Eladio said. "Now that I think about it, it would be improper to ask the bull to pay. He has given enough of himself already."

David pushed himself up from the table, his eyes on Megan. "You talked yourself out of a good deal. I hope you know it."

"That's exactly what it would be," the girl said. "Not a marriage, a deal. After seeing you in action, Sherm, I can't help but be honest with myself. And if I were to explain it or try to say it any other way, I'm afraid it would sound corny."

"Or it would be over his head," Mr. Thornhill said. "Megan, we'll give you a lift to Detroit whenever you're ready."

"Thank you." She looked at Eladio. "You're leaving now, aren't you?"

"I have a ride, thanks." He said then, "Perhaps you'll be coming to Mexico again sometime. Do you think?"

Megan smiled. "To the plaza de toros?"

Eladio nodded. "I'll dedicate a bull to you. I feel I owe you one."

She watched him pick up his coat and suitcase. As he walked off into the darkness, she was half sure she would see him again. She was completely sure she would hear of him again.

Rebel on the Run

1960

THERE WERE UNION SUPPLY wagons passing the house, part of General Sooy Smith's forces, moving through the mist and the chill and the February mud, moving back through Okolona.

Olin Worrel watched them from the front porch. He had knocked on the door and now stood gazing out at the road, at the slowly moving line of gray canvas. *They've got all the time in the world,* he was thinking. *Seven thousand Yankees. They can back off for a while and let Bedford Forrest worry himself sick. Then come back any time they want.*

A company of cavalry came up on the wagons, thinning single file to pass along the tree-lined shoulder of the road. Olin Worrel recognized them by the lieutenant in the lead—part of McCrilli's Brigade—and he waved to them, dropping his arm abruptly and turning away as the last rider filed past the house.

He was about to knock on the door again, but he saw the knob turn. He pulled off his hat and with a quick, self-conscious gesture, smoothed his mustache, brushing it out from the corners of his mouth with thumb and second finger, then dropped his hand as the door opened and said quietly, “Virginia, I wondered if there was anything I could do.”

“I don’t believe so, Olin. Thank you.”

She was dressed in black, a young woman who looked at Worrel calmly and without curiosity. Her features, small and well defined, were accentuated by the pale, drawn appearance of her skin. Her hair, dark and parted in the middle, was combed back into a tight, flat-shaped knot.

Worrel looked beyond her into the hall. “Is there someone with you?”

“The ladies from Okolona were here.”

“I thought I heard somebody.”

“They were here this morning.”

Worrel stood tall to look past her, thrusting out his chin and stretching his neck. *He’s older than thirty-eight,* the girl thought absently, her eyes on the face that was close to hers and looking beyond her. Worrel’s head came down and she lowered her eyes.

“You should have somebody with you,” Worrel said. “I mean all the time, not just for a visit.”

“I’ll be all right.”

“Virginia, I wish there was something I could say.”

She was thinking: *Don’t try to say anything. Just leave.* But she felt the silence lengthening and she said, “Finding words of sympathy is never easy. You don’t have to say anything, Olin; I know how you feel. Everyone has been very kind.”

“You still ought to have somebody.”

“Olin, if you don’t mind.” Her hand moved up the edge of the door. “I’d like to rest now. I’ve been up since five o’clock.”

Worrel moved closer, taking her hand. “I’m sorry. I’m not making it any easier, am I?”

"I'll be all right in a few days, Olin. Let me just rest and think a little bit and I'll be all right."

"You take your time," Worrel said gently. "I know this will delay our plans, but I don't mind. I've waited a long time for you, Virginia; longer than you realize. I watched you even before you were married, so I guess it won't hurt me to wait a little bit longer." He hesitated awkwardly. "Just how long do you think, honey?"

"Please . . . we'll talk about it later."

"I'm always saying the wrong thing. Virginia, sometimes I could cut my tongue out. I mean I can run a business, give people orders that work for me. But I swear, Virginia, I get with you and I'm like a twelve-year-old boy."

"It won't be long," she said patiently.

He patted her hand gently. "You get a good rest and don't worry about anything. I'll keep an eye on the house. With all those Yankees marching through, you just don't know. Oh, they'll be back, I know that; but right now they're skittery, nervous because of Forrest—" He broke off, looking suddenly past her.

"I heard it again. Virginia, there's somebody in your house whether you know it or not."

"Olin, it's all right—"

"I know there is. I heard it." He shifted his position, raising his head and looking beyond the hall into the parlor. "There!" His hand tightened on hers. He was tensed, listening, but now there was only silence and his hand eased open slowly. "Virginia, you heard that," he whispered earnestly. "For Lord sake, like somebody falling to the floor."

He hesitated, studying the girl suspiciously, then brushed past her before she could stop him, hurrying through the front room to the dining room, then through it to the sun parlor. There, in the doorway, he stopped.

A man he had never seen before was lying on the floor with both hands pressed tightly to his side. A Dragoon revolver was on the floor an arm's length away from him, near a basin of rust-colored water. Long strips of cloth, cut from a sheet, were draped over one end of the sofa.

"Virginia, he's a soldier!" Worrel stared at the man's faded gray jacket, unbuttoned but held almost together by a belt that crossed his chest to holster beneath his left arm. His eyes were closed, held tightly closed, and his jaw was clenched so that Olin could see his teeth through the light beard stubble that covered his face. He was a young man, perhaps no older than Virginia.

She moved past him, stooping over the wounded man, then glanced back at Worrel. "Help me get him onto the sofa."

Worrel was frowning. "How'd he get here?"

"He came to the back door, not an hour ago."

They raised him by his shoulder and heard him suck in his breath. But once on the sofa he seemed to relax. His eyes were still closed, but now his face was composed and his chest rose and fell evenly with his breathing. Worrel looked over her shoulder, watching her raise the wounded man's hands from the bloodstained bandage that circled his waist. "It's bleeding again," Virginia murmured. "The bullet went cleanly through his side; but every time he moves it starts bleeding."

Worrel shook his head. "He's got to have a doctor."

Virginia said, "There isn't a doctor in Okolona. You know that."

"Yes there is." Worrel paused. "One in McCrilli's Brigade I know of for sure. He's billeted right down the street from me."

Virginia looked up. "You'd hand him over to the Yankees?"

"I'm thinking about the man's life."

She had unfastened the bloodstained bandage and now pulled it gently from beneath the wounded man. "He wants to get back to his company," Virginia said quietly.

"You talk to him?"

"A little bit. He's been asleep most of the time."

"Who is he?"

"His name is McLean. A lieutenant in Tyree Bell's Brigade."

"That's Forrest," Worrel said. His voice rose nervously. "Virginia, will you tell me why you ever took him in?"

"Olin, the man came to my door bleeding to death."

Worrel stroked his mustache thoughtfully. "We've got to think of something."

Virginia looked up again. "I don't particularly care what happens to him. I don't care much if he lives or dies. But I'm not going to turn him over to the Yankees."

"All right, then send him away. Make him get out the way he came."

"Is that what you'd do?"

"I wouldn't hesitate a minute. Not with seven thousand Yankees in the neighborhood and all of them nervous mean because Forrest is breathing down their necks. No, sir, I wouldn't hesitate even a second."

Virginia began, "If it's certain Forrest will retake Okolona—"

"Listen," Worrel said. "The only thing that's certain is the Yankees are here this minute and that's reason enough to get rid of him."

"He wants somebody to take him through the Union lines."

Worrel stared at her. "Are you serious?"

"It's the only thing he talks about."

Worrel stirred restlessly, frowning, looking from McLean to the girl. "But how'd he ever get here in the first place?"

"Early this morning he was west of town with a scouting party and they ran into Yankees." Virginia was holding a fresh cloth to McLean's side now, not looking at Worrel as she spoke. "Mr. McLean was shot, but he clung to his horse until back somewhere beyond the orchard he dropped off. He said that he passed out; then, just about an hour ago, he came to the back door."

"The Yankees could come here any time," Worrel said absently, glancing toward the drawn curtains of the windows. He was thinking of what he would say next, building the words in his mind. He glanced at McLean and saw his eyes still closed.

"Virginia, listen to me. Listen carefully so you'll understand the situation."

"Olin, I'm aware—"

"Just a minute, Virginia. Listen and think it over like a reasonable person. Here's the thing. General Sooy Smith comes down here from Memphis with over seven thousand Yankees, marches the whole way here in a week and nobody stops him. In the meantime Sherman has marched from Vicksburg clear to Meridian and nobody stops him either. You see what I'm driving at? Two Yankee armies controlling just about the whole of Mississippi."

This isn't real, Virginia thought. *You are going to marry him and you can't even bear his serious, whining voice.*

"All right. Sooy Smith doesn't get all the way down to Meridian like everybody says he was supposed to. He gets as far as West Point and finds Bedford Forrest with his scrawny little brigades pecking at his flanks. Good. But not good enough. Smith doesn't join up with Sherman, but they say he's destroyed a million dollars' worth of corn, cotton, and railroad and picked up three thousand Negroes on the way. Not retreating, Virginia, just backing up now he's done a job. Next thing, Forrest with his brother and Tyree Bell and Richardson and them, they come flying at Sooy Smith's rear, and everybody thinks they got him on the run."

"A moment ago," Virginia said, "you described them being nervous mean, afraid Forrest would overtake them."

"Virginia, listen to me. That's true. A rear guard action isn't the same as fighting head-on. You're at a disadvantage, sure; but it's temporary and it doesn't mean you're going to get licked."

Virginia nodded patiently. "And what does that have to do with Mr. McLean?"

"The point is, the Yankees have Mississippi. Whether we like it or not they're here. And if Sooy Smith pulls out of Okolona today. That doesn't mean he won't come back tomorrow. He could come swinging back before you even unload your Mr. McLean and you'd be worse off than you are now . . . I'm saying, Virginia, accept the facts. The Yankees are here to stay, so you might as well try to get along with them."

Virginia shrugged. "If the Yankees find him here, all right. If he wants to leave here on his own, that's all right too. I don't intend to help him, and I'm past caring about the war or what happens to me or anyone in it."

"What about us, Virginia. You don't care what happens to us?"

"Olin, let's stop." She rose abruptly and walked past him, through the dining room to the front of the house. In the parlor she turned, waiting for him. "Just leave now, Olin. Forget you ever saw him."

Worrel shook his head gravely. "I can't do that. Not while you're in danger for even one minute."

"Don't dramatize it, Olin."

"I'm serious," Worrel said. "I'll find a way to lick this and I'll come back. Just trust me, Virginia."

For some time she stood with her forehead pressed to the door. Worrel's footsteps had faded to nothing, but still she stood listening, gradually becoming aware of the silence and the dim emptiness of the house. *I'm tired,* she thought. *And there's no sense to this.*

But he's still there, she thought then, and moved from the door, passing soundlessly through the soft gray rectangles of light that stretched across the rug from the curtained windows, seeing him then in the sun parlor, beyond the dim length of the dining room, seeing his head turned on the pillow to face her and with his eyes open.

His eyes were clear and held her gaze calmly, though the lines of his face, the beard stubble and lean, drawn expression, told of days with little sleep.

She stooped, picking up the basin of water, and placed it on the side table. She noticed McLean's revolver and stooped again, glancing at him this time, and saw his arm extended.

"How do you feel?" She stepped close enough to hand him the revolver.

"I'm afraid to move to find out." McLean slipped the Dragoon under the pillow. He lowered his eyes then as Virginia kneeled beside him. She pulled open his jacket and gently peeled the bloodstained cloth from his wound.

"You shouldn't have got up."

"You left the door open," McLean said. "I wanted to get out of view, but when I stood up it was like I didn't have any legs. I just fell over and the blood started coming again."

She raised her eyes briefly. "It's stopped now."

With his chin pressed to his chest, McLean studied her profile and the dark gleam of her hair. He watched her fold a strip of the linen and arched his back when she slipped it beneath him and brought it around his waist.

"Who is he?" McLean asked abruptly.

"His name is Olin Worrel."

"He wants to turn me over to the Yankees."

Virginia looked up. "I didn't think you heard."

"Every word."

She shook her head. "He wouldn't do that."

"I hope you're sure."

"I know he wouldn't. He'd be afraid of involving me."

"And himself."

She looked at him coldly now. "Mr. Worrel and I are engaged to be married." She was suddenly sorry she had said it and she lowered her eyes again.

"Oh." McLean paused. "Was he in the war?"

"He doesn't believe in fighting."

"Is that right? You just say you don't believe in fighting and that's all there is to it?"

"A man is entitled to his beliefs," Virginia said.

"Would he help me?"

"I'm sure he'd be against it."

McLean said, "He just waits to see who wins, then goes on like nothing's happened. Is that what he's doing?"

"I don't feel qualified to speak for Mr. Worrel's beliefs."

"Even though you're going to marry him."

"Which doesn't happen to be any of your business."

McLean came up on his elbows. "Listen, my business is to get through the Union lines to the Tombigbee River and I'm trying like almighty hell to find a way!"

Virginia pushed him back gently. "You'll start it bleeding again."

For perhaps a full minute McLean studied her in silence, watching her tie the ends of the bandage now. He said then, "Will you help me?"

"No."

"I don't mean endanger yourself. Just show me a way where I won't have to go near the roads."

"You got here," she said quietly. "Go back the way you came."

"We came from Egypt Station. But my brigade was doubling back across the Tombigbee and we were to rejoin them somewhere just north of Waverly."

"Perhaps they'll be in Okolona tomorrow."

"I can't lay here on a perhaps."

"I'd say you've already done enough."

"Look—all I'm asking is you show me the direction!"

Help me, Virginia. Staring at McLean she heard the words in her mind, looking at his eyes and the lean, hard-boned shape of his face.

She made sure of her words before saying, quietly, without emotion, "Five days ago my brother was here, home on furlough from McCulloch's Brigade. He was here the day the Yankees came, when their cavalry came down the road stopping at every house, and my brother said, 'Help me, Virginia. Talk to them. Do anything, but give me time.' So I helped him. I talked to them while he ran out the back door and was shot seven times before he reached the orchard. Yes, I helped him, Mr. McLean. I helped him die instead of talking sense into him. He could have surrendered and he'd be alive today. But I helped him."

McLean watched her closely. "You stand for Olin Worrel's beliefs but not your brother's, is that it?"

Virginia closed her eyes wearily. "I've had enough, Mr. McLean, if you don't mind."

"Did you stand for your husband's beliefs?" Her eyes came open. "I noticed your ring," McLean said. "He's dead?"

"He was killed at Shiloh, serving with Wirt Adams."

"That's too bad."

"That's too bad," she murmured, staring at him now. "You put it very simply, don't you?"

"I'm sorry." McLean hesitated. "I didn't know what else to say."

"You didn't mention it was too bad about my brother," Virginia said coldly. "Do you think it is? Or my father. My father was killed September 19, 1863, at Chickamauga. Seventeen months and eleven days after my husband was killed. Do you think that's too bad?" Their eyes held, neither of them looking away or moving.

"My mother died exactly nine weeks after my father. How bad do you think that is? She died of pneumonia, though I can tell you the pneumonia had little to do with it. She was a widow nine weeks. On April 8, I'll have been a widow for two years. That's too bad too, isn't it?" She stopped abruptly. Then, more calmly, she said, "If there is anything else you want to say, please say it now. I'd like very much to go lie down."

McLean shook his head slowly. "All you can feel is sorry for yourself."

Virginia's eyes showed quick surprise, but almost in the same moment she was composed, staring at him in stony silence.

"You've had enough war," McLean said mildly. "Like your friend, Worrel, you've washed your hands of it and you sit very quietly asking yourself why did it happen to you, and what is it all about anyway and why don't the Yankees go home, and why don't people stop saying they're sorry and why don't they go home too and just leave you alone to sit and think about all the awful things that've happened . . . First your husband. You started to get over it—and don't tell me you didn't, because you can get over anything. Then your father and your mother, and you even started to get over that. But now your brother. This one is still fresh and right now it's too much because it makes you think of the others, all of them at once, and you say, 'Oh, God, what did I do? Why did it happen to me?' Like you're the only woman in the world who's lost people in the war."

McLean paused, not taking his eyes from hers, holding her with the raw truth of his words.

He went on, "And during this time, Olin came along. The old family friend who's all of a sudden a beau because now you're a widow and twenty years' difference between you doesn't look like so much. He got to be like a fixture, I'll bet, and you leaned on him because he was the only man close by, and one day he asked you to marry him and you said yes because you were thinking of yourself shivering with loneliness and you wanted to be held. You wanted a man to hold you and stroke your hair and say, 'Honey, it's all over. Go ahead, cry if you want. I'll just hold you and I won't let any more awful things happen to you. I'll help you take the terrible sting out of remembering and after a while you'll just have good memories and everything will be fine." McLean watched her. "That's how it is, isn't it?"

Virginia had not moved. She stared at McLean with a look of

patient hatred and said, "You're inhuman. No person with even a shred of feeling could say those things."

McLean shook his head slowly. "Virginia, I'm the realest thing you know. I'm real and human enough to know how you feel. Admit that, Virginia, even if it leaves your pride feeling naked."

Abruptly she wheeled from the sofa and he said, "Virginia!" And as she hesitated he said quietly again, "Virginia, look at my side and see if it's bleeding." He watched her turn to him again, avoiding his eyes. She kneeled and raised his jacket and he said, "That's real, isn't it? I'm lying here holding the thing and I'll testify before God Almighty that it's real."

For a moment her gaze softened beseechingly. "Can't you just leave me alone?"

"I'm running out of time, Virginia."

Her expression tightened. "And I'm running out of patience!" She started to rise, not looking at him—not until he reached for her and pulled her down against him and she felt his arms around her and his hands pressed firmly over her back. She tried to push away, her eyes furiously alive and close to his face now, but he held her tightly against him.

"Listen to me!"

She stopped struggling, stunned by the sudden harshness of his voice.

"Feel sorry for yourself tomorrow," McLean said. "Feel sorry for yourself all you want then. But not today. I don't have time to hold you and comfort you and make the numb feeling go away . . . I could do it though, Virginia, and you know I could. I don't have a wife; I haven't made any promises to anybody; I could comfort you good."

With one hand he began stroking her hair, gently, and he said softly, "Virginia" bringing her face down to his. But said nothing more. He kissed her lingeringly and she did not try to pull away from him. His lips moved to her cheek and she turned her head, burying it against his shoulder.

"You're alive, Virginia"—McLean's words were barely above a whisper—"but you have to do something to stay alive. Something more than just breathe and eat. You have to do something, build toward something, look forward to something; because there's no such thing as just staying in one place. Bringing it down to right now, it's like saying you're either for me or against me, Virginia. There isn't any middle ground—like letting me lie here and not doing anything because you helped your brother try to escape and he was killed. That doesn't make sense, does it? That's an excuse. You don't want to say you feel sorry for yourself, so you make up an excuse that almost sounds like a principle. Do you see that, Virginia?"

She lay against him, listening, hearing the soft-strong sound of his voice, feeling his arms around her and the rough scratch of his cheek and being aware of the damp, faintly sour smell of his coat, but not minding it. She remained in his arms, wondering how she would meet his eyes, then beginning to picture herself in his arms—

McLean was saying, "We'll leave when it's dark. You'll just take me out back through the orchard and show me how to reach the river without going near the road." His hand continued to stroke her hair.

"It's just a matter of making up your mind, Virginia. After you do that it's easy."

She pushed up and away from him, knowing he wasn't expecting it, and ran from the room, feeling his eyes following her and already she was thinking: *You made a fool of yourself! Lying there, showing your weakness—*

She went up the front stairs to her bedroom and sat on the edge of the bed to look out at the gray late afternoon light, at the trees lining the muddy road and the pines that formed a silent dark wall along the far side of the meadow.

She wanted to look at something or do something, anything, but do it quickly to erase the picture still in her mind: seeing herself in McLean's arms, awkwardly half kneeling, half lying over him with his arms around her. She closed her eyes, feeling the restless urge inside of her; then threw herself back on the bed, turning to her side, then to her stomach with an arm up in front of her face.

And now she pictured herself running across the meadow, running with the wind in her face, with the hissing sound of it drowning out McLean's voice, running through the pines and beyond, and beyond that, running and falling and running and finally she would fall and not get up. She would sleep for a long time, lying in a pine grove, and even asleep she would be aware of the clean pine smell and the crisp air that was fresh and brought only whispers of sound.

She would be alone—beyond the solemn serious funeral voices offering sympathy; beyond the irritatingly persistent offerings of Olin Worrel (She told herself that he was a kind, generous, prosperous man who was wise enough to stay out of the war altogether. "Virginia, I'm not angry at those Yankees," he would say. "Why should I go fight them? Just because they talk funny?"); beyond picturing things that used to be and would never be again; beyond the Yankees in Okolona and the silent dark house and the man in the sun parlor; beyond seeing herself in his arms . . .

OLIN WORREL SAID, "VIRGINIA, I'm sorry. Were you asleep?"

She stood with one hand on the door, the other holding a lamp, holding it high so that its light cast a pale yellow glow over Worrel's face, clearly sharpening the drawn expression about his mouth, bringing out the untrimmed, wiry texture of his mustache and the glistening trace of perspiration across his forehead.

Beyond him, the trees lining the road showed ghostly in the

dusk. "I thought I had just dozed off when you knocked," she said. "But I must have slept for hours."

Worrel's gaze darted past her into the darkness of the parlor. "He's still here?"

Virginia nodded. "Yes."

"Is he any better? I mean can he move without it killing him?"

"I suppose—"

"I want to talk to him."

"Why?"

"Virginia, don't waste time, please."

It was in her mind: *He was a way to end this. He's thought it out and made a decision and whatever he does it will be out of your hands and you won't have to think about him or worry about his wound or— That's enough.*

"All right, Olin." She stepped aside to let him in, then closed the door and led him through the dark rooms to the sun parlor. The lamplight spread over McLean and she saw him raise himself on his elbow, saw his body twist suddenly with his left hand crossing over and digging under the pillow.

"Don't move!" Olin's voice. "You bring out a gun, I'll kill you. I swear to heaven I will!"

Virginia had set the lamp on the side table. And now she saw the derringer in Worrel's hand. McLean was on his side, still with his hand beneath the pillow. "Get his gun." Worrel's voice again.

Her eyes went to McLean's now, to his quiet, accusing gaze, and she felt a heat come over her face. "Olin, you said you wanted to talk to him." She said it earnestly, but her tone sounded weakly apologetic.

"I'll talk to him," Worrel said, more sure of himself now. "First get his gun . . . and you sit up." Holding the derringer almost at arm's length, he waved it at McLean. "Come on, swing your legs over."

Slowly McLean pushed himself up. When he was sitting, Virginia moved toward him, keeping her eyes from his; but as her hand went under the pillow, touching the heavy metal of the revolver, McLean murmured, "Now you think it won't be on your conscience." And she glanced at him quickly, seeing the quiet awareness in his eyes and the gaunt hollows of his face.

Worrel waited until she stepped back with the Dragoon revolver in her hand. "Now get up and get out of here," he said to McLean.

McLean looked at Virginia. "You didn't need him. I told you I was going. With your help or without it."

Worrel pointed the derringer threateningly. "I'm warning you. Leave her alone now. She's not about to risk her life for you or anybody like you. If it was me, I'd turn you over to the Yankees in a minute. That's the truth and it would be for your own good whether you know it or not. But Virginia's against that, so I'm giving you one chance to get out of here and never show yourself again. Neither one of us is obligated to help you, and if your being here endangers our lives then you have to get out and that's all there is to it."

Walk away, Virginia thought. *Walk away right now and it will be over, something behind you that Olin did, that Olin was responsible for.* But she thought then, watching Olin and feeling McLean's eyes still on her: *You would have to run. You would have to run and keep running as long as you lived, and the wind would have to be loud, howling loud to keep out the sound of his voice, and if you stopped for one moment, McLean would be with you. No,* she thought. *You couldn't close your eyes tight enough not to see him, or sing or scream loud enough not to hear yourself saying over and over again the things he said. You realize that, don't you? If you don't, try to look at him.*

And try telling yourself you're still going to marry Olin. Try that even without looking at McLean. She thought: *You don't know his first name. You don't even know that much about him. But you still can't run fast enough, can you?*

"Olin, put down that gun." She raised McLean's revolver, pointed it at Worrel, and felt the tension, the tight heaviness, beginning to leave her body. And she remembered McLean saying that it would be easy once she made up her mind.

"Virginia." Worrel's mouth hung open dumbly.

Her left hand came under the barrel to steady it. "Olin, Mr. McLean has to go through the Union lines to the Tombigbee, and we're going to help him."

Worrel watched her closely, trying to understand this sudden change in her. He said then, cautiously, "You're taking advantage of me, Virginia. You know I wouldn't even point this gun at you. Just like I'm sure you wouldn't think of pulling that trigger in my direction. Not even to scare me." He moved toward her, but stopped abruptly as Virginia cocked the revolver.

"You're going to help by giving him your clothes, Olin. That's all you have to do, but it will be something."

"Virginia, just this afternoon you didn't want to have a thing to do with him."

"Olin, take off your clothes or I swear to heaven I'll shoot!"

Worrel hesitated, staring at her in silence; then his arm dropped heavily and he let the derringer fall.

"Virginia," he said tiredly, "I've been a practical man all my life. I apply common sense to everything I do and it's made me a success in business. You know that. Common sense says you don't risk your life without a reason. I mean a good reason. All right, you ask yourself, is this a good reason? You answer, of course not. The Yankees'll be back. You know it and he knows it—look at him. Ask him. All right, even if you're lucky and don't get caught; even if he gets through and even if he's ever well enough to fight again, what's the sense of it? We've lost the war. It's a matter of time now.

"Virginia, I'd gamble my life savings on it, the Yankees'll be back here before you know it and General Forrest will be dead or scattered so thin he'd never find his men again. This could be the last night of the war, Virginia. The last hour. Four years of fighting gone up in smoke and you can almost hear the quietness coming."

Virginia's eyes went to McLean. "Would you risk your life knowing it was the last day of the war?"

McLean shrugged. "The day isn't important. You do what you feel you have to do."

"Olin," Virginia asked, "have you ever believed in anything that strongly?"

"He's a soldier," Worrel said earnestly. "A soldier with an exaggerated sense of duty. But you didn't take an oath. I'm talking about you, Virginia. You haven't even told me why you're helping the man!"

"I'm not sure I can explain it," she said. "And if I could, I doubt if you'd understand."

Worrel closed and opened his eyes wearily. "Virginia, that's a line from a play. But this is real life. There're Yankees outside, all over, and their Springfields are as real as they are. You have to have a reason—and I mean a *reason*—to do what you're talking about. Not just a feeling."

"I have a reason."

"I want to know what it is."

"Though it's a feeling too."

"Virginia, for God's sake—"

Tell him, she thought, and felt a quick excitement through her body. *Tell both of them. Get it out and over with.* And she did, deliberately now, quietly, "I'm helping him because I want to help him, Olin. Not because I feel obligated or feel sorry for him.

"You won't understand it, Olin, because it doesn't sound reasonable. But . . . I'm helping him because he's a man. Because he's so much a man even the house feels different with him inside of it." She almost smiled. "You'd have to be a woman to understand that, Olin." She said then, "I tried closing my eyes to him. I tried closing them so tight that all the things he told me would be squeezed right out of my memory. Then when you came back this evening I thought, *Ah, Olin will do something. Now you don't have to think about him anymore.*

"But I'm thinking about him right this minute, Olin. Because he's something I can believe in, and that's what you don't understand—having a feeling about something so strongly that you believe in it almost the same way you believe in God even without seeing Him."

Virginia's eyes remained on Worrel. "I'll wait for him, too, if he wants. I don't even know his first name; but I think I would wait a very long time just on the chance he might come back."

She waited for the sound of McLean's voice, still not looking at him, afraid to take her eyes from Worrel. McLean was staring at her, sitting on the edge of the sofa with his hands placed ready to push himself up; but he didn't move. He sat with his full attention on her for a long moment before he spoke.

"Virginia," he said finally. "I feel we're going to have a long talk. I feel we're going to learn middle names and nicknames and Confirmation names, and everything there is to know about each other. I've got a feeling as soon as this war is over I'll be back. No matter where I am, I'll come straight here. That's the kind of feeling I have."

Slowly, Virginia let her breath out, as if making the sudden feeling of relief last as long as she could, and she wanted to smile and go into McLean's arms. But there would be time for that. Right now—

"Olin," she said patiently, "take your clothes off."

abruptly, with sudden sounds, it wasn't there. With the swish of the curtain and quick steps in the empty church the Massey boy ~~with the gun~~ was gone.

Father Schwinn watched the sanctuary light flickering silently in the dimness, a small red glow that would be here through the night and through the days, unchanging.

He was tired and content to sit for a while without having to think, without supposing or doubting or half-believing or reasoning; but just knowing now and feeling the actual physical relief that accompanied it. The money was Rindo's. Perhaps he had known it all the time. No, he had felt it; which was not the same as honestly knowing.

Like with the Massey boy. H~~e felt there was hope for him now where he had felt no hope before.~~ there was hope for him; Feeling ~~it~~, not honestly knowing it as you know something is objectively, unquestionably, but being quite sure of it anyway, true. The boy would need help, perhaps more kicks than kind words, and he would have to ~~stay~~ keep away from the older one, which was also part of the feeling; but the boy ~~he~~ still had a conscience and ~~consequently~~ because of it there was hope ~~from~~ for him. Perhaps some other priest's worry, -- God help him.

It ~~was~~ had been close, he thought, thinking of the larger church then and the baptismal font and the new vestments and the cattle for the Aravaipa people and the countless things three-thousand and fifty-five dollars would buy.

But not close enough. It could have happened but it didn't and after supper he would go to Rindo's again; this time with the money. But wouldn't it ~~x~~ have been good, he thought (knowing it ~~would~~ could never have happened but enjoying the thought momentarily), to have used Rindo's money for the church.